BOYS' OWN

BOYS' OWN

An Anthology of Canadian Fiction for Young Readers

Edited by

TIM WYNNE-JONES

PENGUIN

VIKING

VIKING

Published by the Penguin Group

Penguin Books Canada Ltd, 10 Alcorn Avenue, Toronto, Ontario, Canada M4V 3B2

Penguin Books Ltd, 27 Wrights Lane, London W8 5TZ, England

Penguin Putnam Inc., 375 Hudson Street, New York, New York 10014, U.S.A.

Penguin Books Australia Ltd, Ringwood, Victoria, Australia

Penguin Books (NZ) Ltd, cnr Rosedale and Airborne Roads, Albany, Auckland 1310, New Zealand

Penguin Books Ltd, Registered Offices: Harmondsworth, Middlesex, England

First published 2001

10 9 8 7 6 5 4 3 2 1

Printed and bound in Canada on acid free paper ♾

National Library of Canada Cataloguing in Publication Data

Main entry under title:

Boys' own : an anthology of Canadian fiction for young readers

ISBN 0-670-89304-8

1. Boys–Juvenile fiction. 2. Children's stories, Canadian (English)

I. Wynne-Jones, Tim

PS8323.B7B69 2001   jC813´.010892826   C2001-900993-3
PZ5.B69 2001

Visit Penguin Canada's website at www.penguin.ca.

Contents

Introduction

What is a boy's story? Well, it kind of depends on what you think a boy is. Based on personal experience and observation, I would have to say that a boy is, typically, brave and scared, full of strutting self-confidence one moment and as wobbly as a first bike-ride the next. Boys are thoughtful and reckless, amiable and gross, noisy and withdrawn, smart and, sometimes, thick as a brick! So a boy's story, I guess, would have to reflect some of that.

My biggest problem in choosing these stories wasn't really what to choose so much as where to start. I could have easily filled two volumes. Volume One would have started out with the turn-of-the-century nature stories of Sir Charles G. D. Roberts and Ernest Thompson Seton. It might have included glimpses of Mordecai Richler's boyhood Montreal, Stephen Leacock's small-town Ontario, and W. O. Mitchell's windswept prairies. I would have definitely wanted an excerpt from Farley Mowat's *Lost in the Barrens* and a fishing story from Roderick Haig-Brown out on the west coast. These are some of the riches of our literary past. Instead, I opted for Now. Most of the stories in this book were written within the last ten years; the oldest was published in 1986. And there are five brand-new tales written specially for this book.

I *loved* putting this book together, reading a hundred and one stories trying to find just twenty that might appeal especially to boys. *Especially,* not *exclusively.* The subtitle of this collection is *not* "No Girls Allowed." In fact, if you think about it, the elements that make a story really hum and crackle are believable and appealing characters, an intriguing plot, and the right words to do the job. Those characteristics have nothing to do with whether the story is written by John or Joan or intended for Justin or Jennifer.

Which brings me to the first of two confessions:

I have no clear, fixed idea why I chose these particular *Boys' Own* stories, apart from just plain liking them. I didn't start out with some hard and fast rule of what made a story right for boys. Each of the stories hums and crackles in its own way. Beyond that, I found myself thinking, as I read, about all those traditional, noble, boyish heroes and themes: Robinson Crusoe cast ashore, Sir Percival questing for the Holy Grail, Huck Finn hightailing it out of town. I thought about what goes down in the Boy Zone: champs and bullies, strangers in a strange land, the lure of danger, getting lost in the wild, catching the big one, scoring the winning goal, scaring the pants off your brother. I think you'll find most of those themes represented here. There isn't any desert island or a round table. But you can get washed ashore in all kinds of strange places and sometimes the Holy Grail turns out to be an eagle feather.

And my second confession: I like girls. I even slipped one or two into this collection—girl protagonists, I mean. Why? Just to keep you on your toes, I guess. But, truthfully, I think any guy would like these girls. I think any guy could *relate* to what they're doing, what they're going through. Which is one of the truly grand things about reading stories, isn't it? Learning to relate to others.

The thing is, I probably would have had almost as much fun doing a *Girls' Own* collection. I'd have had to change my name, of course, call myself Catriona Smith-Wickware, or something like that, but I would have had a ball. Sarah Ellis got the job, however, of putting together this book's sister anthology, and I'm very glad about it. Looking at her choices, what's not to like: Linda Holeman, Kit Pearson, Teresa Toten, and lots, lots more. You just might want to check it out when you're finished here. It's always good to know what the girls are up to.

Tim Wynne-Jones
Perth, Ontario

A Rafting We Will Go

by
Julie Johnston

"Living on the lake like a pack of savages." That's Father's take on the summer holidays up at Grandpa's cottage, but for sixteen-year-old Fred Dickinson the lake is more than just a getaway—it's almost a sanctuary. He's having trouble living up to his father's expectations of him; he's a bit of a runt, unsure of himself, a stutterer. What's more, the "threat" of a full-time job hangs over his head. In her novel The Only Outcast, *Julie Johnston takes us on a quintessentially Canadian summer holiday that is also a lot more. Based on the real diary of Fred Dickinson, written in 1904, it's kind of* Huck Finn *and* Swallows and Amazons *all rolled into one and set on beautiful Rideau Lake, in eastern Ontario. In chapter four, Fred, his brother Ernie and his cousin Harold, head into the town of Perth for the day. I couldn't resist including this passage—Perth's my hometown!*

1

(Today is my birthday.) This morning we carried water for the ladies to do the washing with. We then finished our job in the grove, and went fishing and sailing. Auntie Lizzie made an enormous cake for our supper and, after we ate it, we made a campfire near the tent and sat around it playing the mouth organ and singing with Ettie and Auntie Min and Mr. McAlpine, a friend of Ettie's, joining in. While we were having this revelry, the large steam yacht Jopl, *towing a barge loaded with cheese boxes, blew for the locks, and immediately we put out the fire and made a beeline for the locks. They let us get on, and we sat on the engine-room windows and watched the engineer at work. Both the pilot and the engineer were friendly and talked with us all the way to the upper lock. They said they were going to stay there all night, and asked us if we wanted to go into Perth with them. They leave at five o'clock in the morning.*

We got an alarm clock from the cottage to wake us up in time. The cottage folk laughed at us and said the *Jopl* would be long gone before we tumbled out of bed. We set the alarm for three o'clock to be on the safe side. When it went off, I was in the middle of a very realistic dream. Ernie fumbled with the clock trying to turn off the alarm, but it wouldn't shut up until he bounced it off the wall of the tent. We all just lay there.

"Come on," I said, finally, "we have to get up." I gave them each an elbow in the back because it was my turn to sleep in the middle. Harold kept on snoring on one side of me, and on the other side, Ernie pulled the covers up over his head and made a snarling sound like a cross dog.

Wedged in, I lay thinking about my dream and trying to get back into it, but I couldn't. Probably just as well as I'm trying to preserve my brain fluid. So I just lay there, thinking about things, about how I was officially sixteen now, and would be out on my own before long. And then I got thinking about the hair I have growing out of my armpits and growing someplace else that you're not supposed to think about too much for fear of either turning into a moron or getting slain by God. This is what I heard anyway in the senior boys Sunday school class from Mr. Lamb, our Sunday school teacher. He preached a sermon to us about somebody in the Bible who spilled his seed on the ground, and God slew him for it. I remember how all the boys started looking out of the corners of their eyes at each other, and Mr. Lamb said, "I know what you're thinking, you boys: that each of you has managed to escape the Wrath of God, so far, but don't be too sure of yourselves. The Worst Is Yet to Come. Every time you have impure thoughts, if God does not slay you outright, He has other ways of Meting out Punishment. You will lose Brain Fluid. That's right boys, Brain Fluid." He told us that every time we waste our seed, we lose a portion of our brain fluid, and the more of it that escapes, the stupider we'll become until we turn into morons, unable to do the simplest sums or spell words like "cat." After this sermon, as soon as anyone did anything stupid, all the senior boys started laughing and pointing at the chap and saying, "What a moron!"

Usually me, unfortunately.

I hate thinking about morons so I crawled out over Harold, who tried to kick me in the ribs, but I was too fast for him. The other boys got up, finally, and we struggled into our clothes, all cold and clammy from the heavy dew during the night.

I got a fire going and we huddled over it, shivering while we waited for our porridge to cook and our eggs to boil. We were in plenty of time. The yacht had the steam up and the barge in place by 5:15, and we were soon underway. We sat in the engine room to keep warm until the sun got up, and asked a lot of questions about the operation of the engine.

If I had a boat like this, with sleeping quarters and a cooking galley, I'd explore all the bays and shoreline. I would search out every shoal and wedge permanent markers into them, so that people would know about the dangers ahead and could avoid them.

I went out to stand on the deck and watch the wildlife. A blue heron, frightened from his fishing spot, spread his ungainly wings and flapped away, with his legs behind him like bent sticks. "Grack! Rackafrack!" he swore at us. In the distance, gray ghosts of trees haunted the drowned lands until the sun, higher now, warmer, brushed them a honey color, bringing them to life just for the moment.

Ernie joined me and the two of us watched the passing scene. We saw a roof washed up against a ridge of land that reared up from the swamp like a dead body. "We should build ourselves a raft and go ex-ex-ex-exploring," I said. A raft would be better than risking damage to the bottom of one of Grandpa's boats.

Harold had come out and was leaning over the railing beside us. "What would we build it out of?"

"Logs," Ernie said, "and planks. There's lots of lumber at the carriage works."

"Unc-Unc-Uncle Will would never part with it. It's new stuff," I said.

Harold said, "Let's take it from that place up across from Rideau Ferry."

"What place?"

"You know, Oliver's place, that the men were talking about. It's going to be sold."

Ernie and I both looked doubtful.

"Why not?" Harold said. "Who would care? It'll probably just get torn down anyway, once it's sold." Neither Ernie nor I said anything. Harold looked right into our eyes. "You don't really believe it's haunted, do you?"

"No," I said.

"No," Ernie said.

"Then ...?"

"Harold, you can't just wal-wal-waltz across the lake and take s-s-s-someone else's property."

"It's an abandoned old shack. No one will care."

Ernie shrugged. I could see him starting to warm to the raft idea. Harold said, "We'll build a huge raft with sides on it and chairs, and take people for tours of the drowned lands and charge them a fare."

"No, wait," Ernie said, "we could build a lean-to on it and live on it. Go where the breeze takes us."

"Why-why-why don't we ask the owner's permission in-in-in case he objects?"

Harold gave me the kind of look you'd give Bessie if she asked a stupid question, although she usually never does. He said, "If you ask, they'll say no. If you just go ahead and do it, no one will be any the wiser. It's the way of the world, Freddie."

I know what Harold thinks: that I never take a risk, never make a move without a plan. But if I don't plan, I end up looking like a moron. I wish I could get a map made of my whole life. Then all I'd have to do is follow it.

By the time we got to Perth, Harold and Ernie had built a raft the size of a Spanish galleon, and I just kept nodding and saying things like, "Don't forget lace curtains on the windows," and "Maybe we should build runners in case the lake freezes over," and they said, "Nobody likes a wiseacre, Freddie."

The *Jopl* tied up in the canal basin in the center of town behind a lot of stores, with their fronts facing Gore Street and their backs facing the water. We helped unload the cheese boxes from the barge onto a wagon, and then set out to walk the short distance to Grandma's house. She and Auntie Ede were clearing up the breakfast dishes, and Uncle Will had already gone to work when we got there.

Grandma insisted on giving us a second breakfast, which we didn't turn down.

We were scraping the last smear of egg yolk and the last crumb of toast down our gullets when the postman arrived. "Looks like a letter from your father," Grandma said, handing it to me. I placed it on the table, dreading its contents. *Frederick must pack up immediately,* it would say. *Summer is over forever. You've got a man-sized job in the city. I'm proud of you.*

"Well, open it!" Ernie said. Instead I shoved it along to him and then leaned over his shoulder as he read out loud, "I hope you are all behaving in a mannerly fashion and not causing your relatives any undue anxiety." We looked at Grandma, whose expression seemed calm enough, so Ernie read on: "I have been thinking of paying a visit to that part of the country so you will not be surprised if I appear on your grandfather's doorstep. I have been developing an interesting plan, which I will explain when I get there, although that may not be for a fortnight as my assistant in the store is holidaying at the moment. In the meantime, Bessie is not to tease, Tom is not to be rough, and Ernie is to be helpful." He saved the last paragraph for me. "I hope Frederick is taking advantage of the outdoor life to build his character and to strengthen his nerves. I expect to see great changes in him."

Ernie still had the letter. "Interesting plan!" he said. "He might at least have given us more information." I took it from him and read it again myself to see if the "interesting plan" could in any way involve my lack of character and weak nerves.

Grandma said, "I think he misses you and doesn't want to admit it."

There was nothing in that letter to indicate that he missed us, and I thought I should set her straight. "He-he-he wants to ch-ch-check on the state of my nerves with a surprise visit."

"There's nothing wrong with your nerves."

I glanced away from her. Grandma is fairly smart, I guess, but she always seems to miss the main point.

"You'll just have to surprise *him*, won't you?"

I shook my head. She believes things are simpler than they are. I sometimes wonder how she managed to raise all her children and not learn anything about human nature in the process. Nothing I could do could possibly surprise my father.

After breakfast we went along the street to the carriage works and poked around the shop looking for old bits of wood to scavenge until Uncle Will kicked us out. Before we left, I managed to have a word with him. "Wh-wh-when will you teach me to drive the *Bessie*, Uncle W-W-W- . . . ?"

"One of these days," he said, "when the time is ripe." This is his usual line. I guess I looked disappointed because he shook his head at me. "You kids, you want everything immediately. Well, listen, you have all summer ahead of you, all your childhood ahead of you, all your long life ahead of you."

So he thinks. I sometimes wonder if he was ever a boy himself. Maybe Grandpa put him to work at the age of three, and he's been forced to be a man ever since.

We walked back to Grandma's, who collared us to do a few errands for her. Walking the sun-filled streets, we breathed in the civilized smell of freshly cut grass, and felt lonesome for the zesty pines and the fishy shore and the smell of the lake evaporating on our arms and backs. We bought some postcards for Tom and Bessie and wandered around town feeling like tourists, watching the men steam drilling and blasting for the new sewerage pipes until it was time to go back to the basin. The *Jopl* had its steam up by the time we arrived, our arms filled with supplies from Grandma: fresh bread for all and a sticky bun just for us campers.

It was mid-afternoon by the time we got back to the upper locks. There were several boats ahead of us. "Ain't in a rush, I hope, for it'll take a while," a man rowing a large skiff called up to the pilot of the *Jopl*. "There's some kind of fuss down at the lower lock."

"Let's go see," Ernie said. We jumped ashore, thanked the captain for our ride, and pitched our supplies under a tree. We ran down to the lower lock where Mr. Buchanan, the lockmaster, had locked in a small rowboat operated by a white-haired old man crouched over his oars. The sluice gates were open; the water was rising. It swirled and eddied, pushing the boat this way and that. Up on the walk rail, Mr. Buchanan called down through a megaphone: "Grab the chain! Hold on to the chain!" But the man didn't seem to see the chains hanging down the stone wall, placed there to steady the boats. He didn't seem to know he was in a lock at all because he kept trying to use the oars, crashing time and again into the high stone walls, nearly capsizing.

We could hear the old man yelling something like, "Get away from me! I'm warning you! Help!" He let go of the oars to shield his head as if he were being attacked. Then he loosened one and brought it down with a crack on the side of the boat. "There!" he yelled. "There's an end of it!" He became calmer then and sat with his face in his hands.

At that moment a younger man appeared on the lock wall. "Grandfather!" he called down, but the old man ignored him, or didn't hear him, and began thrashing about with his oar again, hitting at something or someone unseen.

Mr. Buchanan called across to the younger man, "I'm taking him back down again." To us he called, "Some of you lads come over here to the other side in case he drifts over."

We were not very eager to have our heads whacked by an oar, but we did as we were told and ran across the walk rail. Mr. Buchanan soon had the lock water back down to the level of the lake and, as he opened the gates, the old man seemed to get his wits back. He rowed himself out and brought his boat alongside the wharf opposite us on the other side of the channel, where his grandson grabbed the bow. "He gets confused sometimes," the younger man called up to Mr. Buchanan by way of explanation. "He has delusions. He's all right, now." We all stared at the younger man knowing we'd seen him before, but where, we didn't know. We stayed around long enough to see the young man help the old one into a boat something like the *Bessie* and tow the older man's boat up the lake toward Rideau Ferry.

"Poor old fella," Mr. Buchanan said. "Daft as a loon."

. . .

After supper Beaver Camp held another campfire on the point down near our tent. Tom was not put out about our trip to Perth aboard the steam yacht as he doesn't like getting up early anyhow. We sang for a while. Auntie Lizzie said I have the most musical voice of all the boys. I guess I like to sing because it's the only time I can be sure of getting the words out right.

Ettie and Auntie Min didn't come down because they're in a row over Ettie's friend Mr. McAlpine. Auntie Min thinks he's too old to be forcing his attentions on Ettie, and Ettie says she would be delighted not to have someone minding her business for her constantly. Auntie Lizzie mutters things under her breath like "Moses 'n' Aaron" or "Heaven help us."

Grandpa said he would join us if someone would be kind enough to carry a chair down for him. So we had quite a little crowd, anyway, for our entertainment. Bessie started clamoring for him to tell a ghost story, and Grandpa said he didn't know any. Bessie kept insisting he did so. "Well," he said at last, "the nearest thing I can think of would be the dark and dirty deeds of old John Oliver." We older boys groaned because we'd already heard all that bogeyman stuff.

Tom told us to shut our traps and begged Grandpa to tell it anyway. "And make it the worst story you know," Bessie chimed in, and Grandpa was soon rubbing his hands together, ready to curdle our blood with tall tales.

"Now, don't you dare scare them, Father," Auntie Lizzie broke in. "These smaller ones won't sleep a wink."

"Oh, well, perhaps you're right," Grandpa nodded. He sat there with his arms crossed and his lips shut tight, looking off into the distance as if he had the satisfaction of knowing something gruesome, which we poor suckers would never find out.

"What kind of dirty deeds, exactly?" Bessie asked. She was encouraging a furry caterpillar to walk along a stick, prodding it every so often with her finger. Cross-legged beside her, Tom leaned over his knees and urged, "Come on, Grandpa! Tell!"

"How about some popcorn?" Auntie Lizzie said to change the subject. She had an old fire-blackened saucepan, with a lid and a long handle. She knelt down near the circle of stones surrounding the fire and set it right onto the coals.

Harold said, "Tell the story after Tom and Bessie go to bed. We campers can take anything."

"No fair," Tom said. "We can take anything, too, except for Bessie. Bessie had better go to bed." I waited for Bessie to give him a thump, but she was too busy with her caterpillar.

The corn began to erupt like fifty guns, and after a moment, Auntie Lizzie pulled it away from the heat with a pot holder. Soon we were digging our paws into it and cramming it into our mouths. Bessie put some in her skirt, which formed a little dip, so that she could eat the pieces one by one. Beside her, Tom twitched and shook his shoulders and tried to reach his back to scratch it. We knew we were going to get a story, sooner or later. Whether truth or fiction depended on Grandpa's imagination. So between mouthfuls, we encouraged him to make it a good one and not hold anything back.

"Well," he said, starting off mildly, "I'll tell you this much. People say Oliver was a murderer, but he was never caught and the bodies were never found."

Tom leapt up at this announcement, dancing up and down, reaching down his back, pulling at his shirt.

"Mercy!" Auntie Lizzie said, pulling him away from the fire. "You've given the lad the fits!" The rest of us ignored him, and pretty soon the caterpillar fell out.

"Who did Oliver murder?" Harold asked. "And why didn't they catch him? And when did it happen?"

"How did they know it was Oliver?" Ernie asked.

I said, "How-how-how do they know there was a murder if they didn't find a body?" Grandpa was going to have to come up with some fancy storytelling to keep us sharpshooters interested.

He sat there pulling on his whiskers, his eyes roving over us, back and forth, reveling in our curiosity and our skepticism. It was obviously too much for him. In spite of Auntie Lizzie's protests, he leaned forward over his stick and said in a loud whisper to Tom, "Old John Oliver was the wickedest man ever to live in the county of Lanark." Tom shrank back but sat board straight, glued to Grandpa's every word. "Dead these many years, he is, but his infamy lives after him. A bogeyman if ever there was one."

I glanced around the campfire. The rest of us were sitting hunched over our knees, eyes bright. Tom and Bessie were hardly breathing, hardly daring to crunch down on the popcorn, not wanting to miss any part of the grisly tale. Ernie and Harold caught my glance and leaned back on their elbows, grinning sheepishly.

"Back in the days of the early settlers, back before the Rideau Canal was even built," Grandpa began, "there was only one route overland for people on foot or horseback from the St. Lawrence River to the town of Perth, and that was through bush so dense and dark and ahowl with wolves you'd swear it was the gates of hell, and wish it was, 'cause you'd know at least where you'd got to. And swampland so thick with mosquitoes and black snakes and all manner of slithering creatures that if you were a traveler, you'd wish you could lie down and die and get it over with. And if you ever found your way out to the banks of the Rideau, wild with the heat and the bug bites and the fear of having the flesh torn right off your bones, the first thing you'd see was the devil incarnate in the person of old John Oliver, standing with his back to his ferryboat and his hands on his hips, just awaitin'.

"And, oh, he was a sight indeed! A mean-lookin' beast of a no-neck man, his eyes raw and red, and scarcely a tooth in his slavering mouth. And if it was broad daylight, and after he'd seen your money, he'd set about with the help of his son—a younger version of himself—and together they'd get you and your horse and cart onto a raft the size of a barge. And together they'd ply oars made from the trunks of trees, one either side of the ferryboat, till at last you'd reached the other shore and could skee-daddle as fast as you could out of his sight. And that's the best that could be said.

"And the Rideau was not a lake to be sneezed at, either. Once the wind was up, tossing the waves as high as your head, you'd think twice before attempting a swim across to avoid the ferryman. No, sir, you were for it. It was the ferry or nothing.

" 'Ferryman,' you'd say, 'what will you charge to take me across?' And if it was after the sun'd gone down, he'd answer, 'There's no coin big enough to tempt me out on the water after dark.' And you'd say, 'I've half a crown with your name on it if only you'll ferry me and my goods across the lake, for it may be late, but there's a full moon.'

" 'You must bide with me this night,' he'd say. 'The wife, there, likes a bit of company and she's cooked up a fine pot of vittles. You'll get a soft bed and an early start in the morning.'

"And if you were smart," Grandpa said, "you'd hie yourself out of that place as fast as your legs would carry you and take your chances with the wolves until dawn, for if you were weary and yielded to the ferryman's invitation, you'd never again see the light of day."

"Why not?" Bessie said. She had wriggled herself a little closer to Grandpa and was staring up at him.

Grandpa paused to light his pipe. At last he said in a loud whisper, bending over Bessie, "He liked the taste of blood, so they say."

"Now that's enough, Father," Auntie Lizzie said. Bessie sat back, huddling close to Tom.

Grandpa's whisper grew deeper. "He liked to skewer a man with an icepick and watch him squirm."

"Father!"

"And his missus, sure she'd slit a man from stem to gudgeon and rip out his innards to cook up for the next unsuspecting traveler."

"That's it! Bessie! Tom! Off to bed with you!" Auntie Lizzie was on her feet. She had Bessie by the arm and Tom by the collar of his shirt, but neither one was cooperating.

"I'd fight back," Tom said, wriggling free. "I'd grab the icepick and jab it into him, so I would." He happened to be standing beside me and pounded an invisible icepick into my shoulder. "Then I'd run out the door and swim across the lake."

"You wouldn't be strong enough," said Bessie, ducking under Auntie Lizzie's arm. "Besides, you can't swim."

"Can so."

"Cannot. Don't lie." She crouched at Grandpa's knee again. "What I'd do," she said, "is I'd trick him. I'd tell him someone was at the door, and as soon as he opened it, I'd run out and hide in a tree."

"What if he tied you up first?" Tom asked her. He'd found a length of string in his pocket and was winding it around his fingers to start a ball.

"Cut it out, you kids." This was Ernie. "What I want to know is, how do you know all this, Grandpa?"

"Very good question," Auntie Lizzie said. "Your grandfather likes nothing better than to take some bit of gossip, true or not, embellish it beyond all recognition, and then spew it out for the benefit of your young ears. Remember, first and foremost, he's a storyteller. Take heed."

"Oh, I'm not making it up. People knew, all right. They passed on stories from father to son and so on. Sure they say you could hear the screams clear across the lake. But people 'round here were scared of him. If you asked questions, chances were good that you'd end up in the stew pot yourself. I think there was an investigation at one time, but the local constabulary didn't turn up a thing."

Auntie Lizzie broke in: "Do you see my point?"

Grandpa pursed his lips, nodding at his daughter. "Well, I'm telling you the truth. If somebody's relative went missing, by the time they rounded up enough brave souls to get up a search posse, no track nor trail was left of the person. Gone. Vanished.

"And Oliver, there, he and his family always had the best that money could buy. The son rode a fine horse, and the missus had gold bangles and baubles like she was wife to a duke, more than what could ever come of a ferryman's pittance. And whether there were other offspring, I don't know. They'd have disappeared long before now, for no man alive would admit to being the son of old John Oliver. Even to this day people hereabouts look askance at strangers and wonder, *Now who would that fella's father be do you s'pose?*"

I asked. "But what-what-what happened to Oliver?"

"Murdered," Grandpa said. Our mouths all hung slack. That part we hadn't known.

"And his son?"

"Murdered, the two of them. They disappeared, at any rate. The wife, they say, died of natural causes. And not till then did travelers and local homesteaders dare to breathe the word 'safe.' "

I said, "Ol-Ol-Oliver's place is for sale." Harold nudged me with his foot and both he and Ernie stared at me, giving me the evil eye, willing me not to reveal their plan of liberating the lumber from Oliver's shack.

"Is it?" Grandpa said. "Been abandoned for years, of course. The house should be torn down before it falls on someone, not that anyone goes near the place. Some long-lost relative selling it, no doubt. Good luck to them. It's a blot on the landscape."

"Bessie and Tom!" Auntie Lizzie said in the lull while we contemplated the past. "It's long past your bedtime." Tom scrambled up without much fuss, but when Bessie was at last hauled to her feet, we heard the sound of cotton ripping, and Bessie let out a screech loud enough to make the entire Oliver family sit up in their graves. Tom had tied the skirt of her dress to the bush behind her. He took a running start toward the cottage with Bessie in her petticoat hot on his heels. Auntie Lizzie said something under her breath, bunched up the remains of the skirt, broke the string, and lumbered off after them. "You kids are the absolute limit," we heard her say. "Wouldn't I just like to tan your hides!"

A Mountain Legend

by
Jordan Wheeler

This is another summer outing, but it is also a trip back into mythical time. A vision quest is a powerful thing, an important journey in a boy's life: he sets out as a child and comes home a man, a warrior. That is, if he comes home at all. In Jordan Wheeler's compelling tale, we learn of a legendary Indian lad, Muskawashee, who didn't make it, and of Jason, a city boy, with little sense of his Indian heritage, who decides at the risk of life and limb that he must take up where Muskawashee left off so long ago. The author himself was just out of his teens when he wrote this gripping story. It is collected in Maria Campbell's wonderful anthology, achimoona, *which is Cree for "stories."*

The school bus drove into a small summer camp at the base of a towering mountain. Boys and girls between the ages of eight and twelve, who had signed up for the three-day camping trip, poured out of the bus. Following instructions from counsellors, they began hurriedly preparing their camp as the sunset dripped over the rock walls towering above them. For many, it was their first time away from the city, which they could still see far off in the distance. Tents were put up and sleeping bags unrolled before the last of the twilight rays gave way to the darkness of night.

Roasting marshmallows around a large campfire, the young campers listened intently to stories told by the counsellors. Behind the eager campers, the caretaker of the camp sat on the ground, himself listening to the stories.

As the night grew old, the younger children wearily found their way to their tents, so that by midnight only the twelve-year-olds remained around the fire with one counsellor and the caretaker. Their supply of stories seemingly exhausted, they sat in silence watching the glowing embers of the once fiery blaze shrink into red-hot ash.

"The moon is rising," announced the caretaker in a low, even voice.

All eyes looked up to the glow surrounding the jagged peaks of the mountain. The blackness of the rock formed an eerie silhouette against the gently lit sky.

The caretaker's name was McNabb. He had lived close to the mountain all his life and knew many of the stories the mountain had seen. He threw his long, black braided hair over his shoulders, drew the collar of his faded jean jacket up against the crisp mountain air, and spoke.

"There is a legend about this mountain once told by the mountain itself," he said, paused for a moment, then continued. "People claim that long ago it told of a young boy who tried to climb up to an eagle's nest, which rested somewhere among the many cliffs. He was from a small camp about a day's journey from here and when he was twelve years old, he thought he was ready to become a warrior. His father disagreed, saying he was too young and too small. But the boy was stubborn and one morning before dawn he sneaked out of his family's teepee and set off on foot toward the mountain. There were no horses in North America in his time. They were brought later by the Europeans.

"It took most of the day for him to reach the mountain. The next morning, he set out to find an eagle and seek a vision from the mighty bird, as that was the first step in becoming a warrior. But as he was climbing up the rock cliffs to a nest, he fell to his death, releasing a terrible cry that echoed from the mountain far out across the land. The legend says the boy's spirit still wanders the mountain today."

A coyote howled in the distance, and the campers jumped.

"Is it true?" asked one of the boys, with worry and fear in his voice.

"Some people say so, and they also say you can still hear his scream every once in a while."

All around the dying fire, eyes were straining up at the menacing rock peaks. The caretaker, McNabb, however, wasn't looking at the mountain, he was watching one of the young campers. He was an Indian boy, smaller than the others, with short braided hair that fell down his back. The boy was gazing up at the mountain, his curiosity obviously blended with fear. Turning his head, his eyes met those of McNabb. For a fleeting moment, they locked stares, then McNabb relaxed, a knowing expression spreading over his face, while the boy continued to stare at him, wide-eyed and nervous.

There were small discussions around the fire, debating the story's truth before the counsellor told them it was time for sleep. Both tired and excited, they retreated to their tent and crawled into their sleeping bags.

The boy Jason lay in a tent he shared with two other boys, who lay talking in the dark. As Jason waited for the heat of his body to warm his sleeping bag, he thought of that long ago boy. He felt a closeness to him and imagined himself in his place.

"Hey, Jason, why don't you climb up that mountain tomorrow morning and try to catch an eagle?" It was Ralph, who was against the far wall of the tent on the other side of Barry.

"Why?" asked Jason.

"You're Indian aren't you? Don't you want to become a warrior?"

True, Jason was Indian, but he knew nothing of becoming a warrior. He had spent all his life in the city. All he knew of his heritage was what his grandmother told him from time to time, which wasn't much. He had been to three pow wows in his life, all at a large hall not far from his house, but he never learned very much. His time was spent eating hot dogs, drinking pop, and watching the older boys play pool in the adjoining rooms. Little as he knew, though, he wanted Ralph and Barry to think he knew a lot.

"No. It's not time for me to be a warrior yet," he told them.

"Why not?" Barry asked.

"It just isn't, that's all," Jason said, not knowing a better answer.

"You're chicken. You couldn't climb that mountain if you tried," Ralph charged.

"I'm not chicken! I could climb that mountain, no problem. It just isn't time yet."

"You're chicken," Ralph said again.

"Go to sleep!" boomed a voice across the campground.

Ralph gave out three chicken clucks and rolled over to sleep.

Jason lay there in mild anger. He hated being called a chicken and if the counsellor hadn't shouted at that moment, he would have given Ralph a swift punch. But Ralph was right. The mountain did scare him.

With his anger subsiding, he drifted into a haunting sleep, filled with dreams. Dreams the wind swept through the camp, gently spreading the mountain spirit's stories throughout. A coyote's piercing howl echoed down the rocky cliffs, making Jason flinch in his sleep.

The following morning, Ralph, Barry, and Jason were the first ones up. As they emerged from the tent into the chilled morning air, their attention was immediately grasped by the huge rock peaks looming high above. Ralph's searching eyes spanned the mountain. A light blanket of mist enveloped its lower reaches.

Pointing up he said, "See that ledge up there?" Jason and Barry followed Ralph's arm to a cliff along one of the rock walls just above the tree line. "I bet you can't get to it," he dared Jason.

"I could so," Jason responded.

"Prove it," Ralph said.

Jason was trapped and he knew it. If he said no, he would be admitting he was scared. And there was another challenge in Ralph's voice, unsaid, but Jason heard it. Ralph was daring him to prove himself an Indian. Jason had lived his whole life in a city on cement ground and among concrete mountains where climbing was as easy as walking up stairs or pressing an elevator button. To prove to Ralph and himself that he was Indian, Jason had to climb to that ledge. He knew that mountain climbing could end a life. And there were wild animals he might have to deal with. How was he supposed to react? How would he react? He was afraid. He didn't want to go. But if he didn't?

"What's the matter?" Ralph taunted. "Indian scared?"

At that point, Jason decided he would face the mountain and he would reach that ledge. "Okay," he conceded.

At first, the climbing was easy, but his progress became slow and clumsy as he got higher up. Struggling over uneven ground and through trees, he came across a large flat rock. In need of a rest, he sat down and looked down at the campground he had left right after breakfast an hour ago. He could see bodies scurrying about. If they hadn't noticed by now that he was missing, he thought, no doubt they would soon.

Looking up, he could just see the ledge above the tree line. It wasn't much farther, he thought. He could get to it, wave down at the camp to show he had made it, and be back in time for lunch. Raising himself up, he started to climb again, marching through the trees and up the steep slope, over the rough terrain.

A few moments later he heard a loud howl that seemed to come from somewhere above. At first, he thought it was a coyote, but it sounded more like a human. Nervously, he kept going.

In the camp, Ralph and Barry were getting ready to help prepare lunch. McNabb was starting a fire not far away. They, too, heard the howl.

"I never knew coyotes did that during the day," Ralph said to Barry.

Overhearing them, McNabb responded, "That was no coyote."

Half an hour later, Jason stood just above the tree line. The ledge, his goal, was thirty feet above, but what lay ahead was treacherous climbing, nearly straight up the rock wall. He scrutinized the rock face, planned his route, and began to pick his way up the last stretch.

The mountain saw the boy encroaching and whispered a warning to the wind sweeping strongly down its face as it remembered a similar event long ago. Jason felt the wind grow stronger, driving high-pitched sound into his ears. Gripping the rock harder, he pulled himself up a bit at a time. The wind seemed to be pushing him back. But he felt something else, too, something urging him on.

When he was about twenty feet up the rock face, with his feet firmly on a small ledge, he chanced a look down between his legs. He could see that if he slipped, he would plummet straight down for that twenty feet and after hitting the rocks below, he would tumble a great distance farther. He knew it would spell death, and for a split second, he considered going back down. But once again he felt an outside force pushing him to go on. It gave him comfort and courage. His face reddened, his heart pounded, and beads of sweat poured from him as he inched his way higher. Straight above, an eagle flew in great circles, slowly moving closer to Jason and the ledge.

Far down the mountain the search for Jason was well underway, but the counsellors had no way of knowing where he was, as Ralph and Barry hadn't told. McNabb also knew where Jason was, but he, too, remained silent.

An eight-year-old girl in the camp lay quietly in her tent, staring up through the screen window at the sky. The search for Jason had been tiring and she had come back for a rest. She was watching a cloud slowly change shape when a large black bird flew by high above. Out of curiosity, she unzipped the tent door and went outside to get a better look. She watched the bird fly in smaller and smaller circles, getting closer and closer to the mountain. She took her eyes off the bird for a moment to look at the huge rock wall, and there, high above the trees and only a few feet below a ledge, she saw the boy climbing. Right away she knew the boy was in danger. After hesitating for a moment, she ran to tell a counsellor.

Jason paused from climbing, just a few feet below the ledge. He was exhausted and the insides of his hands were raw, the skin having been scraped off by the rough rock. The ledge was so close. He pulled himself up to it, placing his feet inside a crack in the rock for support. Reaching over the edge, he swept one arm along the ledge, found another spot for his feet, hoisted his body up, rolled onto the ledge, and got to his feet. There, an arm's length away on the ledge, were two young eagles in a large nest. For several minutes he just remained there looking at the baby eagles. He had never seen an eagle's nest before. He was so interested in the two young eagles he didn't notice the mother eagle circling high overhead, nor did he hear her swoop down towards him and her nest. She landed in front of him, spread her wings, and let out a loud screech. Jason was so terrified, he instinctively jumped and in doing so, lost his balance. Both feet stepped out into air as he grabbed the rock.

His hands clung desperately to the ledge as the sharp rock dug into his skin. He looked down and saw his feet dangling in the air. The wind swung him, making it impossible to get his feet back on the rock where they had been moments earlier. A coyote howled and Jason's terror grew. Again he looked down at the rocks below. Tears began streaming down his face. He didn't want to die. He wished he had never accepted Ralph's dare. He could picture them coming up the mountain, finding his dead body among the rocks, and crying over him. He began crying out loud and heard it echoing off the rock. Or he thought it was an echo. He stopped and listened. There was more crying, but not from him. Again he felt the presence of something or someone else. The wind swirled in and whispered to Jason the mountain's legend.

Though running swiftly, the boy Muskawashee had paced himself expertly for the day's journey. He would arrive at the base of the mountain far earlier than he had expected and would have plenty of daylight left to catch his supper and find a spot for a good night's sleep. Though small and having seen only twelve summers, his young body was strong. He would be able to reach the mountain in only two runs, pausing in between to catch a rabbit for lunch.

As his powerful legs moved him gracefully across the prairie, he thought back to the conversation with his father the day before. He had explained how most of his friends were already in preparation for manhood and he felt he was ready also. He did not want to wait for the next summer.

When some of his friends came back later that day from a successful buffalo hunt, he decided he would go to the mountain alone and seek a vision from the eagle.

He knew he would have to rise before the sun to get out of camp without being seen.

When he reached the base of the mountain, the sun was still well above the horizon. He sat down in a sheltered area for a rest. He decided this was where he would sleep for the night.

After a few minutes, he got up and made himself a trap for a rabbit and planted it. After laying the trap, he wandered off to look for some berries to eat while preparing his mind for the following day when he would climb the mountain. After some time, he returned to his trap and found a rabbit in it. He skinned it with a well-sharpened stone knife he had brought with him, and built a fire to cook his meal. He would keep the fire burning all night to keep away the wild animals while he slept.

Finishing his meal, he thanked the creator for his food and safe journey and prayed for good fortune in his quest for a vision. Then he lay down in the soft moss and fell asleep to the music of the coyote's howls and the whispering wind.

The next morning, he awoke to the sun's warming shine. The still-smouldering fire added an aroma of burnt wood to the fresh air. He again prayed to the creator for good fortune in his quest for a vision and for a safe journey up the mountain. When he finished, he looked up, high above, and saw eagles flying to and from a rock ledge. This would be his goal.

Half an hour later, he stood where the trees stopped growing and the bare rock began. His powerful body had moved steadily through the trees even though he wasn't used to uphill running. Without resting, he continued his climb, knowing he would have to be careful ahead. The mountain could be dangerous and its spirit could be evil.

As he pulled himself up the face of the rock, he heard the mountain spirit warning him to stay away. Its voice was the whispering wind, which grew stronger and seemed to be trying to push him back. With determination, Muskawashee climbed. High above, the powerful eagle circled its nest.

Just five feet below the ledge, Muskawashee paused. He was dripping with perspiration from fighting the wind and the mountain. Though scared, he would not let fear overcome him. His desire for manhood was stronger. His hands were hurting and covered in blood from the climb, but he reached out again. After several scrabbling attempts, he was able to grab hold of the ledge and pull himself up onto the narrow, flat edge. Eye to eye with two baby eagles, he stopped. He felt great pride and relief in having reached his goal and stood there savouring those feelings. He didn't hear the approach of the mother eagle. As she landed on the ledge in front of him, she let out a loud screech and spread her wings wide. Muskawashee was startled, stepped back and lost his footing. A gust of wind shoved him farther and he could feel his body in the air as he tried to get a foot back on the rock. He grabbed the edge, but his arms were trembling and he could not pull himself back up. His fingers ached and began slipping from the edge. Knowing he would soon fall, he began whimpering. He looked up, into the eyes of the eagle. One day, he thought to himself, he would be back.

His fingers let go and he fell, releasing a loud, terrifying scream that echoed from the mountain, far out across the land, and down through time.

McNabb and one of the counsellors left the camp when the eight-year-old girl told them what she had seen. Both experienced hikers and mountain-climbers, they were able to cover the distance in a third of the time it took Jason. When they heard the scream, they quickened their pace. Minutes later, they reached the edge of the tree line and looked up at the ledge.

Jason, who had been hanging there for several minutes, also heard the scream and looked down into the eyes of Muskawashee as he fell. Jason felt the tension in his fingers, but sensed there were greater forces keeping him hanging there, perhaps the mountain itself was hanging on to him. Whatever it was, Jason remained high above McNabb and the counsellor, who were watching from the tree line. The wind died down and the eagle stepped back, making room for him on the ledge. Jason hoisted a foot back onto the ledge and tried again to haul himself onto the shelf.

Suddenly, he saw Muskawashee standing on the ledge, extending a hand down to him. Jason grabbed his hand and Muskawashee pulled. The two boys faced one another, looking into each other's eyes. The descendent gaining pride in being Indian, and the ancestor completing the quest he had begun hundreds of years earlier. A powerful swirl of wind swept Muskawashee away, leaving Jason alone before the eagle's nest. Jason reached down and picked up a feather out of the nest.

Below him stood the counsellor and McNabb. They had witnessed Jason's rescue.

"Who was that other kid up there?" asked the counsellor in disbelief.

McNabb smiled and answered. "Muskawashee. He will wander this mountain no more." Then, unravelling a long line of heavy rope he said, "Come on, let's get Jason down."

Spin Master

by
Sheldon Oberman

*When I was a kid, I loved fishing. Happily, I have recently
rediscovered the joy of fishing. I would like to say that I'm
happy just to be up and outside sitting by the lake on a beautiful summer morning, but that wouldn't be entirely true.
I still hope, every time, I'm going to catch* THE BIG ONE.
*Sheldon Oberman does, and it's a lot more fish than he bar-
gained for. In this dynamite story, Daniel, the scrawny protagonist, ends up catching a whopper and nearly losing his
life in the process. Apart from this story's surprising turn of
events, I love the word-pictures Sheldon paints, the images. I
can't resist saying it: when it comes to telling a story, he certainly is a spin master.*

No brakes. That's the way to do it, I told the country road that blurred beneath my feet.

I spread my legs, feet free of pedals, and let my five-speed glide. This time I'd show them all, especially my father.

I rumbled down the dawn-grey hill, gravel tearing at my tires. I felt older than eleven. And not skinny at all. Or short. Or anything like a loser.

Not while I had my father's fishing rod—aimed like a lance at the wooden bridge, my bridge, where I'd biked with just a hook and line every August morning, rising early enough to miss my uncle and aunt grumbling awake on the other side of the panelboard partition, and to miss my mother fussing over the cottage stove, burning porridge that my cousins would poke and my father would drown in cream, mixing it into a sweet soup; this day I'd risen in darkness, dressed in shadows, a shadow myself, sifting cereal into a bowl already filled with milk, muffling the falling flakes, hushing shut the fridge door, the cabinet door, the screen door so I'd be gone before even my mother woke, my mother who said she couldn't sleep because of "nerves," who clip-clopped onto the porch in frayed pink slippers sighing, "Daniel! Are you going out again? I don't know what you're doing anymore."

My uncle's summer cottage was worse than home; I had to share everything with my cousins, which simply meant giving in, giving up, and constantly apologizing because everyone was so cranky and so cramped. I got so jumpy that I made even more mistakes: I tore the screen, bent the lawnmower blade, moved the candle to where it set the curtain into flames so that my aunt would chime at every chance, "It's a good thing your Uncle Steve was there to stamp it out. We could have all been burned alive!" And my uncle would grunt back, "We have to watch that kid every minute of the day. He doesn't have a clue." While my mother looked to my father for some kind of answer and my father stared darkly over rows of cottage roofs.

It was better to bike away, past sleeping lawns and curtained windows. Only this time I had the Bradley Spin Master, the fishing rod that I gave my father for his birthday, bought with my own money from my own bank account.

"What do I know about fishing?" I later heard him ask my mother. "No one gets in shape by fishing and wishing and sitting in some boat."

Still, I'd pressed him into bringing it with us to the cottage. He warned me, "I'll pack it, Danny, but you're responsible for it." Wasn't that almost saying I could use it at the bridge?

I was sure the rod would do it. I had practised behind my parents' store with old Mr. Werner, casting for pages of his *Jewish Post*. Kitefish, we called them as they fluttered in the wind, hooked and struggling to escape into the clouds.

The Spin Master was far better than my hand-held hook and line that only pulled in sour catfish. Or sauger. Or toss-away perch. The Spin Master would catch a fighting fish so huge, that would be so heavy I would have to grip with both my hands to haul it waist-high through the cottage doorway shouting, "Here's supper, Dad! I got the Big One!" as my father, uncle, cousins, the whole lot would jump to their feet, astounded.

"No brakes, no brakes," I whispered, the bike shaking out my words, vowing to the hill, the road, the tires—let hill, road, tires decide; my feet will fly, or break on stones, but they wouldn't touch the pedals. Not till I was there.

And just before grace and courage failed, the merciful hill levelled out, steadying my heart, and carried me onto the rumbling planks.

A single clap applauded from the river—the sound of a broaching fish, ten yards out.

"The next one belongs to me. I swear it."

I tested the rod in the air. It was strong, alive and eager in the rising sun. I gripped it between my thighs and tied on a red devil lure. The rod swayed, tip trembling in the air, divining for the Big One.

Another splash, rings widening from its bull's eye centre. The rod couldn't wait. I cast the line. Reel whined, lure sang through sky toward the rings on water that were broadening in a welcome.

But the reel seized, clogged. The lure jerked and faltered. I choked a cry as it spiralled, dead into the water.

The spool had become a snarl. I tucked the handle under my arm and worried at the line with both hands feeding it out until it hung in a loose tangle at my knees. The more I tried to separate the loops, the more it clenched into a mass of knots.

I felt a familiar scurrying in my chest, a draining in my limbs that told me this day was already ruined like so many others and I would not free the line, and if I did, I would not catch a fish, and if I did, something else would go wrong, something I should have seen coming from the start.

I lifted the tangle, a mad cat's cradle that was netting sky, bridge, river, everything.

"Not fair!" I moaned.

Not then and there. Not after school was finally over and I was free of fractions, history, graphs of grammar, free from my own handwriting that coiled and cramped so badly that both I and my teacher were worn almost to yelling.

I sucked in my breath and picked at a knot. It loosened so the line looped out but only to crow in other loops that all pulled tight. This way, that way, every way was impossible.

I bit my lip, tasting the saltiness of blood, and remembered how I'd gotten myself slugged by the rusty-haired kid, the one named Riley. I'd tried to be his sidekick, to joke around, but Riley had gotten me wrong and called me "dope." So I swore at him and kids circled shouting, "Fight! Fight!" till I had to hit him, and Riley had to punch me back, but he slugged me hard and in my face, and my lip began to bleed.

I stared up at the telephone line stretching across the river—a sagging horizon, draped with lures and sinkers twisting in the sun's first light.

"Next time I'll probably snag up there." I lowered the tangle, reel, all of it onto the railing and mourned into the mess: "Dad's going to know I took it. What'll he say when he sees the rod like this?"

An explosion answered me, a hollow eruption twenty yards up the river. Huge. Furious. The explosion ripped the river into an open wound. It raised a heavy pillar five yards high of churning mud and spray. It shook me and I dropped the rod.

Rod, reel, line struck the water's surface.

I leaped forward, stretched over the railing, crying for my arms to reach, but it was gone, with only rings wavering where it sank. A sudden spray and the rings were swamped by the first angry wave.

Lost. It's lost, I told myself as the bridge shuddered under me. But how could the river explode? And how could I have dropped the rod? The waves still rolled, proof that the river did explode, but the waves wouldn't last and even proof wouldn't matter. The rod mattered and the rod was lost.

I twisted around to search but the rod did not miraculously reappear on land and no hand rose with it from the water.

"I can't go back." I imagined hiding in the woods, hitching to the city, or living on the road, travelling on forever. Yet I knew I would go back. Just as I knew how my father and Uncle Steve would stare from the enamelled kitchen table, and how I'd look or rather how I'd look away, hesitating at the doorway, as they laid down their cribbage hands. I'd begin some defence before I explained anything, while my aunt entered to make coffee but really to note my signs

of guilt, and my cousins, delighted by the show, would con-
spire on the couch. I'd describe this impossible thing that
struck the river as if it was something out of my comic
books but with no white word bubble reading BOOM! no
cartooned border to keep it separate from the world. All
the while I'd be slouching, and mumbling, knowing that
Uncle Steve always said a mumble means a lie. Dad would
tighten around his coffee cup, my mother would drift to the
sink for a dishrag to rub against the worn counter, both of
them wincing as my words tangled in confusion, while
everyone decided what really must have happened.

"Ha! That gave it to her good!" The voice broke from a
thicket on the river bank. Bushes shook and the silhouettes
of two men dragged a long shadow into the water—a rowboat. The lean one sprang into it saying, "Get your ass in
gear, jerk!"

The other one standing in the mud grunted the boat
into deeper water, then stumbled in. "Oh, yeah, I'm the jerk.
You think I don't know nothing about boats?" he whined,
as he pulled off his cap to run his hand through thinning
hair. "You're the one who's standing!"

"Okay, sailor, get it moving."

"You got to sit down, Jack."

"Damn it! They're rising."

Who were "they"? I wondered. Was he talking about
others like himself? Was the explosion some kind of signal?

The two men, the water, the river banks on either side
focussed into vivid colour. I hid and watched.

"Over to the right!" Jack shouted. "Some sailor; you can't even row."

"How about you doing something, eh?"

"Dig the oar in the water, the left oar. Row with your left one."

I kept low, scrambling into the weeds at the end of the bridge while the men manoeuvred into midstream. I slid down the embankment into the bushes, thrilled to be a witness, a reporter like Jimmy Olsen, Superman's young pal.

"Nothing's happening, Jack. You said they'd come up. I got to be in Riverton by nine to open the garage. Hinkley's coming for a valve job."

Jack snapped back, "Stuff it, will ye?"

"Says who? Eh? Says who?" Even his anger sounded like a sulk.

Jack ignored him as he scanned the water. Eventually, he answered, "Hinkley's going to leave the truck on the lot and your boss never gets in till ten—so what's he going to know?"

"But, Jack . . ."

"Just shut up. You're bugging me."

Closer to the bridge, the sun touched their upper bodies. Light haloed Jack's bleached hair, the faintness of a moustache. He looked sixteen but could have been older, even twenty, with features that were were almost feminine, except they were set into a sneer as if he meant to ruin anything delicate about himself. I knew enough to fear this kind of angry mannish boy.

I wasn't worried about the other one, who kept whining. He was pimply and clumsy as an overgrown kid. He seemed to be more like me, helpless, somehow innocent. I was already planning to tell the police that "Whiner" was bullied into whatever they were doing.

"Here they come. They're rising!" Jack shouted.

"Look, Jack, they're everywhere!"

Jack slapped the water with his hands, "Come on! You're floating up to heaven. Come to Daddy."

I saw only clouds beneath the surface, slow dreaming ghost clouds seeking the real clouds that were reflected on the water. At first I thought it was one large fish, like some great whale rising. Then I saw there were many fish, mostly pickerel, surfacing everywhere, white stomachs and gleaming scales bobbing under a skin of water. Some were dead. Others twitched in surrender. Stunned, drowned, they'd been dynamited.

My heart was firing in short wild bursts. I crouched lower in the weeds, the sides of my corduroys rubbing at thistles, my chin sliding along the cool stem of a bullrush. I was trying to recall what my Uncle Steve had said about dynamite and rivers. "Those poachers, they don't care," he'd said. "They dynamite a whole bloody river and kill ten fish for every one they get."

Jack scooped fish with a long-handled net. Whiner held the plastic bags. The boat and the fish were being carried by the current, drifting so close to where I hid that I could see the sweat on Whiner's lip as he wiped his forehead with his sleeve. He spit into the water and I watched the spittle float towards me and finally ease against the pebbles of the shore. So very close. The boat scraped an outlying rock. A dozen pickerel bobbed along the shore. They would come for them.

I tried to think. Should I run or stay? Or pretend I didn't know anything? Say I'm here by accident? Act blind. Unconscious.

"Who the hell are you?" Jack stood balanced in the boat with his feet spread against the inner ribbing. "What, are you deaf?"

I rose from the weeds, caught by Jack's stare, slipping in the mud towards him. I made myself look away, focussing on a pickerel's wide dead eye.

"Maybe you're some kind of retard."

I stayed mute, choking on the wrongness of his words and staring down, fixed on the fish's eye, then on an eye-shaped pebble wet with the water's tongue, green pebbles, blue ones, many pebbles white and brown. Jack jumped to shore, his work boots grinding pebbles underfoot. "Hey, you look at me when I'm talking."

"Jack, he saw!" Whiner rocked in the boat as if cradling himself. "That's all we need! They're going to find out how we got the dynamite and . . ."

"Just shut up!"

Whiner clamoured from the boat, desperate with an idea. "Hey, kid, how about some fish? Lots of fish!" Stumbling out, he grabbed Jack's jacket for support, pulling him backwards into water.

"Hey, let me go!"

My chance. I skittered up the bank, breaking through the bushes to the road. I raced over wooden planks, the bridge a roller-coaster blur, with Jack behind, pounding, panting, "Goddam, goddam!" Words lost and stretching out. Whiner crying far behind, "Hey! Hey!" as Jack was getting closer.

I was caught, yanked back; shirt ripped, legs twisted, scraped on gravel. Jack towered overhead.

"You . . . you little . . ." Jack was breathless, his face was swollen and dark. "Want to get away, huh? . . . I'll fry your ass!" I was lifted and dropped, dangling by my collar. Sky, river, clouds, fields crashing about my ears.

"Thought you'd be smart, eh? . . . play around?" His words broke over me.

"No, Jack . . . don't hurt him!" Whiner yelled from somewhere.

My knees were scraped, one felt warm and wet through the corduroy. My head throbbed. Suddenly my back struck something hard. Jack had slammed me against the railing and I collapsed against him, the two of us, one in fear, the other furious, were panting into each other.

I heard Whiner saying, "Jack, listen . . . he don't know us from . . . don't know a thing."

Yet I spit out, "You're Jack and you're . . . you're from Riverton . . . the garage . . . and you made me lose my rod . . . It's your fault, not mine!"

Too late. The words were out, all the worst ones, and already Jack was fiercer and he was laughing.

"You're really looking for it, aren't you?" As he closed in, I saw his lips stretching back from small white teeth. "If you think you're telling anybody anything . . ." He bounced me against the railing in a slow, even motion, again and again. I wanted to fall onto him, cling to the softness of his denim jacket, to touch his boyish face, to sob, "No! No, please! Don't hurt me," into the heart of that mannish boy. But he propped me against a post and clenched both his fists.

"Don't, Jack," Whiner was pleading and I felt oddly sorry for him. "You'll just make it worse, Jack. You always make it worse."

Jack kicked the post, barely missing me. "Damn! It won't just be the warden, it'll be Sergeant Vanier." He smirked as if to taunt himself. "He's been after me ever since that game in Ericksdale when I got him against the boards. He's going to love this. He'll come cruising into my folks' farmyard with his Mountie lights flashing and he'll take me like a goddam trophy!"

Whiner hovered at the edge of my vision, blocking out the sun. "Kid, how about some fish? For the old man, maybe?" I couldn't focus on the face, only his smells of sweat, gum, gasoline as I felt my knees dissolving.

A shadow hoisted me up and leaned me against the railing. Then something flickered in the sun—a fishing knife with its row of teeth grinning into my eyes, and Jack's own bitter voice. "Want this? . . . sharp . . . if you know what's good . . . worth ten bucks."

I leaped over the railing. Something in me as powerful as Jack pulled me up, thrust out my hands and feet, manoeuvred me off the dark barrier of bridge, to toss me, with my shirt flapping like broken wings, headfirst into the reflecting blaze of sun.

And crashing through.

To be hugged by water. Dragged down by water until my eyes could open and see again—green shafts of light and mossy pilings. Dead fish, the ones that did not rise but stayed below, each one a marker on some wide path. No words. No sound. My lungs ached but I stayed. The fish seemed to want me. They waved, nodding with the current. *Come with us. With shadows. It's quiet here and you can stay.* It seemed so easy to be carried by the cool dark flow.

Until my lungs screamed out and my arms grabbed towards the air. The upper light broke against my face. Sky blue. Field green. The wooden bridge all light and shadow. I swallowed air and water, choking as my hands reached for a cable wrapped around the pilings.

Dust and voices sifted down.

"You see him?"

"Jeez, Jack, he's been down too long."

"You looking or talking?"

"There must be lots of junk down there. He could be stuck on something."

"I was letting him keep the goddam knife. He was crazy or a retard or something."

"Jack, what if he doesn't come up?"

Down again. Slowing my heart, my mind. Rowing downward like a water beetle along a shaft of light, I reached the grey riverbed speckled in greens and whites. My clothing swelled into fins. My cheeks filled, my throat blocked water as I floated with dead fish, so many more than had risen to the surface, suspended in a murky light curtained by darkness.

I stroked forward and back, a bowing stroke with my eyes open, my lips mouthing water, shaping some sort of song for the dead. Without words or sound I was nodding, chanting to them.

Arms and legs forced me up a second time, gasping and crying, until I could let the waves rock and calm me. And the sighing of wind.

I was jarred by a scraping far away, the metal hull of the rowboat pulled over rock. Then a break of voices. I submerged, merged, stroking through the weeds, then turned in a dead man's float, letting my face bob among the lily pads near to shore. Eventually, after the bridge rumbled with the weight of heavy tires and the distant hill ground with gears, I understood that the men were gone. Yet I remained, gazing at the clouds, as they shaped and re-shaped themselves, dissolving even as they formed.

I broke the spell myself, with a deliberate plunge. This time I stroked to the river bottom to search for what I'd lost. First I retrieved my runners, kicked off in the dive, where they were dangling like two more fish along the base of the pilings. I moved along the pilings to find my father's rod stuck upright in the silt. Its golden label, SPIN MAS-TER, gleamed in some trick of light. I gripped it as I rose and swam to the closer bank.

I crawled out across a bed of mud. My body was weak, trembling with its own weight, so I steadied myself on a flat large rock. Two legs, I thought, still streaming water. I'm some kind of creature with two legs.

My steps became firmer on the bridge, solid once I saw that my bike and tackle box were safe. I dropped the runners, leaned the fishing rod against the railing and whipped water from my sleeves. My back, especially my neck, felt stretched, and a tingling at the base of my skull seemed to brighten everything before my eyes.

Something gleamed beside the box, like a long thin mirror, a shard of sky and cloud—it was the blade of Jack's fishing knife. Forgotten or left as a threat, a bribe, a prize.

I held it in my right hand, felt the sun's heat on it and its own hard weight. It had belonged to Jack; now it belonged to me. I didn't feel proud or excited or even tired. I only felt removed, as if I'd become a part of some great and distant order.

I tested the blade with the flat of my thumb, then looked to the tangle hanging from the rod. A stroke of the knife. Another. The tangle sailed off the rod. It floated down, collapsing on the water. I watched it sag into the current and my chest released something that sounded like a laugh, as the tangle drifted with the dead fish into the shining river.

from

Blaine's Way

by

Monica Hughes

*Monica Hughes is best known for her many science fiction
stories, such novels as* The Keeper of the Isis Light, Ring-
Rise, Ring-Set, *and one of my very favourites,* Devil on My
Back. *But I have chosen to represent her in this collection
with an excerpt from one of her equally readable true-life
adventures,* Blaine's Way. *Set during the Second World War,
this is the story of Blaine Williams, an eighteen-year-old
rural-Ontario lad who has lied about his age in order to fight
overseas. As this passage begins, he has been in combat training for weeks on the Isle of Wight, off the coast of England, in
preparation for the invasion of France. The soldiers will be
put ashore from infantry landing craft, flat metal barges. If
you've seen* Saving Private Ryan, *then you know what Blaine
has in store. But Spielberg's movie recounts the Normandy
invasion, which wasn't going to happen for another two
years. What Blaine is setting out upon one dark and early*

August morning is the raid on Dieppe. It was meant to be a kind of rehearsal, a chance to see how good the Nazis' defences were. They were very good! Dieppe was one of the great disasters of the war and one in which half the Canadian soldiers involved were either killed or taken prisoner.

On Tuesday, August 18th, we were suddenly told to get our full battle gear together. Then we were bundled into lorries and driven down in convoy to Southampton.

"Another stupid exercise," was Jim's opinion.

"Maybe this time it'll be the real thing."

"Blaine, you're a hopeless dreamer. Bet you a week's pay we're off to the Island again."

At the docks we mustered by companies and waited. And waited. Finally we were marched onto a couple of little ships, the *Prince Charles* and the *Prince Leopold*. We got the *Leopold*—what a name! As we were herded below decks I saw the familiar LCIs swinging from the davits. Well, at least now it's August the water should be a bit warmer, I thought.

At four o'clock Lieutenant-Colonel McKay stood up in the crowded mess.

"Well, this is it, boys. No turning back this time. Next stop Dieppe."

After the first cheer there was no time for celebration. As we began to break out our gear we found that the idiots in stores had sent us boxes and boxes of new Sten guns, straight from the factory, still in their packing grease.

"Why the hell couldn't they have let us keep our own guns? We'd just about got them ready to fire without jamming."

"These are bloody useless. How are we going to fight with them?"

Our platoon leader looked kind of white. I guess officer training had never prepared him for this kind of stupidity.

"We'll just have to spend the night cleaning them and adjusting them."

"Without firing them? Kind of difficult," Alex grumbled.

At least we weren't as badly off as one of the other battalions. It seems that some of the men, fed up with all these practice invasions, had dumped the ammo back at base and carried aboard dozens of empty boxes. They weren't laughing now. Nor were their officers. Lieutenant-Colonel McKay went to the captain and begged and borrowed every gun and spare bit of ammo from ship's stores.

And that wasn't the last of what went wrong. Whoever had loaded the machine gun belts had forgotten to insert tracer bullets. This meant that the soldiers firing them would have no idea if they were aiming correctly. What a way to start an invasion, I thought, even a little one. That evening in the crowded ship was an exercise in controlled panic.

"Wonder what else can go wrong?" Steve asked gloomily.

"Maybe it's like the rehearsal. When we get there it'll go like clockwork," I suggested hopefully. My stomach was like a leaden lump, and I hoped I wouldn't disgrace myself. I got permission to go up on deck for a breather.

We had just cast off. It was 9:30 by Nancy's watch. Five hours' difference ... or would it be six with double summer time? It would be late afternoon and she'd be helping her mom cook supper. Around us was the shadowy bulk of other ships. As I watched, the sailors hoisted canvas super-structures and false funnels to make us look like an inno-cent merchant convoy, heading out of Southampton Water. In case of spies? That made me think a bit. Suppose they were waiting for us when we got to Dieppe? The whole point of the landing was that it should be a surprise. But suppose it wasn't?

I swallowed my panic and took a deep breath. It was a warm evening, the sky clear, the last rosy light of the sun reflecting off the downs. It had been a peaceful twilight much like this three weeks before, when John had gone down in the Channel somewhere east of here.

I went below. I needed companionship. We ate sand-wiches and dozed a bit, or lay thinking of what the morn-ing was going to bring, going over in our heads everything we were supposed to do.

At three o'clock on the morning of the 19th, that cold hour when your blood runs slow and your brain feels empty and courage has fled, we went up on deck and got into the landing craft. It was still very calm, with the sea just breathing a little, silky looking with the light of the setting moon dancing on it.

Packed like sardines, thirty or so of us to a craft, we squatted on the benches. Steve and Mike were over in the centre nearest the ramp; and Jim, Alex, Pete and I were against the metal bulwark on the left. We sat silently, not moving, though now and then you could catch the flash of a man's eyes. Someone dropped a tin mug on the iron deck and it was like a bomb going off. We all jumped and swore.

"Watch it, you careless oaf!"

Ahead of us Motor Launch 291 chugged fussily along, showing us the way to Red Beach, the left half of the crescent lying immediately below the town of Dieppe, while to our right other launches were leading in the assault landing craft with the Hamilton Light Infantry aboard.

I stuck my head up and took a quick look. It was just like the photographs we'd been shown. There were the long moles of the harbour running out to sea to the east, and the white mass of the casino to the west. As we got closer the cliffs on either side of the city looked more imposing. Could they be climbed? The Royal Regiment and the South Saskatchewans and the Cameron Highlanders should be up there by now putting the guns on the headlands out of action. Without their help, we guys coming in on the open beaches would be sitting ducks.

I ducked as the destroyers behind us began to barrage the shoreline. The shells whistled overhead and burst in clouds of dust and smoke among the buildings across the esplanade.

5:10 a.m. Every moment our landing craft crept closer. By now we'd forgotten the chill and the wet spray and the early morning miseries. We were ready and raring to go. Now the east headland was wreathed in white smoke. Flames spat from exploding cannon as Hurricanes swooped low ahead of us. The naval salvos from behind burst in clouds of red and orange, and flak and tracers criss-crossed the clear dawn sky.

We stood up and yelled. This was exciting! Then sudden spouts of water shot up around us and fell like rain on our shoulders. The air was bitter with the smell of cordite. I heard a sudden patter like hail on the water and a cry of pain from the assault craft next to us. Shrapnel! We ducked down and crouched against the comparative safety of the bulwarks. That was *us* they were shooting at!

Three hundred yards off shore. Crouched, ready to go as soon as the ramp slammed down. I clutched my Sten gun so hard my fingers went numb. I let go and flexed them and tried to relax, to breathe slowly and evenly, pretending this was just another exercise.

Three red Verey lights suddenly lit the sky. The Hurricanes peeled off and headed back to England. The bombardment of the destroyers was turned off as suddenly as a door slamming. What was going on? Two hundred yards still to go and the only sound was the pounding of the shore guns at our tiny craft. This wasn't what we'd been told was to happen.

A hundred yards to go. Next to me Jim Aitken swore on and on in a monotonous undertone.

"The bastards. They've left us in the lurch. The bastards . . ."

The mortars in the bow of the landing craft lobbed smoke bombs along the shoreline. Our LCI nosed in to the beach. 5:20 a.m. on the button. For the first time we'd done it perfectly. The ramp swung down and there, ahead of us, was the shore of occupied France.

Steve and Mike charged ahead of me to the right. I saw them land and begin to run. Pete and Alex were directly in front of me. I leapt down the ramp behind them, thinking, *Today is for you, John.* And I tripped and went full length. Pete and Alex had thrown themselves flat on the beach and I'd fallen over them.

"Come on, you idiots," I tugged at Alex's shoulder. "Don't stop here. Get up to the seawall."

Everything seemed to slow down as Alex rolled onto his back. His eyes were glazed, staring at the sky. Pete was dead too. Pete and Alex. All along the beach, wherever the landing craft had beached, men were dropping.

I ran, or tried to run, and sprawled flat again. This wasn't just a pebble beach like the one in Dorset. These shingles were as big as your hand and they were smooth and round and they slithered against each other so your feet couldn't get a grip.

From up on the eastern headland the shells pounded down. Somewhere across the esplanade I heard machine gun and rifle fire. A ricochet broke a pebble in two and the stone leaped up and cut my cheekbone just under my eye. The little sting of pain cleared my head and I got back on my feet and slithered and scrambled up the slope to the first row of barbed wire.

Someone had already thrown himself across its coils, and two more had died as they had crossed. I swallowed and then pounded over their dead backs and up the last steep slope to the seawall.

Crouching out of the line of fire, I couldn't see a thing, but over to my right the pebbles were piled until they were only three feet below the top of the wall. I crawled over and peered across the esplanade. A bullet whined over my head and I dropped and pressed my face against the cold pebbles, sweating with fear.

But in that quick glimpse I had seen the barbed wire along the top of the sea wall, huge festoons of it, running right along the front from the harbour to the casino. I looked around for help. The regiment was scattered along a thousand yards of beach, some of us under the safety of the seawall, others dead or pinned under fire on the beach itself.

Then, according to plan, the tank landing craft crunched onto the beach. Now things will go better, I told myself. They'll be able to get up onto the esplanade, and behind their firepower we can demolish the barbed wire and get into the town.

The sun had just risen. It was a clear beautiful day, just the kind of day we'd hoped for. The first tank trundled down the ramp, its guns angled up to direct its fire over the seawall at the hidden enemy. The second and third were right behind it. Before they'd even reached the crest of the beach their treads had been torn off by the merciless shingle. The first two were destroyed by fire from the headland. The third was stranded, but could still fire its guns.

Behind the tanks came more of the Essex Scottish, B company. It was dreadful to watch helplessly as they tried to run towards the shelter of the seawall, to see them spin and fall, or stagger blindly on with blood pouring from them.

"Come on, men!" Lieutenant-Colonel McKay yelled. "Let's get that bangalore torpedo up here. If we can just shove it through the barbed wire and blow it up, it's a short run across the esplanade."

We pushed the bangalore torpedo into the coils of wire and crouched while it blew. But when we scrambled over the wall we found that the torpedo was faulty. Only the first three feet of wire had gone. There was another three feet to get through. We fought at it with wirecutters and our bare hands, while all the time the hail of machine gun bullets and rifle fire from the far side of the esplanade cut us down.

Someone thudded onto my back and I fell onto the wire, unable to move.

"Get off me," I yelled. "Come on, you creep, move!" I managed to wriggle sideways and found myself face to face with Jim Aitken. His eyes were shut.

"Jim!" I wriggled slowly back to shelter, pulling him after me. His battle blouse caught on the wire and I tugged at it furiously. Lieutenant-Colonel McKay caught me by the leg and pulled me down.

"Not without Jim, sir," I yelled.

"He's dead, son. Can't you see? Come on. Get down."

Battered and bleeding, we crouched beneath the wall to get our breath. By now almost half the regiment was either dead or too badly wounded to fight. Some of us began going down the beach and hauling up to safety anyone who was still moving. Even then the bastards didn't leave us alone. Their fire raked the whole beach, and as often as not the wounded were brought to safety by those now almost as badly wounded.

Our company sergeant-major finally got a bangalore torpedo to explode properly right inside the barbed wire. Through the gap he and fifteen men rushed across the esplanade and zigzagged to the houses on the far side.

The rest of us who were still mobile stood under the wall and fired incendiary grenades across their heads at the houses. One big building, with two chimneys, slap in the middle of the row, exploded into flames. We cheered and watched the men duck out of sight behind the houses. Faintly, above the constant din of cannon, we could hear the chatter of their Sten guns.

It seemed forever before they came running back, dodging the snipers across the esplanade and rolling over the seawall on top of us.

"Couldn't get far, sir. There's a lot of Jerry troops coming into town by bus. They know we're here now and no mistake."

I leaned against the wall, my Sten gun at the ready, staring through the smoke and dust. My right hand was beginning to throb where I'd torn it on the barbed wire, and my eye was swollen from a flying stone, but not enough to spoil my aim.

I pinpointed a sniper up on the roof of a building over to the right and blazed away at him until my fool gun jammed. I threw it down in disgust and looked around for another. There was one, up on a drift of shingle only a few yards out into the open. The guy whose gun it had been was lying face down and it was still in his right hand. I figured it would take me about three seconds to nip up that shingle slope and grab the gun, and about two seconds to roll down to safety again.

The shingle slithered round my feet as I scrambled up. I reached out and grabbed the gun with my right hand and rolled back down the slope, deafened by a nearby shell. But dammit, I didn't have the gun. I couldn't believe my stupidity. I stared up the slope, blinking a sudden dizziness out of my eyes. There it lay, with the dead guy's hand still on the butt and another hand grasping the barrel. Mine.

Dazedly I looked down at the sleeve of my battle blouse, at the awful mangled mess dangling from the cuff. I slithered down against the wall with a kind of croak. I guess the man next to me must have turned and seen what had happened, because the next thing I knew he was grabbing my arm and wrapping a tourniquet around it and yelling for a medic.

He saved my life, I guess. I was so dazed and surprised I think I'd have just sat there and peacefully bled to death. I never got a chance to thank him. I never saw him again.

Whether he died on the way down to the boats or in the crimson sea, or whether he finished up in a POW camp I just don't know.

Things got muddled for a while. The next thing I was really sure of was lying on my back under the wall with the sun in my eyes, listening to someone moaning. It was an awful noise and I wanted to tell the guy to button up, but I was too tired.

"Hold on, son. Here's some morphine." That was Lieutenant-Colonel McKay's face floating over me. The moaning stopped and I realized that it must have been me.

There was a dogfight overhead. Hurricanes and Spitfires against the Luftwaffe. A lazy dance high up in this incredibly blue sky. Like seagulls. Or maybe pigeons . . .

I saw the pigeons swoop and soar between the rafters of the barn. One of them fell out of the sky. No, not a pigeon, a Spitfire. Down towards the sea, turning and twisting like a maple seed. John had finished like that. *Splat.* "Not a whole bone left in his body," Dad had said. I shut my eyes, but the picture of the ground coming closer and closer, twisting round and round, wouldn't go away.

Bam. Bam. The noise shook the beach. Mortar fire from the headlands, rifle fire and machine guns from the town and from the pillboxes on the esplanade. From our guys, too, and the couple of tanks that were still operational. *Clatter, slash, shake.* "You've got to watch out," Mom had warned me. "You could lose an arm in that old thresher. What good would you be then? Without an arm?"

A mortar from the east headland hit one of the stranded tanks square on. It went up in a sheet of flame and billowing black smoke. The poor devils inside didn't stand a chance. Trapped. Like the chickens in the barn. Fool chickens clucking their heads off and running back into the flames. Grandpa never did find out how the fire started. A cigarette, he guessed. A careless cigarette from a farm hand. "A moment's stupidity and there's a year's work up in smoke."

Yes, Grandpa. I nodded. *A year's work. Or a life's...*

Someone was shaking me.

"Huh?"

"If I help you, can you make it down to the landing craft?"

"Hell, yes." I shook the mist out of my eyes. "My legs are okay."

"Wait till I say, then, and we'll make a run for it."

I saw that it wasn't just the mistiness in my eyes. They'd put up a smokescreen along the shoreline to cover our retreat. Maybe it made sense, but it also signalled to the gunners up on the headlands what was happening. At once they turned their guns from the beach to pound the shoreline. You could tell exactly where the landing craft had come in. That's where all the bodies were. Lying at the edge of the sea, the tide reddening with Canadian blood.

"Now!"

His arm round my waist. My good arm over his shoulder. We pounded down that slithery slipping beach and I was dumped like a sack of wheat into a landing craft already packed with men, most of them wounded, some already dead, I think. I tried to thank my rescuer, but he'd turned back and was wading knee deep through the water, going back for another man.

The shells were landing in the sea on either side of us, sending up great salt water spouts. I could hear shrapnel spatter against the metal sides of our craft and I prayed we'd make it back to the assault ship without sinking.

I blacked out for a bit. The next thing I'm sure of was being on the deck of a ship. It was pitching and tossing, rolling from side to side like a porpoise. Turned out it wasn't an assault ship at all, but a destroyer that had nipped in and picked us out of our sinking landing craft. Our lucky day, I guess.

The pain was really bad. I could feel it down my arm and clean into my fingertips. I remember thinking: *That's crazy. I don't have any fingertips.*

Someone wiped the sweat off my face and gave me a sip of water. One of the seamen, I think. I could feel the heavy serge of his uniform against my cheek. And someone said—or was that later? I'm not sure—"How old are you, son? You don't look old enough to be fighting."

"I'm eighteen, sir," I said without thinking, being high on pain and morphine. "May 17th, 1924."

"Why the hell did you get into this mess if you didn't have to?"

"It was the train." I could hear my voice as if it were a stranger's, a long way off, like an old-fashioned radio. "I thought I could get the train out of there. But I picked the wrong train."

"What d'you mean, son?"

"I thought it was the passenger train through to Detroit and Chicago. But was just the old Toonerville Trolley."

Blood all along the line, I thought. *Or were they just Grandpa's tomatoes for the canning factory?*

Gore

by

Sarah Ellis

Sarah Ellis is very smart. She is also very funny. She trusts her reader; she knows you're going to get the joke, so she doesn't explain it. That's a good thing to know if you're going to be a writer. I also like the way she squeezes lots of great-sounding words into short sentences. "Gore" is pure Sarah; it is very smart and very funny with lots of good words in it. It's a satire of sorts, a take-off on the popular Fear Street books. In Sarah's story, the horror writer's name is R. L. Tankard. Choice. It's taken from her short story collection, Back of Beyond, *which offers up a dozen imaginative tales of the unexplained, the startling, and things that go bump in the night.*

Twins have a very special bond. Together from their earliest moments of consciousness, they are true soulmates. Linked by feelings of deep kinship and love, mutually attuned with an almost magic sensitivity, they often feel like two halves of the same person.

Twins separated at birth who meet as adults often discover amazing coincidences in their lives. They both have wives named Linda and sons called Hamish. At their weddings both of their best men wore kilts. They both have Maine coon cats and use an obscure Finnish brand of aftershave. This proves that the twin relationship is one of the strongest in the world, overriding individual personality and the forces of upbringing and environment.

Horse patooties.

Soulmates? Sometimes I can't believe that Lucas and I are in the same family, much less twins. In fact, there have been times when I've wondered if Lucas and I are even of the same species. I'm pretty much a basic homo sapiens. Lucas is more like an unevolved thugoid. I've heard that there are some photos of twins in the womb that show them hugging. If someone had taken a photo of Lucas and me in there I'll bet dollars to doughnuts it would have shown him bashing me on the head.

Lucas must have grabbed all the good nutrition in there, too, because he's a lot bigger, faster and stronger than I am. I don't stand a chance on the bashing, kicking, running away, immobilizing-your-opponent-in-a-half-nelson front. As the years have passed, my two areas of superior firepower, an extensive vocabulary and a gift for voice impersonation, have sometimes proved inadequate. I have been forced to take up psychological warfare.

Lucas attacks without provocation. The other day, for example, I'm sitting reading. I finally got the new R. L. Tankard out of the library and it is extremely choice. There's this girl and she has a babysitting job in this glam apartment building, on the twenty-sixth floor. When she arrives, the baby is already asleep so she hasn't actually seen it. She's watching TV in a darkened room and she thinks she hears a noise from the baby.

"*She muted the TV for a minute and in the sudden silence she heard the noise again, but louder. It was a heavy wet noise, like the sound of a big piece of raw meat being flung to the floor. She stared at the door to the nursery. It was outlined in a thin band of crepuscular light. She stood up and, with her heart pounding in her ears, she approached the room . . .*"

Isn't that excellent? I read it again. Sometimes I like to do that with R. L. Tankard—slow it down by reading the best parts twice before I turn the page. "Crepuscular." I roll the word around in my mouth like a hard candy. Who cares what it means? ". . . like a big piece of raw meat being flung to the floor." Choice.

Then, WHAP! Lucas leans over the back of the chair, rips the book from my hands, runs into the bathroom and slams the door. I'm after him in a second but of course by the time I get there he has it locked. I learned years ago that you can click open our bathroom door with a knife. I learned this about two minutes after Lucas learned that you can wedge the bathroom door shut by pulling open the top drawer of the vanity.

I kick the door. "Give me my book back, you grommethead."

"Make me."

I just hate that, the way Lucas can sound so smug. If possible I would appeal to a higher authority. I have no shame about finking, whining, telling, etc., when it comes to Lucas. I use whatever counter-weapons I have at my disposal. With Lucas as a brother it is sometimes necessary to have referees. I'm not ashamed to stand behind an adult peacekeeping force. Lucas regards this as an act of cowardice and wimpiness. He tries to shame me. "Why don't you run to Mummy?" But I don't care. I figure it is like some small but extremely valuable country calling on the United Nations when attacked by an aggressor. Unfortunately, in this case, the peacekeeping forces are out at Mega-Foods doing the Saturday shop.

I try to plan a strategy. At least it keeps my mind off what is happening behind the door of that baby's room, in that crepuscular light. The carrot or the stick? Or, to put it another way, the chocolate cheesecake or the uzi? I could try the chocolate cheesecake or false bribery. Such as, "Lucas, just give me my book and I'll do your poop-scooping in the backyard this week." This technique has lost its effectiveness through overuse, however. Even Lucas, microbrain that he is, doesn't fall for that one anymore.

So what about the uzi. "Lucas, if you don't give me back my book this minute, I'm going to tell Dad that you . . ."

What? I've used up the fact that Lucas was the one who let the rabbit into Mum's office where he ate through her modem cord. I've already gotten my mileage out of the time he tried to photocopy his bum on the photocopier at the public library. I've used up everything I know about Lucas's sins, crimes, misdemeanours and shady dealings.

I collapse on the couch in despair. I am a stealth bomber with no aviation fuel. I am a pioneer with no powder for my musket. I am a merry man (well, okay, merry woman) with an empty quiver. I am weaponless.

Not quite.

"Rats. Lucas, there's someone at the door. I'll get it but I'm warning you, Lucas, if you're not out of there by the time I get back, you're toast."

"Yeah, with peanut butter."

I run to the door. The doorbell gives three loud blats.

"Just a minute. Coming!" I open the door.

There are two, no, three of them. The faces are hooded and I only catch a glimpse but it is enough to make me step back in horror, as though a huge hand has given me a push. This is my first mistake, leaving me a split second too late to push the door shut.

They are inside. They are silent.

"Hey, hold it, you can't do that. Get out of here. Help!"

I pull myself together and try to fool them. "Dad!"

The front door clicks quietly shut behind them. I race around the corner into the hall and fall against the bathroom door. I strain to hear.

Nothing.

"Lucas," I yell-whisper.

Lucas's bored voice makes its way out of the bathroom. "Forget it, Amy, you're not fooling anybody."

"Lucas, I mean it. Let me in. Please. Those faces. They're not . . . aagh." A shadow falls into the hallway. I grab the doorknob and screw my eyes shut.

The first thing is the smell. The fetid stench. The noxious reek. It is the smell of something dead, sweet and rotten. It rolls into the hall like a huge wave, breaking over my head, flowing into my mouth and nose until it becomes a taste. I am drowning. I gasp, dragging the air painfully into my lungs.

"Very dramatic, Lady Macbeth."

I find a voice. "Lucas, can't you smell it?"

Lucas giggles and flushes the toilet. "Now I can't."

Then something ice-cold and soft and damp fixes itself around my wrist like a bracelet and begins to pull my fingers away from the door. I hold on, unable to talk, unable to breathe.

And then the voice. The voice as dry and white as paper. "Come with us. We need you. We need your being."

A cold sweat breaks out over my entire body. I grab at the door one last time as my slippery fingers slide off the knob. I grasp at anything. My fingernails scratch across the shiny surface. The door rattles.

"Lucas!"

Lucas laughs.

The thing moves me to the living room. Not roughly. Like a powerful, persistent and silent wind. I force my eyes open but I can't seem to focus. The room is shimmering like a mirage on a hot road. I am lying on the floor and the ceiling is pulsing slowly. The strong, crepuscular wind pushes me to the floor. I am pinned, paralyzed, frozen with terror. My heartbeat pounds in my ears.

The paper voice is louder. "Eat. Of. Our. Food." Each word is a little island of sound, a pebble dropped into a pool.

The ceiling disappears and a face looms above me. A smooth white mask, skin stretched across sharp bones. Bright yellow eyes that stare unblinking, like a baby or a reptile. Thick shiny brown hair. The echo of the smell of decay. I feel something being held to my lips. I lock my jaw and squeeze my lips shut.

The voice is louder, booming. "Eat. Of. Our. Food."

I see movement in the shiny brown hair. Movement that ceases the moment I look directly at it. I want to close my eyes but my eyelids are stiff and wooden. The movement increases. Shiny, brown, undulating, dancing like a thing alive.

Or many things alive.

Pink rat's eyes. A scream consumes me, vomiting up from every part of my body. And into my open mouth falls a greasy, slimy gobbet of ooze. I flail my head from side to side and try to spit it out but it turns to a thick, viscous, glutinous, sticky liquid that coats my mouth, rises up the back of my nose and clings to my teeth. I retch. I gag.

The mask floats once more above me. Its smoothness has now exploded into a cobweb of wrinkles, an old crazed china plate. The hair has turned dead-rat grey. Beads of milky liquid ooze out of the yellow eyes, now dull and bloodshot, and begin to rain down upon my face. They are warm, then cold and solid. The quavery, rusty voice floats down to me, "You. Are. The. New. One. Now."

With a strength I didn't know I had, I force myself up. I beat away the mask face and push aside the shimmering air of the room through which my scream is still echoing. Chairs and side tables fall as I crash past them. Magazines fly through the air and crash against the walls.

"Hey, fink-face! What are you doing out there? Demolition derby?" I have no voice to answer Lucas.

I reach the phone in the hall just outside the bathroom door. I grab the receiver. I dial Emergency. I wait through a century of rings. Finally someone answers.

"Do you wish police, ambulance or fire?"

My voice is choked with sobs. "Police, oh, police. Please, hurry."

Click. The line goes dead. Cold, gentle fingers touch the back of my neck. I drop the receiver, which swings like a pendulum, banging against the wall, a dull, hollow sound.

I fall to the ground like a stone, like a piece of raw meat, and bury my face in my hands. My hands smell like skunk cabbage, no, like swamp water, no, like the bacon that somebody forgot in the back of the fridge. My face is smooth and cold and becoming more solid every second. My hair begins to move on my scalp.

They have me. I am becoming one of them. I feel my brain hardening inside my head.

I hold onto one thought. My dear twin. My brother. My boon companion. Fellow traveller on the road of life. Oh, God, don't let them take Lucas.

I try to picture the bathroom window. Oh, please, let him be skinny enough to get through it. My mouth is becoming rigid. I use up my last human words. "Lucas, break the window. Get out. For pity's sake, don't come out here."

Then silence. The only sound is the telephone receiver thudding against the wall.

"Amy? You're just kidding, aren't you? That was pretty good. You know if you weren't so funny-looking you could probably become an actress."

Silence.

Lucas's voice shrinks. "Amy? Amy, come on. Quit it."

Beep, beep, beep. The telephone's humanoid voice rings out in the silent hall. "Please hang up and try your call again. If you need assistance dial your operator. Please hang up now." *Beep, beep, beep.*

The bathroom door opens slowly. I'm curled up behind it. I hold my breath. Two steps, that's all I need. Two measly steps.

"Amy?"

Two steps it is. I grab the door, swing around it, jump into the bathroom and turn the lock.

Success! Triumph! Oh, happiness, oh, joy! I shake my own hand.

I slurp some cold water from the tap. My throat hurts a bit from that final scream. But it was worth it. It was one of the better screams of my career. There's something to be said for really scaring yourself.

R. L. Tankard is sitting on the back of the toilet. I open him up. R. L. Tankard is such a good writer that he can make you forget all about what's going on around you. He can make you forget, for example, a flipped-out twin brother using inappropriate language on the other side of the bathroom door. Listen. He's already repeating himself. Really, his repertoire of invective is pathetically inadequate. He should do more reading to increase his word power.

I settle down on the bathmat and find my page. So—what *was* in that baby's room?

Looking Down, I Can Just See

by

Richard Scrimger

Richard Scrimger burst onto the children's book scene with his hilarious novel, The Nose From Jupiter. *So, I was thinking noses when I asked him to write something for this collection. Or thumbs, maybe. Something, well ... funny. But there is more, it seems, to Richard than terminal nuttiness. Which is not to say that there isn't any humour in "Looking Down, I Can Just See." There's a scene, in fact, on the Toronto subway that is knock-down, laugh-out-loud, riotously funny. But there is also mystery here, and very real suspense. And at the end, something quite extraordinary, an epiphany, a moment of revelation.*

Looking down, I can just see the tops of the pine trees in the courtyard. I lean out to get a better look.

"Careful, Jacko!" says my brother Stephen.

"I'm fine," I say. Grandad's apartment is on the twentieth floor. I love coming to the city to visit Grandad. How many buildings in our little town are twenty stories tall? None, that's how many.

"You know what Mom said," says Stephen. He's a worrier. He takes after Mom. She's a worrier too. She finds all kinds of crazy things to worry about. That we'll get sick from eating too many cookies. That we'll fall in the river and get muddy. I can't see why she worries so much. So you get sick, or muddy, so what? She was even worried about Grandad taking us to the museum this morning while she went shopping. Kept telling us stay close to Grandad, stay together, be on our best behaviour.

"Grandad's waiting," said Stephen.

Mom says I take after Dad. Not just my red hair and blue eyes, but the way I go rushing off in all directions without thinking. I don't remember my dad. He died in a traffic accident when I was small. Stephen grabs my hand and pulls me away from the edge of the balcony. "Come on!" he says.

Grandad is at the door jingling his keys in his pocket. I dash past him into the hall. The elevator door is open to let a little old lady off. Really little. Her head is on a level with mine. "Hi there," I say, dashing past her into the elevator.

I press G for ground. The elevator door starts to close. Slowly.

"Jacko—wait!" bellows Grandad. He runs to the elevator and slides his hand in the open space. The door stops closing. Grandad and Stephen step into the elevator. They're both frowning at me. "You almost went without us," says Grandad.

"Uh-huh," I say.

"You'd have been alone in the elevator," he says. "What would you have done then?"

"I would have waited for you at the bottom," I say.

Grandad sighs.

"Isn't that the right thing to do?" I ask. "If I'm all alone on the elevator, isn't that the right thing to do?"

"Yes, it's the right thing. But you shouldn't be all alone on the elevator." He sighs again.

"Is it time for your heart medicine?" I ask. When he sighs a lot, it means that his heart is acting up.

"No," he says. The frown lines around his mouth deepen.

Stephen sighs too. Not that he needs heart medicine. Grandad is looking at the elevator numbers counting down. 20, 19, 18. I kick Stephen. He sighs again.

Stephen doesn't get mad. He gets superior.

The elevator doors open on the ground floor. "Keep close to me," says Grandad.

"Uh-huh," I say. But of course, when we get outside a dog comes bounding up, wanting to play. "Hi there!" I say to the dog, and I pat it on the head and chase after it. It runs to the tree and runs around it barking. I follow.

"Come back, Daisy!"

"Come back, Jacko!"

We look at each other, the dog and I. Then Daisy trots back to her mistress and I trot back to Grandad. "Honestly," says Grandad.

We walk to the subway station. It isn't far. When we cross the street, Grandad grabs my hand and holds on tight. Stephen takes Grandad's other hand.

"What do you want to see at the museum today?" Grandad asks us.

"Mummies," I say quickly. "Dead people with their faces all dried up."

Grandad smiles. I always want to see the mummies. "What about you, Stephen?"

I open the heavy glass door to the subway station. WHOOOSH! The rush of air from a fast-moving train drowns out Stephen's answer.

"Yippee!" I shout.

"Careful, Jacko!" calls Grandad.

There's an old man ahead of us. A tired old man with a coat on, even though it's a hot day. His face has wrinkles, like Grandad's, but Grandad's wrinkles are freshly shaved. This man's aren't. He carries a white stick, and taps his way forward.

I love the busyness of a subway station. The noise and the smell and the speed. I even like waiting for the train. I clatter down the stairs, racing past the man with the cane.

"Careful, Jacko," the man calls after me. I turn. How did he know my name? He taps his way past me. I follow, carefully.

"That's better," he says.

I don't say anything.

The platform is crowded. Lots of people going downtown on a Saturday morning. I hope they're not all going to the museum, or there won't be any room in front of the mummies.

The wind always comes first. The hot wind, from in front of the subway train. Grandad and Stephen are nowhere near the edge of the subway platform, but they take a step back anyway. The subway snakes down the tunnel towards us, its light shining. The wind blows stronger, stronger. I stand just behind the yellow safety line with my arms wide open. The train goes right past me.

"Careful!" Grandad calls over the noise.

I nod. I know to be careful. There's a crowd of people waiting to get on. I feel Grandad's hand on my shoulder. Stephen is beside me. The subway doors open. The crowd surges forward. I don't have to push myself. I can stand still and let myself be carried along. I'm floating. It's magical.

I've had this feeling before. It's as if a movie is taking place all around me, and I'm watching the movie from the inside. Magical, like I said. I don't think Stephen gets this feeling.

I hear the three dings that say the doors are closing. Stephen and I are on the train now. I turn around to tell Grandad how exciting it all is, how much fun I'm having, only—it's not Grandad who has his hand on my shoulder. It's a stranger, who pushes onto the train just as the doors close. I look around but can't see—actually I can't see *anything* except other people's backs and shirts. I fight my way back to the doors and finally see Grandad. On the other side. He's still on the platform. He sees me and shouts. I can't hear what he's saying.

The subway starts to move. Grandad moves with it, staying right beside the doors. He shouts some more. I can't hear him, but I can read his lips. MUSEUM, he says. WAIT AT THE MUSEUM STOP. I smile, and give him the thumbs up. He's scared but I'm not. The train moves faster, and Grandad is left behind.

Stephen is in the middle of the subway car. "Grandad!" he calls. "Where are you?" He sees me and waves. "Jacko, where's Grandad?"

I go over to where Stephen is standing. The train lurches. I fall against a stranger. "Sorry," I say.

"Where's Grandad?" asks Stephen. He's looking around frantically.

I tell him. His face screws up like he's going to cry or make a wish. Or like he's trying not to wet his pants.

"It's okay," I say. "Don't worry. I know what to do."

"What?"

"Go to the Museum subway stop. Grandad is going to meet us there. He said so. We just have to get ourselves to Museum."

"And how are we going to do that? How are we going to get to the museum by ourselves?"

The train lurches again. I grab on to a pole to keep myself upright. Stephen falls over. I laugh. "How can you laugh?" he asks, picking himself up. "We're in an awful mess. How can you laugh?"

"I don't know," I say. "But I can."

Lights up ahead. The train slows down. We're coming to our first stop. The signs on the walls of the station say Summerhill. The doors open.

"What do we do now?" says Stephen. "Should we get off?"

"Why?" I ask.

Stephen is trembling. His head goes back and forth like he's watching a tennis game. He stares at me, and then the door. Then me. Then the door.

Not too many people get on or off. The doors close almost as soon as they open. Stephen moves towards the door, but by then it's too late.

"Maybe we should get off and wait for Grandad," he says.

"No," I say. "Stay on the train."

"Are you sure?"

"Remember when I almost got in the elevator by myself? He said the right thing to do was go to the bottom and then wait. Now he's expecting us to go to Museum."

"And how do we do that?"

The train is jouncing through the tunnel. The darkness makes the window into a mirror. Stephen's face is a mask of worry. "I want Mom," he whimpers. My big brother.

The subway lurches again. I fall against a different guy this time. He's sitting down by himself. "Sorry," I say.

"That's all right, Jacko." It's the old blind guy from our station. I didn't realize that he was in our car.

"Hi," I say. And then we're out of the subway tunnel and in the open air.

Two stops later, at Bloor, the train almost empties. I don't know what to do.

"Do you think we should ask directions?" I say to Stephen, who shakes his head emphatically.

"You know what Mom thinks about talking to strangers," he says.

I know. Believe me, I know. We live in a small town, where there almost aren't any strangers, but we still get the lecture.

"I just want to know how to get to Museum," I say.

"Look at the map over the door, Jacko," says the blind guy.

Oh, yeah. I should have remembered that. There's maps in every car. I peer up at the nearest one, and find Bloor. That's where we are now. The door closes, and the train lurches forward. I lurch backward, but stay up.

"I can't find the Museum stop," I say.

Stephen is sitting very still with his hands in his lap. He is making himself as inconspicuous as possible. He doesn't want anyone to notice him. Not me. I want people to notice me. I look around for help. There are other people on the car, but they turn away so they don't catch my eye.

"Follow the green line west from Bloor and you'll see Museum in a couple of stops," says the blind guy. "You could change at Bloor to get to Museum."

"That's great," I say, "only we just passed Bloor. Too late."

Stephen beckons to me. "Jacko, stop it," he whispers.

I don't move. "Stop what?"

"What you're doing. Sit down."

"What do you mean, Stephen?" I ask him out loud. He looks away, like he doesn't know me. Like it wasn't him talking.

"Your brother is shy," says the blind man. "That's okay."

"So what should we do now?"

"Stay on this car, Jacko," he says. "Go all the way around the loop."

A few more stops pass. The colours of the subway platforms change from green to gray to yellow. There are pictures of hockey players. More people get on.

It's kind of funny. Really it is. Two kids lost in the subway, and the person who is helping them read the map is blind. No one else wants to.

The map isn't really a loop—it's shaped more like a capital U. As we go down one side of the U, I notice that the people getting on the subway look poorer and poorer. Their faces look unhappier. There's a crying kid. Her mom tries to stop her from crying by yelling at her, and then slapping her. Doesn't work. I could have told her that. The mom leans way back in her seat because she's pregnant. I hope the baby doesn't turn out to be a crier.

"Hi there," I say to the crying little girl. She cries even harder. And clutches at her mom. Oh, well.

"You sure this is where we should be going?" I say to the blind guy. I'm standing next to his seat. I can see the top of his head. He's almost bald. White hairs sprout like weeds in pavement cracks.

"Oh, yes," he says. "Don't get off this train. It's a longer trip, but you'll get there. And you'll see your dad at the other end."

For a second, hope flares up inside me like a match. Which is stupid, because I wouldn't recognize Dad if I saw him. The little picture on Mom's dressing table is from when they were married—years and years and years ago. I don't even miss my dad. How can you miss someone you don't remember?

"You mean my grandad," I say. "My dad is dead."

The train lurches into a turn. I almost fall. The blind guy nods. "Union next," he says. "Bottom of the loop. Watch out."

"Watch out?" I say. "For what?" And then the train stops.

He stands up, points his stick at the door. "This is where I get off," he says.

"Bye," I say. He waves, for all the world as if he can see me, and then taps his way off.

Two of the toughest-looking people I've ever seen get on our car. Neither of them has any hair. One of them is pierced all over the place. He has a stud in his nose, and bolts in his forehead and chin, and a million earrings, going all around the outside of his ears like stitching. His head looks like a pincushion. His friend has tattoos crawling up his arms. Snakes and knives and skulls and swords. I can see the tattoos because his shirt has no sleeves anymore. Maybe he popped his sleeves with his muscles. He has huge muscles. They both do.

I stare. I can't help it. There's a line where cool turns into gross, and they had crossed over the line, but I could still see that they might have been cool a ways back.

I sit down. Stephen comes over to sit beside me. He stares too, then shuts up inside himself, like a folding chair. He turns away from the tough guys and makes himself small.

The two tough guys walk up and down the subway car. They hold their arms wide, and swagger when they walk. They seem to take up more room than they need. And they make odd growling noises in the back of their throats. Like dogs. They frown all the time. They look mad. Mad at—I don't know. Mad at everything. I'm glad the crying little girl has gone. I think if they heard her crying they'd get even madder.

They throw themselves into the seat beside a couple of businessmen with glasses and topcoats and briefcases. The businessmen look a little out of place. The tough guys stare and growl. The businessmen don't stare back. Don't talk. The tough guys keep staring and growling. The businessmen get off at the next stop. So do a few other people. No one gets on.

"Let's get off," whispers Stephen.

"Look, we're at St. Andrew. Only ... four more stops."

"We can wait here and take the next train," says Stephen. "Come on, Jacko. I don't like this. I'm scared."

"But we can't get off. The blind man said to stay on this train."

"What blind man?"

"I was talking to him."

Stephen frowns. "You were talking to a little girl."

"He was sitting right there." I point to his seat. How could Stephen not have seen him? "An old guy with a coat and a white stick."

"Jacko, are you making things up again? You know what Mom says about that."

The tough guys get up and wander over to a group of teenagers—guys and girls chatting about a party last night. They stop talking. The tough guys stare. And growl. The teenagers frown. One of the girls—she has freckles and jet black hair and fingernails—says, "What is *your* problem?"

The tough guys don't reply, except to growl louder.

The teenagers get off at the next stop. So do an older couple. The tough guys follow them to the doors. They're like a pair of sheepdogs herding everyone out of the car.

Everyone but us. Stephen and I are alone in the car with the two tough guys.

The train moves off, picks up speed. "Three more stops," whispers Stephen.

The tough guys check out the empty car. They see us. Stephen's face crumples like balled-up paper. They come over to where we're sitting. The pincushion guy has a pierced lip. He pulls back his lip to growl, baring his teeth.

The other guy stretches his arms over his head, the way a cat stretches on the couch after taking a nap—showing off his tattoos and muscles. He bends down so his head is next to ours. Stephen is quivering like a life-sized Jell-O mould.

The subway train is slowing down. It's not our stop. I don't want to get off. But maybe, just maybe, we'd better.

We stand up. The two tough guys get out of the way so we can move towards the door. Their growls are loud, like the roar of a waterfall when you're standing right beside it.

The train stops. The doors open. People are waiting to get on. A dozen or more men and women all dressed the same. Men and women, small and tall. White faces, dark lips and eyes, striped shirts, white pants, ballet shoes. They crowd onto the train, making it impossible for us to get off. We keep trying to push ourselves forward, but there are so many of them that we can't get off. Next thing I know the doors are closing, and we're still inside with the tough guys and an entire troupe of mimes.

Of course they don't say anything. Mimes never do. They must be from a mime convention. They wear those little tags that say HELLO, MY NAME IS ...

Stephen and I stare at them. Pincushion and Tattoo stare at them. They stop growling. My ears clear.

The train starts. Stephen and I take seats near to the door.

The two mimes nearest to me sit down—but not on seats. They sit down on the air. I don't know how they do it, but they look like they're sitting down. Their legs are crossed and their knees are bent, but they're in the air. They smile at us. One of them holds out his wrist to check the time on his watch—only he isn't wearing a watch. The other one unfolds a newspaper—only of course she doesn't have a newspaper. But she makes all the gestures about unfolding this huge newspaper. And all the time they're sitting there, in mid-air.

The mime beside Pincushion has his arm out, so that he can hang on to the pole for support—only he's not hanging on to any pole. He's hanging on to mid-air. The train goes over a bump, and the mime hangs on to the invisible pole even tighter. His body bounces up and down with the train. He doesn't fall.

The mimes act like regular subway passengers. They're sitting, standing, leaning—but they're not sitting or standing or leaning on anything. They turn invisible pages of invisible books, they chew invisible gum. One guy near me unwraps and eats a candy bar. I swear I can smell the chocolate. It's an Oh Henry! I know it. Only it's invisible.

The two tough guys stare and stare.

The train comes to the next stop. No one gets off or on. The train starts up again. The tough guys keep staring. They go over to the mime leaning against an invisible doorway. His name tag says his name is Vince.

"Hey!" says the tattoo guy. "What's going on?"

He has a voice like an old attic staircase, high up and kind of creaky.

Vince the mime smiles up at him. Reaches into where his shirt pocket would be if he had a pocket. Unwraps and offers a piece of gum.

It's such a real gesture that the tattoo guy believes it, and reaches out. Then he catches himself, and moves to slap

Vince's hand, but Vince has already taken his hand away. The tattoo guy hits only air.

He swears.

None of the other mimes are noticing. They're busy doing their mime things. One of them appears to have fallen asleep. His head is back against the—well, against nothing, and he's snoring silently away.

Pincushion makes a fist. At my side I can hear Stephen whimper.

Vince doesn't pay any attention. Pincushion cocks his arm, ready to throw a punch. He draws back his arm, and ...

Does the subway train swing extra wide? Does it hit a bump? Does it jerk suddenly, slowing down? I don't know. But Vince, the invisible-gum-chewing mime, bounces suddenly in his invisible chair. So does the mime beside him. So do all the other mimes. All at once, and all in perfect time. They bounce up and down as if the subway had hit a bump. The illusion is perfect—so perfect that Pincushion staggers and falls over. Tattoo falls on top of him.

So convincing is this performance that I can't even tell if it is a performance. There's no sound of brakes, no sound at all except the regular *clackety clack* of the train wheels. They don't miss a beat. And yet, watching the mimes, I feel the bump myself—so strongly that I grab on to Stephen to steady myself.

"Did you feel that?" I ask.

"What?" he says. He isn't watching the mimes. He stares down at the floor of the subway car, where Pincushion and Tattoo are scrambling to their feet.

"Didn't you feel anything? Did you . . ." I stop talking. The subway car is slowing for the next stop. Cream-coloured bricks, with dark lettering. Museum. I forget about the mimes and the meanies. I think about what the blind man said to me before he left. I stare out at the platform. Funny, we're going slower and slower, but my heart is beating fast.

Stephen is on his feet, in front of the doors. An old man is standing on the platform, bent forward, peering intently into the passing cars. He's way over the yellow line, too close to the tracks for safety. A worried old man with a bad heart. Grandad.

The doors open. We get off.

I look hard up and down the platform, but I can't see anyone else. Not a young man in a wedding costume. Not even a dashing stranger. All I see is Grandad.

Stephen waves frantically. His face is bright with new life: first green after a long hard winter. He's relieved. Grandad is relieved. So why am I disappointed?

We both keep close to Grandad as we walk up the stairs to street level. And what a street! Six lanes across, and every one of them full and fast-moving. It's a huge river of traffic, flowing in two directions at once.

The museum looms in front of us, gray and dirty. Across the street is a park. The trees are waving their branches in the wind. The leaves flutter like handkerchiefs.

A man stands near us with one foot on the busy street, waiting to cross over to the park. He's whistling. A happy guy in sandals and blue jeans, with long hair, red as mine, tied behind him in a ponytail. He turns to smile at us, naturally, the way he smiles at everyone, and then stops and smiles even wider. For all the world like he recognizes us. He waves.

Then he walks out into the street.

I stare after him. My heart thuds in my chest. "Who's that?" I say.

"Who?" asks Grandad.

"The man with the ponytail."

"What man?" Grandad pulls me towards the museum. I stare back over my shoulder. The man crosses one lane of traffic. Then another. The cars are whizzing by so fast I'm sure he's going to get hit. Why would he decide to cross right in the middle of the block? It's dangerous to cross in the middle of a busy street. There's a set of lights down the road.

The cars keep moving. He dodges across another lane of traffic.

"I don't see anyone with a ponytail," says Grandad.

"Do you see him, Stephen?" I ask.

But my brother isn't paying attention to me. "Look, Grandad! An ice cream cart ..."

His voice is lost in a sudden squeal of brakes, a crash, and the sound of a horn blaring. We're near the steps of the museum now. I turn around and stare. Grandad doesn't. Neither does Stephen. It's as if they don't notice any of this.

I get that floating inside-the-movie feeling again. I'm not worried about the feeling. But this is a scary movie.

There's a car pointing in the wrong direction. Another car has run into it. Doors are open. People are running around. The man with the ponytail is down. I can see him clearly. He looks small. He's all curled up with his knees pressed against his chest, like a little baby. The noise of the horn cuts out suddenly. I can hear a woman sobbing. I look away.

I'm trembling as I walk towards the museum. I can't get him out of my mind. A careless man, smiling, crossing a busy street. You'll see your dad, said the blind man on the subway. My dad died when I was very young. In a traffic accident.

"Did my father ever wear a ponytail?" I ask.

Now Grandad turns around. "What was that, Jacko?"

"Did he?"

Of course it's all crazy. There's no reason to think the man with the ponytail is my father. Was my father. But I can't help thinking about him.

"So, could we get some ice cream?" asks Stephen. He's standing in front of the cart. "Please, Grandad."

"I suppose so," says Grandad.

I run to the top of the steps with my treat. I can see more clearly looking down. Stephen stays on the sidewalk. I open my mouth to take a bite of ice cream, and then forget about it. My mouth stays open.

I don't know how to put this. The man with the ponytail is on his feet, dusting himself off. He doesn't even look hurt. Traffic is back to normal. All the cars are facing the right way and moving fast. The man with the ponytail straightens up and walks calmly through the river of traffic. He never looks left or right. He's sure of himself. When he arrives at the other side of the street, I'm so relieved I want to cry. He's in the park now, among the trees. He turns to look up at me. My heart fills. I wave to him.

"Careful with your ice cream," calls Grandad. His voice is very faint, as if it is coming from a long way off.

The man waves back. I'm sure he's waving at me. At us. "Grandad, come quick! Do you see? Stephen, Stephen, come up here!" I call. "He's waving to you too. I know it."

Grandad is climbing. Stephen is eating his ice cream down at the bottom of the stairs.

I wave at the man with the ponytail. He waves back. He's on the other side of the street from me, with six lanes of traffic between us, but I feel very close to him. I am filled with a sense of peace. Everything is all right. That's what he is saying. I know this. I don't know how I know, but I do. I stare so long that I can feel tears pooling in my eyes. The man begins to blur. I wave harder.

"Careful, Jacko!" cries Grandad.

Oh, dear. The scoop of ice cream has fallen off my cone. Fudge ribbon—I should mind, but I don't. I'm crying, but not about the ice cream. I'm crying because I'm so happy. It's the strangest thing.

I look across the street. There are people in the park, but none of them has a red ponytail. The tree branches wave in the wind.

The movie's over. And it wasn't scary after all. It was wonderful.

"What is it, Jacko? What's wrong?"

"Nothing," I say. "Nothing at all."

The first mummy on display isn't what you'd expect. There's no big wooden casket, no trailing bandages, no gold. The first mummy is a poor guy who'd been buried in the ground. He's on his side, all curled up. The writing on the side of the display case explains that bodies take up less space when they're all curled up.

Looking down at this poor dead guy, I think about the man with the ponytail all curled up on the road. I think about all the dead people in the world, curled up on their sides, like millions and millions of babies waiting to be born. I think of them all in the park, waving. And I smile.

"What's so funny?" Stephen asks me.

"Nothing."

I smile and smile.

Pincher

by

Brian Doyle

My all-time favourite Canadian children's book is Brian Doyle's Angel Square. *I've probably read it a dozen times. "How does he do it?" I ask myself. I've read everything else Brian has published. And I've watched him break up a room packed with people—grown-ups—telling them a story. Seen tears in their eyes, seen grown people in their go-to-meeting clothes roll around on the floor. Brian's that funny. But "Pincher" isn't funny. "Pincher" is stunning. You'll probably read it a dozen times, trying to figure out how he does it.*

Pincher thought that if he could keep his face from hitting the floor he wouldn't die. If he could put his hands out to break his fall and turn his head so his nose and teeth wouldn't smash into the terrazzo, he'd be OK.

He was surprised how far forward he'd been pitched by the impact of the bullet.

Funny how he knew it was going to happen.

It was something to do with the way Alexander was handling the gun, showing it to Pincher, leaning into his locker so nobody'd see. Showing him it was loaded, showing him the safety catch, his hands shaking.

Clumsy, uncoordinated Alexander. Pincher had a premonition as he turned to walk away after he slammed his locker closed and clicked the lock shut. Wouldn't you know it, clumsy Alexander. The gun is going to go off—an accident. He knew it.

Sure enough, now he was flying through the air, hit in the back.

Hardly felt it—just a touch, like something tugged his shirt—but the force of it!

And now, go down.

This slow motion stuff is easy, he thought, just put out your hands and break your fall, turn your head aside. There. Simple.

Done!

That was easy. Here's the floor.

Pincher decided not to try to get up as the gunshot exploded in echoes up and down the hall.

Even as the rolling thunder died away, doors were being ripped open, teachers came running, students, cries of alarm, screams of shock.

I'll wake up in the hospital, he thought, as the vibrations of running feet tickled his ear on the polished floor.

I'm not going to die, he thought.

I'm going to live.

And he was right.

Ever since he woke up, all they could talk about was what a miracle it was. How the bullet went right through him without touching anything. Missed his spine, vital organs, arteries. Just tore some muscles, lost some blood, be sore for a while, up and around in no time!

And all the attention, the flowers, the visitors, the jokes, the tears, the kisses, the cards.

Of course, Alexander was kicked out of school. Zero tolerance policy.

It didn't seem to bother him much, though. Said he was looking for a job. Face didn't look as pasty as it usually did. And his hands weren't shaking as he apologized for what happened. And he wasn't as clumsy looking, the way he sat on the edge of the bed.

Shooting somebody in the back must have agreed with him, Pincher smiled to himself.

But the surprise visit was from Carol. Carol wouldn't talk to Pincher or have anything to do with him up until now. She told him why, too, when he called her on the phone that time last summer.

"It's your friends," she said. "The people you hang with. They're scum. And your name. Pincher. Doesn't that mean you're a thief?"

But now, in the hospital, not only visiting but being very friendly. Brought him a book, held his hand! Leaned over to say goodbye, almost kissed him, he thought. He felt a rush with the smell of her hair as it tumbled onto his chest when she leaned over him.

"We're glad you're going to be OK," she said. We're glad. Who's we? Pincher felt like asking. But he didn't.

He just wanted to drown in her eyes.

He was home from the hospital in three days and back to school the next week.

Everybody was all over him. Never had so many friends, so much attention.

He and Carol, going down the hall between classes, sitting in the cafeteria, walking around after school, always together, celebrity status.

At home, his parents were back together. His mother moved back in right after the accident. In fact, although they didn't come right out and say it, it was the accident that brought his parents back together.

"Good things can come from bad things," his father said.

And no more hitting like before.

And the shouting even stopped. And the all-of-a-sudden meanness.

They were so pleasant to each other, so loving, it was weird.

Actually sitting down together to eat, even! Pass the butter please. Thank you. How was your day? Pardon me. Stuff like that. Pincher would sometimes stop chewing and look at them both, marvelling, maybe shaking his head at it all. And his parents, both looking up at him, innocent eyes, saying, "What!" smiling.

Then there was the hilarious thing with the geometry. In the previous geometry exam, before the accident, Pincher came last in the class with the ridiculously low mark of four. Four out of a hundred. The teacher dropped his exam paper out the window. The geometry teacher, Isosceles they called him, had this method of handing back the papers that he considered to be extremely witty. He'd hand out the papers in order of the marks. He'd take the first paper, the highest mark, and hold it away up as far as he could reach, standing on his toes, and call out the name and the mark. "Whatsyourface—95!" Holding it away up there. Then the next mark would be held a little lower. Still up there but not on tiptoe this time. "Whats-yourname—92!"

And on, down.

Down to the lowest marks, which he'd hold away down near the floor. And the last paper, the lowest mark, which he'd toss into the basket.

With Pincher's four percent, he walked over to the window, called Pincher's name to the street, and yelled out the mark and dropped his paper out the window into the wind.

Hilarious.

This time around, though, Pincher couldn't wait for the papers to be handed back. Something had happened to him during the exam.

Everything fell into place, all the angles, the planes, everything fit. He nailed all the theorems and solved the problems so easily that he could almost hear the clicking and snapping of the shapes as they slid together and spring-locked on each other like parts of a clean new weapon.

He got 99 on the exam.

Missed a little bit of math. Added a number wrong, a misprint really. Lost one lousy mark.

Isosceles climbed up on his desk, stood tiptoe on top of his desk, impaled the paper on his pointer, held it up over the ceiling lights, called out Pincher's name and the number. "99."

Mayhem in the class.

Geometry is like that, Isosceles told them after; you can suddenly get it. It's the kind of stuff that can dawn on you. It can all come to you in a big minute. Make sense all at once. Like getting a joke you didn't get at first.

A weird feeling. Quick as a flash you see everything.

It happened once when he was just a kid. It was at his grandmother's funeral. Everybody standing around the funeral parlour and the coffin open with all the flowers. But something was wrong. Some of the aunts were whispering about something embarrassing. Pincher finally overheard.

His grandmother's dress was on backwards! The undertakers, or whoever, had put the black silk dress on

Granny with the white trimmed V-neck at the back and the buttons down the front. That was wrong. The buttons go down the back. How awful.

That was OK, though, Pincher thought. Just forget about it. She looked horrible anyway. What's the difference?

But it was what his grandfather did that caused him to see everything. Caused everything to dawn on him.

The aunts were trying to keep the grandfather from noticing the dress. But he overheard the whispering and one of the meeker of the aunts spilled it to him and he marched noisily over to the casket and stared down and turned purple with rage. Then he raised his clenched white fist and brought it down hard into her dead face.

"Mildred!" he screamed. "You stupid cow!" That look on the old man's face. Pincher had seen the look many times on his own father.

Everybody was shaking, terrified.

Pincher could see then where his father had learned all this screaming and hitting.

Grandfather to father to son to grandson? He could see it all as his grandfather's bony fist mashed the waxy head in the coffin.

Remembering, too, those times at the cabin with his father. His father and the three other men he played cards with. He was just a kid then. Nine or ten.

Remembering the time his father humiliated him.

His father had been so loving and friendly that day. Praising him up for going to the well to get the beer and returning so quickly, the beer bottles clean and cold, getting the other card players to give him dimes and quarters each time he went, stroking him with encouragement, winking at him, nudging him secretly, squeezing his arm, saying how strong he was, ruffling his curly hair, saying what a good lad he was, how proud he was to be the father of such a good and talented little man.

The feeling was all warmth and the heart was full.

That day, after many trips to the well for beer, Pincher was showing them the trick he'd learned. A back bend. He could bend over backwards, touch the floor, then kick over. Very supple back. His father got him to show the trick to his friends. They were playing cards. There was a blanket spread over the table where the cards and the money sat. And the beer bottles and the ashtrays.

When he was halfway through the trick, bent over backwards like that, Pincher had his pants pulled down by his father.

He didn't complete the trick.

He collapsed in shock. Tears came. His face screwed up in hurt and heartbreak as they all laughed.

Then, his father, sarcastic out of the side of his mouth, growling, mad now, telling Pincher not to be such a big baby. Crybaby, can't take a joke. What a sissy. What a useless tit. "Get up off the floor, you useless tit. Be a man! Go down to the well and get us four cold beers. Make yourself useful! Be good for something for a change."

The rain tapping the tarpaper roof of the cabin. Pincher once again making his way down the steep, greasy clay path into the swamp where the spring-fed well was.

Pincher, plunging his arm into the icy water up to his shoulder to reach the first bottle of beer.

Pincher was remembering how numb his arm always got, plunged into the ice cold water, water bubbling up into the box from way down under there somewhere.

Remembering how clear the water was until he pulled the first bottle of beer from the bottom. Disturbing the bottom would cloud the water. The next three bottles he would have to feel for.

The clear water was suddenly swirling, clouded with mud.

Pincher, remembering stopping on the path on the way back and putting down the beer against a rotten log.

In front of him, facing ahead, sat a green frog, blinking in the rain. Pincher caught it easily and lifted it up and squeezed it until its mouth opened with a squawk and its eyes popped.

Then he raised the frog high, and with all of his strength, he smashed it to the clay, splatting it flat with a cruel slapping whack.

Pincher remembered that he'd like to kill a person like that—pick them up and slam them to the clay, squash them with the impact. The way the frog burst on the clay path when he slammed it into its death.

The remembered feeling grew violently inside him like an exploding airbag. The rage pushed up into his throat like puke.

But that was a long time ago, he warned himself.

Since the accident, everything had changed.

Everything was great now.

That spring he made the school track team. For the first time in his life he was chosen to be on a sports team.

His specialty was the pole vault.

In the city final he placed second in the junior category. He cleared just over four metres. The feeling was full inside him. The ecstasy of the attention. He was the best junior pole vaulter in his school. And only this much away from being the best junior in the city. He gulped down the success like he would gulp down a dipper of cold well water on a hot day in August.

It all came together, just like the geometry. The pole carried at the proper angle. The tip lowered and slid perfectly into the box. The left foot slammed into the exact mark every time. The right leg kicked. The left hand sliding up the pole to join the right hand. The head back, the hips high over the shoulders, the bending of the pole, now the push, and the pole pauses and falls casually back and now the delicious sight of the bar in front of your face as you laugh and relax and fall, sprawl onto your back into the bag.

As they pinned his ribbon onto his sweater, his father jogged over.

He hugged his son and asked him to go up to the cabin with him. Just the two of them, no card players, catch a few fish, cut some wood maybe, just relax. Things would be different.

Guaranteed.

At the cabin, Pincher was pumping the Coleman lamp. His father put his hand over his and helped pump. The touch was gentle. Not like the times past when he'd put his hand over and squeezed so tight that the boy's flesh would grind against the metal, and the bones of his fingers would be like dry sticks about to crack, and tears would fill his eyes.

But this time it was the father's tears. He was so sorry. Say it slow.

So, so, very, very sorry.

And the father told of his own father and how he had been tormented, tortured and abused by the old man, and how he had passed it on to his son without knowing what he was doing, and how much he loved his son now and how it was all over now, the cruelty, the meanness, the hurt.

Their lives were new now.

And the father's tears poured down on their joined hands and wet the lamp and the table and flowed with such volume that Pincher was becoming alarmed.

This could be a world record for tears, he thought. And he smiled and then laughed at the idea how the tears could cover the floor of the cabin, rise up in the small cabin to the level of the little windows and flow out the forced door, and in a river of tears of regret and sorrow, table, chairs, lamp, father and son would be carried out on the flood, the river of hot tears, tears of oh, I'm so sorry for the hurt that I caused . . .

A guidance teacher and a phys ed teacher were keeping the crowd back for the ambulance people and the police in the school hallway.

The guidance guy thought he might have talked to this kid at one time about family problems, or the gang he was running with—or maybe it was some other kid. Hard to tell them apart sometimes these days.

The guidance guy was trying again to remember if he'd ever talked to this kid. Pincher, they were saying his name was. The nickname sounded vaguely familiar but he couldn't place him.

He was a little ashamed. It was his job to be on top of these things.

Some of these kids are almost invisible. They just don't give you anything to help you remember them, he thought.

Kid from nowhere, going nowhere.

Now, the kid with the gun, Alexander. He knew him for sure. Bad news. Something was bound to happen with that kid. But the other one, Pincher.

Couldn't place him, really.

Have a conversation. Cut the tension a bit. The horror of it. A kid lying shot dead in a large pool of blood in a school hallway. What's the world coming to, anyway?

The guidance guy, pale and frightened.

The phys ed guy, not shocked by this, has seen it all before. Used to drive an ambulance.

The guidance guy spoke first. "Do you think he suffered?"

The phys ed guy, gruff, out of the side of his mouth. "I don't think so."

"You think he died quickly, then?"

"Very definitely. Look at the position of his arms. Straight down by his sides. And his hands. Look at them. Palms up."

"Which means?"

"He didn't try to reach out to break his fall."

"I see."

"And look at the way his face is flat into the floor. And the blood there from the broken nose and teeth. Not blood from the bullet damage."

"He didn't even turn his face away?"

"That's right. The way I see it, I bet they'll establish he was done before he hit the floor."

Done, thought the guidance guy. What an odd way to put it.

Done.

The Ghost of Eddy Longo

by

Tim Wynne-Jones

What collection of Canadian stories for boys would be complete without a hockey story? Not surprisingly, Canadians have written some super hockey books for kids: Scott Young's popular hockey trilogy, beginning with Scrubs on Skates, *for instance, and more recently, Roy MacGregor's entertaining* Screech Owl *series. It was hard, however, to find just the right excerpt to suit my needs, so I decided to include a story of my own. Like many boys in this country, I dreamed of becoming a hockey star when I grew up. The fact that I was one of the world's most porous goalies didn't stop me dreaming. I based the character of Tyler Taylor in "The Ghost of Eddy Longo" on a Grade Five hero of mine. When Joel follows Tyler, trying to walk like he does—that's me. So this is a hockey story, but it's also a scary story about the perils of winning!*

See that guy coming towards us? The one in the yellow and green jacket? You can't tell from here, but it says "Christ the King" on the front. The guy's not bragging. That's the school he goes to. His name's Tyler Taylor. He's sixteen.

Watch him walk. His feet stick out sideways. He kind of swaggers like a pirate. It's freezing but his jacket is open. He's cool—the coolest—and not just because his jacket is open.

He's passing by. Look down. Now look up quick. See what it says on the back of the jacket? "Goalie." He's the goalie for Christ the King. They've played six games this season and his goals-against average is zero. That's right. Nobody has put a puck past Tyler Taylor all season. It might be a world record.

See the guy following him? That's my best friend, Joel. Joel is walking like Tyler, his feet sticking out sideways. Only Joel has his jacket zipped up on account of his asthma. Joel thinks if he walks like Tyler, it will make him a better goalie.

"It's the swagger," he whispers as he walks up alongside me. I join him. We both walk like Tyler, feet sticking out, arms swinging free. "It makes him more limber or something." Joel's been watching Tyler a lot. We both try to feel what it must be like to be inside that sixteen-year-old body, so loose-limbed and quick. Nothing gets by him.

"He's possessed," says Joel. We both laugh our guts out.

· · ·

You might be wondering what kind of parents name their kid Tyler Taylor. Well, the fact is, it isn't his original name. He was born Tyler Longo, but when Tyler was about five, his father disappeared and never came back. So Mrs. Longo remarried somebody named Frank Taylor who adopted Tyler and gave him his name. She might have met someone named Brown or Le Maitre or Grabowski but no. She married a guy named Taylor, and so Tyler is stuck with being Tyler Taylor.

"Too many T's," says Joel.

"Too many Y's," says me. We've had this conversation a million times. "But by the time he makes it to the NHL he'll be called Buzz-saw Taylor, or something like that." I'm thinking of how vicious he is protecting his goal crease, swinging his big stick like a weapon—like some Dungeons and Dragons monster it's going to take you three lives to get past.

"I bet he'll take back his father's name," says Joel. And this, though it has never occurred to us before, seems most likely. Longo is a big hockey name in our town, but not because of Tyler's disappearing father.

It was Eddy Longo, Tyler's great-grandfather, who was the famous one. He was a centre with the old Montreal Maroons back in the twenties and thirties. Won all kinds of trophies. He was fast and his hair was white so they called him the Ghost. Whoosh, he was past you, just like that. Like something in the night.

Tyler's grandfather played professional, too, with the Leafs. They just called him Carl; he never earned a nickname. He was good, lasted fifteen seasons, but he didn't live up to the legend that the Ghost had carved out for himself.

Then came Tyler's father, Randy. Randy played in the pros a bit, but mostly he played around. That's what they say. Randy earned himself plenty of nicknames, most of them ones you couldn't print in the newspaper. Tyler's father was a gambler and a low-life. That's what everybody at the rink says, though they don't say it around Tyler.

Randy Longo disappeared—never heard from again. There's all kinds of speculation as to what happened to him, but it's been eleven years now since he took off and nobody talks about it much, except some of the old-timers who hang around the rink to watch our local Junior B team. The Junior B team is called the Ghosts in honour of Eddy Longo. They're pretty good.

But these days no one is as good as Christ the King. A lot of the old-timers will be at the rink this afternoon to see the school take on Mary Magdalene from Tressourville. They wouldn't normally come out for a high-school game, but they'll be there to see Tyler defend his zero goals-against average. So will Joel and I. There's a rumour that a TV crew from the city will be up to catch the game. There are those—you hear them around the snack bar in the arena—who believe that Tyler will go on to be the greatest Longo of them all, even if his name is Taylor.

"In a couple of years he won't be able to walk anywhere with just two guys following him," says Joel.

"There'll be crowds chasing him," says me. "And they won't all be guys."

Outside the arena, Tyler stops at a bronze statue that rises four metres from its concrete base. It's the Ghost, his stick poised for the face-off, his knees bent, his head up. Apparently Eddy Longo was little—wiry and fast—so the statue fools a lot of little kids who think the Ghost was a giant. It fooled me when I was little. Then again, he *was* a giant, kind of—a legend.

We watch Tyler as he passes the statue. Swipe—he rubs one of the bronze skates with his hand for good luck. He doesn't look up at the statue; he just keeps moving, like someone scooping up some holy water on the way into church or something. Then he heads into the arena. We stop at the statue and give the skate a good hard rub as well. We aren't the only ones. Most of the bronze statue is grungy green with age, and there's usually pigeon poop on the Ghost's shoulders, but the toe glints and shines from all the good luck that's been rubbed out of it.

"I wonder if the guys from Mary Magdalene rubbed the toe," says Joel.

"They're gonna need it," says me. Then we swagger into the arena, our feet sticking out to either side, silent now, caught up in expectation, imagining strapping on a goalie's trappings, imagining a goal-less season.

"The boy's cracking," says a woman sitting about four seats away from Joel and me. Tyler has just missed blocking a shot that, luckily, hit the goal post. Mary Magdalene is coming on hard. The arena is about half full, which is impressive for an afternoon game.

"Have you seen her before?" Joel whispers. I shake my head and steal another glance. She's about my mom's age but she's not anything like my mom. She's got about a ton of make-up on and she's smoking. There is no smoking allowed in the arena, but everybody's too caught up with the game to care. Besides, she doesn't look like someone you'd want to cross. She's wearing a fur coat and the fur still has its head on; looks like it might bite your head off if you got too close.

"Somebody'd better score on him soon or the poor kid's gonna crack," she says to no one in particular.

I look at Joel. His face is mad, but he doesn't say anything.

"Maybe she's a teacher at Mary Magdalene," I whisper. Joel cracks up.

Then Christ the King gets a penalty and Mary Magdalene puts on the pressure. They fire off a couple of fast ones from the point. Tyler handles them with ease. The crowd cheers, but it's a strained kind of sound, as if a huge fist has closed around the arena. Christ the King kills the penalty and turns the game around, taking the action back down the ice.

"Who's he think he is? God?" says the woman. She isn't talking to us, though we're the closest people to her.

"I think she's drunk," says Joel.

"I think she's wacko."

I don't think she heard us, but suddenly she turns to look our way. We just watch the game, trying not to laugh. We're waiting for her to say something to us. Then the buzzer goes and it's intermission. It's 1-0 for Christ the King. The buzzer stops but the buzzing in the arena doesn't.

Joel and I slip out for a Coke. We get back to our seats and are sitting there talking, when suddenly the woman is right behind us, leaning forward. Up close, her fur looks pretty flea-bitten.

"You think I don't know?" she says. "You think I don't know what I'm saying?"

It isn't really a question, so we don't answer.

"His old man was just the same," she says. " 'Cept his game was for higher stakes."

The teams are skating onto the rink. Joel and I turn our attention to the ice surface, clean and shining after the Zamboni. We concentrate on Tyler, roughing up the surface in front of his net so he'll have more traction. The woman doesn't move. She lights another cigarette. Joel coughs. Tyler bangs his goal posts with his stick. *Bang, bang.*

"Bah, superstition," says the woman. "That ain't gonna help him." She laughs a sandpapery laugh. She blows out a long line of smoke. Joel coughs again. His asthma is getting to him.

"Do you mind," I say to her.

She looks at us as if she hadn't really noticed anyone was there. It takes her a minute to figure out what I'm saying. Then she looks at her cigarette, and dropping it to the floor, she puts it out with the pointy toe of her high-heeled boot. They're black leather but salt-stained and ratty.

"Thanks," says Joel.

"You know the Longo boy?" she asks.

We don't answer. The action has started. Tyler is at the far end of the rink now, and Mary Magdalene gets a break-away. The player loses the puck, though, and all Tyler has to do is fall on it. Still, he jumps up screaming at the skater, who has glided too close by him.

"He's strung way out," says the woman. Then she leans forward again. "You friends of Tyler Longo?"

Joel looks sideways at me. As if.

"His name's Taylor," I say to her. She laughs.

"Tyler Taylor," she says, chuckling. "Randy woulda loved that."

I keep my eyes on the game, but my mind can't let go of what the woman said. I steal a peek at Joel. He heard it, too.

Just then, Mary Magdalene poke-checks the puck from Christ the King and takes a ferocious slapshot from in close. Like magic, Tyler throws out his glove arm and plucks the puck out of the air. The crowd goes wild.

"He's amazing!" says Joel reverently.

"You wanna know somethin'?" says our uninvited neighbour.

I'm just about to say no when she coughs loudly—badly—and doubles up, gathering her flea-bitten coat around her as if she's trying to keep her lungs inside her skinny body. One of the creatures who make up her coat is staring at me with a flat brown stare.

"He's only human," she says finally in a hoarse whisper.

Joel is angry. "Yeah, maybe," he says, "but he's a lot better than some humans." He doesn't turn towards her, but she knows who the comment is intended for.

I make a grimace. I'm afraid she might start kicking us with those pointy boots. But she sits there, still as can be. It's as if the combination of her coughing spree and Joel's insult has knocked the breath out of her.

I can't help it; I feel sorry for her. Once, when the action comes down to our end, I steal a glance at her again. I notice she's shivering. She's sick, I think. She doesn't look quite so scary anymore.

Then Christ the King scores again.

"You see," says Joel, turning to her as we jump up and down. "Nobody's going to beat him. Nobody."

It's a dumb thing to say, really. Tyler didn't score the goal. But I sort of know what Joel means. Christ the King has gotten its second wind and the other team is folding.

The woman smiles at Joel, almost sweetly. "Maybe not today," she says, calmly now. "But, for his sake, I hope soon."

Our faces must have looked pretty confused. She smiles again, chuckling her gravelly chuckle. Then she looks at us very seriously as if she is weighing up whether or not she can trust us.

"The boy is possessed," she says.

Joel and I sit down, and now we're the ones who are shaking. Nobody has said anything about Tyler being possessed except us on the way to the rink.

We watch the game in silence for a bit, glancing back and forth at each other. A fight breaks out at the other end of the rink, catching everyone's attention. Tyler, his temper getting the better of him, gets a penalty for being the third man in. When we turn to see what the woman will say about this, she's gone.

"It's not such a big deal," says Joel. "I mean, somebody always says geniuses are possessed sooner or later. We said it sooner and she said it later."

But he knows and I know that that isn't what's bothering us. There was something about the look on her face and the way she said it that wasn't the same as the way we had, joking about it on the way to the game. She meant it.

"Hit me with your best shot," says Joel. He's suited up on the mini-rink in his backyard. I put everything I've got into a drive. *Thwack.* The puck lifts and lifts, sailing over Joel's head and over the fence into his neighbour's yard. A dog back there barks. Joel glares.

"You're possessed," he says, banging his stick against the goal posts.

"It's the puck," I say.

"Right," says Joel. "The puck is now possessed by Sparky. He's got more pucks than we do."

"Hey," I tell him. "You've got a zero goals-against. What're you complaining about?"

"You only got three shots on the net," he says, pulling off his helmet.

It's cold so we head inside. Joel's dad is filling a lunch pail with about twelve roast-beef sandwiches. He works the night shift at a factory.

"Gonna catch the big game tonight?" he asks. We both nod. Sacred Heart is coming into town. And Tyler Taylor is now on a seven-game shut-out streak. It's a rare night game for a high-school team, rescheduled so more folks can come out.

"There's talk that *Sports Illustrated* has sent up a reporter," says Joel's dad, cutting up some pickles. "Wish I could be there."

"There'll probably be NHL scouts," says Joel as he zaps us a couple of Cup-a-Soups.

"What do you know about Tyler's father?" I ask.

Joel's dad shakes his head. "A real hard case," he says. "I went to school with Randy."

"What happened to him?"

I watch Joel's dad take a pie out of the fridge and cut himself a large hunk. Cherry. He licks the flat of the knife and chucks it in the sink. There's a bit of cherry on the corner of his lip. It looks like blood.

"Well, most people figure he was wiped out by the mob for his gambling debts. Oh, it was big-time stuff for a small town like this. There's no proof, mind you. They never found his body. Some people figure he just ran out on Carrie and the boy and didn't leave a forwarding address."

"What do you think?"

Joel's dad thinks for a minute. "I think the mob got him," he says. "You wanna know why?" He checks the clock and then leans back on the counter, cleaning off his hands.

We're sitting at the breakfast table with our Cup-a-Soups at our lips, just waiting.

"Because—mean scum-bucket that Randy could be—I can't see how he would have missed the big ceremony even if he'd had to crawl to it."

"The big ceremony?"

"The unveiling of the Ghost."

Joel and I remember the photographs up in the snack area of the arena. But we've never looked very closely at them.

"You mean," says Joel, "that's when he disappeared?"

His dad nods. "I'll never forget it. Boy, the talent that was here in town. The Rocket, Howe, Stasiak, Bathgate, Armstrong, Lindberger. Some of the oldtimers and some of the new stars—the Great One himself."

Joel and I can hardly believe our ears. Gretzky!

Joel's dad laughs. "It was the off-season. A lot of guys wanted to pay tribute to the Ghost. Eddy Longo was a guy who really loved hockey—had a good time. It was a game to him. I remember Howe sayin' that at the ceremony.

"Eddy looked great that day. A real gentleman, in his eighties by then but pretty chipper. You should have seen it. Actually, you did, Joelly, now that I remember. You were there."

Joel just about chokes on that one. "I was?"

His dad looks pleased. "Yeppers," he says. "In a pack on my back."

"I saw the Great One here in town?" Joel has put his cup down. You can see by the look in his eye that he's trying hard to remember it.

"I oughta know," says his dad. "I was the one lugging you around. You were just over one year old."

Joel's dad takes a king-sized Thermos and fills it with coffee from the perc. "I remember seeing young Tyler there. He'd have been about four or five. He was holding Carrie's hand—cute little tyke—and every now and then his granddad Carl would pick him up and show him off. When the Ghost pulled the rope that unveiled the statue, I think Carl handed the boy to him. Yeah, it was in the papers. This spry old hockey legend beaming out at the crowd, holding his great-grandson. Made a lovely picture. The only thing that ruined the picture was Randy not being there. I guess the family tried not to notice."

There is silence for a minute or so. I take a slurp of soup. "I heard some guys at the rink say the mob guys dragged Randy away from the dinner table, right in front of Mrs. Longo and Tyler."

"There's all kinds of tales about what happened," says Joel's dad, packing up his midnight lunch. "He wasn't in town much in those days. He was playing for one of the new expansion teams—Philly, maybe. He and Carrie weren't really together anymore, but he had come up for the ceremony. I saw him myself in town a day or two before the unveiling. Seemed pretty strung out. And then—poof—he was gone. That's why I think they got him."

Joel and I stand looking up at the big bronze of Eddy Longo. It's about half an hour to game time. The arena lights give the Ghost a long shadow that stretches down the path towards the parking lot. He's bigger than ever in this light.

Then we see Tyler coming across the lot, his feet sticking out, his arms swinging, his jacket wide open. He's got his own shadow swaggering along behind him, head down. He passes through his great-grandfather's shadow and comes out into the light, where he reaches out to rub the cold shiny toe.

Suddenly he notices us and his eyes get shifty, as if we might just have a puck or two on us somewhere, maybe hidden in a pocket ready to hurl in his direction, and he's got to be ready to snag it. Anytime, anywhere. It suddenly feels a lot colder, and Joel and I head inside.

And she is there again. In the same flea-bitten furs. She doesn't look like she's changed her make-up since last week. She's sitting alone. We wave as we take our seats, sort of as a joke. She turns away.

The place is packed. Sacred Heart is in second place in the county. They lost to Christ the King 1-0 in the first game of the season. They haven't lost since.

The game starts fast and tough. Before five minutes are up, the Hearts have had four solid shots on Tyler.

"He looks scared to death," says Joel to me nervously, as we watch the goalie regroup after a close call.

"TY-*LER*, TY-*LER*, TY-*LER*." The whole arena is chanting. Maybe it's because of all that foot-stamping that we didn't notice the weird woman moving. Suddenly she's poking her face between Joel and me again.

"As scared as if he's seen a ghost," she says.

Joel and I just about jump out of our skins.

"Who are you?" I ask, before I can stop myself.

She looks at us closely. We can hear the game start up behind us again, but she seems to hold us hypnotized. She's sizing us up.

"His old man's got a hold on him," she says. "He did the same to me, but I got over it. Something's gotta be done."

By now Joel has recovered a bit from the surprise attack. He says, "Well, I hope no one ever tries to unpossess me from being the greatest goalie in the world."

She stares at Joel as if she can't comprehend what he's talking about.

"What do you mean exactly?" I ask her. Behind us the game goes on, back and forth. Back and forth. But something has been on my mind since the first time we met the woman, and suddenly I know what it is. "Tyler's real father—is he back?"

The woman looks at me keenly, then at Joel. "He never left," she says. I feel a chill climb up my spine. She doesn't seem drunk tonight. "His father has been around this arena ever since he vanished." She throws her hands up into the air like a magician, as if she's just scattered Randy Longo all over us in tiny invisible pieces of confetti. I pull back, startled, and actually look around in the air for something. Then I feel stupid.

"This is crazy," says Joel. He turns back to the game, but I can't.

"In the arena?" I ask her.

"Watching," she says. "Watching."

I nod as if I understand. What I think I understand is that this woman is really and truly nuts, and it might be a good idea to play along with her until the intermission and then find somewhere else to sit. Still nodding, I turn slowly towards the ice, catching Joel's eye as I do. He raises his eyebrows.

I try to tune in the game, but it seems far away somehow. I can feel the woman behind us. I can hear her raspy breathing if I listen close enough. Then she starts to talk— mumble, more like. She's going on about Randy Longo. About Randy and her. About the fun of it, at first, when he was still playing. Then about his temper. I watch Sacred Heart passing the puck, shooting on net. I watch Tyler block his twelfth shot, his thirteenth. And all the time the woman behind us carries on without raising her voice.

"Then he started gambling," she says. "That's what got him. Not just in the ordinary way. Sure he lost money now and then—that wasn't so bad. But he was not a man who could stand losing. That was his big problem. He refused to see it. He got himself in deep with all the wrong kinds of people. People who only know one way to solve a problem."

The puck is out to centre ice, but Sacred Heart is on a roll. They steal the puck back from Christ the King.

"In order to be truly great," says the woman, "you have to be able to lose now and then. The great ones learn early. They play to win but they can handle losing. Put it behind them. Separate the bad moments out. They can smile about it. Not right away, but the next day. You see?"

Even as she is saying it, Sacred Heart is all around the net, with less than a minute in the period, swinging and chopping at the loose puck. The crowd is on its feet. I rise with them in time to see Tyler scoop the puck off the ice and, at the same time, take a mighty swipe with his goalie stick at the nearest Heart, hitting him hard across the back of his legs. I watch the player crumple like a water buffalo with a lion on its back. The whistle blows.

"This is the greatest goalie in the world?" The woman says it quietly but loud enough for Joel and me to hear over the hollering of the home-town crowd as Tyler Taylor is ejected from the game.

That's when Joel loses it. "See what you did!" he shouts at her. "You unpossessed him, all right—you *hexed* him. What are you, a witch or something?"

"No," she says.

"Well, you look like one," says Joel.

I know Joel pretty well. I bet the second he said it, he wished he hadn't. I sure did. But I can't think of anything to say. The woman looks down at her hands. Her nails are gross—too long and too red and all exactly the same shape. Suddenly she just looks pathetic.

"I'm sorry," says Joel. "It's just that . . . it's just that . . ." But he can't think what it just is. The buzzer buzzes noisily to end the period. There is no score in the game but with the unsportsmanlike penalty to Tyler, with him out of the game, it might as well be 6-0 for Sacred Heart.

"I'll get out of your hair, boys," says the woman. Neither of us says anything to stop her. "But I'd like you to do something for me."

"What?" I ask. Somehow I feel we owe her.

"You tell your friend Tyler Taylor next time you see him that if he's going to go getting himself possessed, he better dump the spirit of that rascal father of his and let the spirit of the Ghost get inside him and do the job *right*."

It takes a minute for Joel and me to figure it out.

"He rubs the Ghost's toe every time he comes to play," says Joel.

The woman nods. "I seen him," she says. "I seen him. But that's idol worship. Don't people know the difference anymore? Don't you boys know your Bible? Idol worship is all wrong. You gotta look up. If that boy looked up at that statue of Eddy out there, he'd see the old man smiling. He's having himself one whale of a time, Eddy Longo. But Tyler's too much like his own father. He never looked up either. That's how he got blind-sided."

She smiles a little as she gathers herself up to leave, but it's a sad smile. "He couldn't fill his grandfather's skates," she says. "So they went and did it for him." Now she laughs out loud—big and loud—and that brings on a fit of coughing. She doubles over and we back off, afraid she's going to spew. When she recovers, she doesn't even look back at us, just wobbles out of the bleachers on her salt-stained heels.

I want to say that we don't even know Tyler and there's no way we're going to pass on some message from a crazy lady, but she's leaving and that's really what I want now. For her to go. It's stupid, but it's like Joel and I want to blame her for what happened to Tyler, as if she really did hex him in some way. Something did.

Then I remember the look on his face before the game. He'd been spooked all along.

We watch the rest of the game in a kind of glum silence. The back-up goalie for Christ the King is good but not good enough. Sacred Heart wins the game 1-0. Tyler still has himself a zero goals-against average, but it's just not the same anymore.

We hang around in the lobby watching the crowd file out into the winter's night. It has started snowing. Joel and I wander over to look at the photographs of the Ghost. There are pictures of him playing and holding trophies. There are pictures of him with his son Carl and even of the three generations all in uniform, although by the time Randy was professional, Eddy was retired.

There's a group of pictures about the making of the statue. Pictures of it being cast, then one of the bottom half of it mounted on the concrete block. Just from the skates to the top of the hockey pants. It looks funny. The upper half is lying on its side in a big crate ready to be welded on to the bottom half.

And then there are photos of the big ceremony, as Joel's dad called it, when the statue, now all together, was presented to the public. There's even the photo of Eddy holding Tyler. I've seen it before but I've never read the captions so I've always thought it was any old kid. I didn't know it was Tyler. He's not smiling. I can pick out Carrie Longo from the crowd. She's not smiling either. No Randy.

He never left.

I find myself scanning the crowd at the big ceremony, as if maybe Randy was there all along like Huck Finn at his own funeral.

Watching. Watching.

I look around at the lobby, almost completely empty now.

"What is it?" says Joel.

"Maybe he's like the Phantom of the Opera," says me. "Maybe he's in the building in some secret hideout watching every game Tyler plays." My eyes scan the rafters.

"Now she's got you spooked," says Joel. But he looks around, too.

"Maybe if we stayed after they close—"

"Forget it!" says Joel. "Anyway, she didn't say he was *in* the arena. Just *around* it, whatever that means." Joel's as spooked as I am.

We're the last ones to leave. A janitor locks the door behind us. We stand there for a moment, watching the snow swirl around. We head up the path to the Ghost. It's hard to tell with the snow in our eyes and the spotlights pointing up—throwing weird shadows—but, like the woman said, the Ghost seems to be smiling.

"Looks kind of devilish to me," says Joel.

I'm not sure if it's the cold, but I find myself shivering.

He couldn't fill his grandfather's skates so they did it for him.

I lower my eyes. There around the top of the pants, like a corded belt, is a bead where the two parts of the statue were welded together.

Before I can even think, I let out a string of swear words.

"What is it?" asks Joel. He looks scared.

"Those pictures in there," I say. "The statue—"

"What?" says Joel. He grabs my arm.

"The statue's hollow," I say.

"Yeah," he says. "So—"

Then he begins to know, too. He looks at the line where the statue was joined together. "Randy was in town that week. That's what Dad said. Then he was gone. *They never found his body.*"

I can't take my eyes off the Ghost. He's smiling like the woman said, but lit from below his smile looks truly evil.

Then Joel is grabbing on to me. Tightly. "*He's in there?*"

It all makes a gruesome kind of sense—everything the weird lady was saying. And yet, who put the statue together? Joel must be thinking the same thing as I am.

"The mob," he says.

For another minute we try to imagine it. Then Joel punches me in the arm. "Let's get out of here," he says.

But even as we turn to leave, we hear a door open somewhere in the dark behind us, and out from the side of the building a shadowy figure appears. Even before we can see him clearly, we both know who it is. We've been watching this guy all winter.

"Bet he waited so no one would talk to him," whispers Joel. I nod excitedly. And maybe we've guessed something like this might happen. This meeting, I mean.

"Are you gonna say something?" whispers Joel.

"About this?" I whisper, pointing at the statue. But Joel is watching Tyler walk away, and he makes up his mind for us.

"Tough call," he cries. He wants it to sound friendly, like we're on his side. Mostly it just sounds nervous.

Tyler turns around and looks our way. He doesn't say a thing, just stares. He doesn't move.

"Your zero goals-against is still intact," says Joel. I can't believe he's doing this.

"What do you want?" Tyler says.

We don't move. I look at Joel. He can't think of anything more to say.

Then Tyler comes towards us. He squints through the snowflakes on his lashes. "You guys again," he says.

"We were looking at the statue of the Ghost," I say. It sounds pretty dumb. I wonder if Tyler can hear the shaking in my voice. He doesn't look at the statue.

"Coach says I had it coming," says Tyler. He doesn't sound angry, just kind of dull on the edges, like last year's skates. We kind of shrug.

"Coach says I'm lucky they didn't throw me out for the season." We shrug again. I have the feeling Tyler really wants to talk but I can't think of what to say. I feel dizzy.

Tyler looks puzzled, then he turns to go.

"Do something," says Joel.

"No!"

"You've got to!" he whispers frantically.

"Tell a guy I know where his dad's dead body is?"

Tyler couldn't have heard what I said, but he stops and turns around. "What's going on?" he says.

"This is a great statue," I say before I know what I'm doing.

Tyler is coming back and Joel is grabbing my arm so hard that I can feel his fingernails right through my jacket. Right through his gloves.

"Have you ever noticed how he smiles?" I say. "The Ghost, I mean."

I can almost feel Joel wince. I look up. I look back at Tyler. But he's still not interested in looking up. He looks like he's more interested in punching out my lights.

"Who are you guys?" he says. "You making fun of me?"

His face looks angry, but there's something else there. He's tired; that's part of it. And sad or something. Like he's got an ache in his gut. I take a quick glance back up at the statue.

"They say the Ghost loved the game." I almost choke on that. I look at Joel. He looks at me, at Tyler, at the statue, panic-stricken. Then nobody speaks. There's hardly any sound. Just the four of us standing there—Tyler, Joel, me and the Ghost—in the thickly falling snow.

And in the silence I think I hear a sound. Not the traffic up on Delaney. Nearby. I look at Joel. He looks at me. There it is again, and it's coming from the statue. Like a finger on a window.

Tap, tap.

Joel crowds close to me, almost knocking me over.

Tap, tap.

We both look at Tyler to see if he's heard it, but it seems like he's in a trance. He's looking up, trying to make out the smile on his great-grandfather's cold bronze face.

"I don't," he murmurs. I'm not even sure he's talking to us.

"Don't what?" I ask.

"Don't love hockey."

Tap. Tap. Tap.

There is no mistaking it this time. Joel groans. Tyler doesn't seem to notice. He seems far away. He's looking up into the snow.

"So give yourself a break," I tell him. "Lighten up."

"Yeah," says Joel. "Lighten up."

Suddenly, it's as if Tyler has remembered where he is and who he's talking to—a couple of nobodies. "You're telling *me* to lighten up?" he says.

Tap, tap. Tap, tap.

He must have heard it that time. But he's smiling. Smiling at us.

"You're the guys who should lighten up," he says. "You look like you've seen a ghost."

"Not seen," mumbles Joel, but the words are lost in my shoulder where his face is buried.

Tyler chuckles, and before I know what's happening, he reaches out and grabs me by the arm.

And I scream.

I don't mean to scream. It's the suddenness of it. I scream and then Joel screams and we both jump away from him as if he's got a blow torch in his hands.

He steps back. He holds up his hands. "Hey," he says. "What is it with you two?"

That's when Joel loses it for the second time that night.

"It's you," he says. "You scared us. You're a scary guy, Tyler."

Tyler does nothing for a moment. Then he nods. He looks down.

"He didn't really mean that," I say. "We're just a little freaked out. Must have been the game."

"Yeah," says Joel. "The game."

Tyler looks at us again. At Joel. His face looks a bit calmer. "You know, this is weird," he says. "But you're the second person's said that to me tonight. About being scary, I mean."

Joel and I are thinking the same thing. But we're wrong.

"The coach said it to me," he says. "Maybe he's right."

He looks up at Eddy Longo. I can feel my heart going crazy. Joel and I are holding our breath.

"Eddy," says Tyler. "Is this thing all getting too scary?"

Tap, tap, tap, tap.

We all hear it this time. Tyler looks at us, startled. We stare back at him. "Can you beat that," he says. "He talked to me."

Then he laughs out loud.

Joel and I exchange glances.

"The Ghost talked to me," he laughs. "I guess I should listen, eh?"

Joel and I nod. Then Tyler laughs again. He reaches out and rubs the shiny toe. We all laugh a bit. Then the laughter peters away.

"Will you guys be at the next game?" he says. We nod.

"St. John's," says Joel. He knows the schedule off by heart.

Tyler nods. He looks down and kicks at the snow a bit. "If only I knew how to let the pressure off," he says. "Should we ask the Ghost what he thinks?"

"No!" says Joel.

"I think one message is enough," I add quickly. "I mean, for one night."

Tyler suddenly shivers and pulls his jacket together. He buttons it up, brushes the snow off his Christ the King crest. "Maybe it's time to let one get by me," he says. He looks at us suspiciously, as if we might think what he has said is weird. But it doesn't sound weird to us. Not tonight.

"One for the Ghost," says Joel.

"Right." He's glad we understand. "Don't tell anyone I said that."

"No way," says Joel. I second the motion.

Then Tyler Taylor smiles at us. It's not a great smile. He could use some lessons. He turns and walks across the parking lot, his feet sticking out, his arms swinging, swaggering like a pirate until he disappears into the snowy dark. We pause only for a second, but it turns out to be one second too long.

Tap, tap, tap.

And we're out of there! Arms swinging like mad.

Later, when we talk about it, we both agree that the laugh that followed us *must* have been our imagination.

Tennis Champion

by

Ken Roberts

If the last story was about the perils of winning, here's a sports story about a particularly weird way of becoming a winner. Not that Marc Bouchard is any weirder than the rest of us, really; it's just that his mastering of the game of tennis—or certain aspects of it—is unconventional, to say the least. Ken Roberts is a master of crazy ideas. In fact, that's the title of one of his books. Hiccup Champion of the World *is another. In Ken's stories, there is always the sense that everybody has the chance to be a champion at something.*

After the mine closed in Lac Vert, Quebec, the federal government built a tennis court.

The federal government built the tennis court in Lac Vert, Quebec, as part of a national fitness campaign. Lac Vert qualified for one single concrete tennis court, complete with net and a chain-link fence. No lights. Lac Vert would have needed a population of four hundred to qualify for lights.

After the mine closed, the population of Lac Vert dropped to 173. If the government had used this figure, Lac Vert would only have qualified for a horseshoe pit. People might have used a horseshoe pit more than the tennis court.

There were two tennis racquets in all of Lac Vert, Quebec, old racquets Marc Bouchard found in the garage. They had been left behind by a miner years ago.

Marc, who was nine years old, found those tennis racquets and borrowed some money from his mother to buy three new tennis balls from Gabe Macaluso's groceteria. Monsieur Macaluso had purchased fifteen bright yellow tennis balls after the federal government built the tennis courts. He was hoping that people would play, which they didn't, so Marc was able to buy three balls on sale.

"Would you like to play tennis?" Marc asked friends at school, who sneered because they only wanted to play hockey and to someday star in the NHL.

"Would you like to play tennis?" Marc asked his mom and dad and his older sister, all of whom had lists of several dozen things they'd rather do.

"Would you like to play tennis?" Marc even asked old Mrs. Winters, who travelled through town in a motorized wheelchair, and the mayor, Monsieur Leduc, whom nobody had ever seen without a suit and tie.

Nobody wanted to play tennis with Marc.

So, Marc played by himself.

He served to nobody for two hours a day. He hit his three tennis balls and then walked around the net, picked up all three balls, put them into a wicker basket, placed the basket by his feet and then served his three tennis balls back to the other side.

For four years Marc practised all by himself almost every day, even during winter months when the court was clear of snow. Each spring Gabe Macaluso ordered more yellow tennis balls and sold them to Marc.

Marc liked serving, and he learned that if he threw the ball higher, giving himself time to put the weight of his body into the swing, then he could hit the ball harder. He learned that if he hit the ball with the racquet held at just the right angle, the ball would hit the concrete and skid to one side instead of travelling straight.

Marc never would have applied to play in the provincial junior championships if someone—anyone—in Lac Vert, Quebec, had picked up that second racquet and hit some tennis balls back to him. He wanted the chance to play tennis, to have somebody stand on the other side of the net.

The championships were being held in Hull the same day Marc's parents wanted to visit Tante Hélène, so he filled out an application and wrote that he was the junior tennis champion of Lac Vert, Quebec.

Monsieur Macaluso co-signed the form, after putting up a notice in his store window stating that the town's championships would be held that afternoon at 4:00 p.m. and that anybody wanting to play should show up at the court. When nobody except Marc showed up, Gabe

Macaluso declared Marc champion by default. He was accepted as a tournament entry since he was the only registered tennis champion for about 100,000 square miles of northern Quebec bush country.

Marc's parents didn't mind if he played in the championship. They even bought him an outfit so he'd look like a tennis player. Marc's dad drove him from Tante Hélène's house to the country club where the championships were to be held.

"Can you hit the ball at all?" asked his father as he opened the door for Marc. Marc's dad didn't plan to stay.

"I don't know," answered Marc.

"Then why are you playing?" asked his father.

"Because I want to serve to somebody. I want somebody to try to return what I hit them. I want to find out if I can hit the ball."

"Well, have fun. Call me when you're ready to come home. I guess it might be early."

"I guess," said Marc, closing the car door behind him.

Marc watched his father drive away and then walked past fourteen perfect, freshly painted tennis courts. On each court stood three or four boys his age, hitting yellow tennis balls back and forth, warming up.

Marc stared for a few minutes, his fingers gripping the fence, and then he walked over to the athlete's sign-in desk and told them his name.

"First four rounds are single set knockouts," said the woman who handed Marc his schedule. "If you lose, you get to play in the consolation rounds until you lose again."

Marc nodded. He knew how to score a set. He'd read the rules that morning. There was no rule book in Lac Vert but his tante lived down the street from a library and Marc had borrowed a book.

To prove he knew the rules, Marc said, "In a set the first player to win six games gets the victory so long as the player wins by at least two games, or if the score in games becomes tied at six each, then the first player to win a seven-point tie breaker by two points wins the set."

"Right," said the woman, glancing at Marc's old racquet and his high-top basketball shoes. She directed Marc to the court where he was supposed to play.

The first person who was going to stand on the other side of a tennis net and hit a ball at Marc was Nicolas Fournier, the junior tennis champion of Gaspé. Nicolas Fournier asked if Marc wanted to warm up and Marc shook his head no. He didn't figure it would do him any good.

Marc won the toss and elected to serve first. He stood behind the serving line, told the umpire that he didn't need any practice serves, waited for Nicolas to get into position, tossed a yellow tennis ball into the air and then smacked it.

Nicolas's head swivelled around to watch the ball fly past but his legs never moved.

"Ace," shouted the umpire. "Server's point."

Marc made four straight aces and won the first game. Then he stood, as he had seen Nicolas stand, behind the serving area and waited for Nicolas Fournier to become the first person to hit a tennis ball across the net so that he could try to hit it.

Nicolas hit four straight serves and Marc made four swings but missed the ball each time.

"One game each," said the umpire.

Marc and Nicolas traded games until they'd each won six. Neither had returned one single serve.

"Tiebreaker," shouted the umpire.

Marc won the tiebreaker after Nicolas double faulted two straight serves.

Marc won his second-round match and his third-round match and then his fourth-round match, putting him into the finals. In all of his matches Marc had connected with seven balls hit to him, only one of which went back over the net and won him a point. His opponent was too surprised to swing.

A huge crowd sat in the stands for the final three-set championship match. Players and parents gathered to watch Marc serve, the best serve anyone had ever seen a junior tennis player smack, and they came to see if the great Jean Houle, junior tennis champion of Quebec City, could figure out how to return that serve.

Marc won the first set on a tiebreaker. He even managed to hit a few balls back, mostly by sticking out his racquet so a hard-hit ball might ricochet across the net.

Marc won the second set and the match on a tiebreaker, after Jean double faulted on the twenty-third tiebreaker point. Marc's father, who had come to pick him up, watched his son win the match and receive, to shocked and puzzled applause, the largest trophy anyone in Lac Vert, Quebec, had ever won, even the midget hockey team when it won the provincial championships twenty-four years ago.

"Was it fun?" Marc's father asked as he carefully wrapped the tall trophy in a spare blanket and gently nestled it next to the spare tire in the trunk.

"Sure," said Marc. "I liked it."

"Are you going to play any more of these tournaments?"

"Nope. One's enough."

Six months later a federal government employee happened to notice that the junior tennis champion of the entire province of Quebec had come from the town of Lac Vert, a place where the government had built a tennis court.

"Oh good," thought the federal government employee, "our fitness program was a success. Why, I'll bet they need another tennis court."

He was right. Lac Vert, Quebec, did need another tennis court. Marc Bouchard wanted to build rockets and needed a place to launch them.

The Book of Days

by
Lesley Choyce

Welcome to the weird and wonderful middle part of the book.

Lesley Choyce surfs, and I'm not talking about the Net, either. Lesley surfs on the ocean. He lives on the beach not far from Halifax and he surfs just about all the time. Including winter. I'm not kidding. He's also one of the busiest people I've ever met: writing books, running his own publishing company, and hosting his own TV show. And surfing.

I didn't ask him, but I like to imagine it was out on the Atlantic on a blustery winter's day, waiting for just the right wave, that he came up with this bizarre science fiction story. Like Reese, the fisherman protagonist of "The Book of Days," I like to think of Lesley all alone out there—who else would be around? Maybe he saw something bobbing on the tide or washed up on the shore, a little mysterious fragment of someone else's life. And maybe he found himself wondering, just as you or I might do, Where did this come from? Who sent out this "message in a bottle"?

The People did not have very many laws about fishing. Usually anything at all that was found in space could be kept. In fact, there wasn't a great deal out there to find. Once you left the neighbourhood of the outer planets, in fact, space was very empty. Maybe you'd find one molecule of oxygen or, if you were lucky, a speck of silicon dust. But even that was something to a true fisherman.

The People were great collectors of anything found in space. Every home had a special room for fishing trophies. But almost everyone on the planet admitted that their sun system was just about fished out. Some got lucky and discovered a very small asteroid that they could take home. Others continued to collect silicon dust or radioactive particles of anything just for sport.

But there was the one law that everyone had to abide by: if you caught anything in space that belonged to anyone else, you had to give it back. The People were great givers and takers. Lending and borrowing was the most sacred thing in their world. They had all kinds of ancient laws about lending and borrowing. But none were ever enforced because it was unnecessary. You gave away whatever you had and it was always returned in one way or another. It happened automatically.

Since nothing was hardly ever found in space that belonged to anyone, however, fishermen were free to keep their catch. But then came the problem with Reese.

Reese had found plenty of nothing in space for years and years. He was one of the worst fishermen ever to live among the People. And it was probably Reese's own fault. He fished remote areas that were far from the sun. He was bored by cosmic dust and molecule dusters of trace elements. Reese liked deep space and didn't mind scads and scads of nothing. He liked fishing for fishing's sake.

And then one day, Reese was out cruising, looking for anything that presented itself, but happy to be companion to all the emptiness, when he found something.

The something was a probe. A small roundish vault with spikes sticking out. It was maybe a metre across. Reese couldn't believe that he was so lucky. He circled the probe, then came up behind it and slowed down to follow it at its own speed. The speed of the vault was almost zero. It was drifting. Reese knew that in deep space speed was rather relative. But he calculated that the probe had long since run out of whatever fuelled it. Now it just kept going because nothing had got in its way to stop it. And here it was. In his own backyard.

So Reese reeled it in without a fight.

During the last years of life on Earth, folks began to become real interested in leaving some chronicle of who they were. For posterity, one would say. They wanted to leave evidence: a record of who they were as individuals, about what their jobs were, and about what they had learned and thought about life in their neighbourhood and on Earth.

Some rented lockers in old mines that tunnelled very far down into the earth because they hoped that someday another generation would excavate and find the evidence of their existence. Writers sent books down into the earth, filling up old coal mines; film directors paid vast sums of money to store movies down there. All the old mines were filling up.

This was after everyone gave up the idea of saving themselves and their families. Oh, a few folks tried to chase off into space and find another place to live on. But it was very expensive and it didn't work out. And at first, the mines seemed like a possibility for human retreat when the big moment came, but the new weapons took care of that.

When the Deep Threat system was approved for development on one side, it was also approved on the other. And so there was no place left to stick your head in the sand. Either you went off into space and died up there in a tin can or you just hung around and made the best of things until the end. Even space seemed an unlikely place to survive. So far, all of the colonists had ended up dead or returned home, preferring to take their chances on the good old surface of the planet after all.

Christopher Day lived a quiet life in the suburbs of New York, five hundred miles from Manhattan. He had a good job as a research scientist. His main specialty was trees and why they died. All the trees were dying and there hadn't even been a war yet. He pondered on this for a living.

Chris Day had a really nice wife, Camille, and two kids. Hickory, his son, was nine and Willow, his daughter, was eight. They were a sort of new breed of happy-right-up-to-the-end family because that's the sort of folks they were.

The earth was a mess and everything was irreversible, or so it seemed. The oceans had risen as predicted. The New Manhattan sat on the water and would rise with the new levels. There were no trees left there, of course—no room in the new city, no soil.

All of the professionals in the sciences these days studied the end of things. The Save the Whales, Save the Seals, Save the Frogs, Save the Flowers, Save the Trees movements had all died off. People were becoming more realistic. There was much to be learned about the way things stopped existing.

Of course, the men and women who came up with new weapons were still around, dreaming up Deep Threat or Space Chasers and a whole bunch of other things up their sleeves. Everybody was in one way or another working on or studying the end of things and watching the news at night to see if anybody had lit the first firecracker that would call for the curtain.

When the entrepreneurs came up with the idea of sending family probes into space, the public loved the idea. They weren't really probes, because they weren't going to find anything. Except maybe an audience. Or so everyone hoped. But who or what?

Now Chris Day came home with the paper one day and showed the ad to Camille.

"It looks like a lot of money," Camille said.

"We have a lot of money," said Chris. "Besides, what are we saving it for?" This was a common thing for all of the elders to say. The end of the world was doing great things for the consumer economy. Nobody saved money at all any more. What would be the point? Many people (but not the Days) spent well beyond their credit limits, counting on the end of the world before full payment was due. The banks didn't even seem to mind.

But the Days had saved a little and could borrow a lot. They were waiting for something just like this. A chance to send a record of the existence of their family off into deep space.

The price was high: all of Day's salary from day one up to the end except for a small subsistence allowance. But in return, the Days would be able to send a half-hour video disk, a documentary of the daily life of their family, off into the frontiers of space.

It would be like living on forever. Long after the end.

So Chris Day picked a Saturday in May. He got out the home video camera, popped in a fresh platinum disk and started filming Hickory and Willow on the swing set. (Hickory and Willow had been given those names because hickory and willow were two of the species of trees still alive. At least they were when Hickory and Willow were born.)

Chris Day filmed Camille in a new dress smiling up at the sun. He took five minutes of Willow walking along a balance beam and falling off only twice. He then filmed Hickory riding his bicycle all over the lawn where the grass had all died. The grass in the video, however, was sprayed with that rubbery green grass preserver that made any lawn look almost as good as the real thing.

Chris started feeling real creative and he climbed up onto the roof of the house and filmed his backyard with his family just sitting down at a patio table playing Monopoly. Then he climbed down, set up a tripod and filmed himself kissing his wife. Behind them the two kids were doing handstands on the permanent green grass.

Camille suggested they should take a picture of everything they owned, so Chris started filming some footage of his car in the driveway. He was just zooming in on the steering wheel when Camille yelled something, told him to stop.

"I changed my mind," she said. "Let's just do us. Forget the car and the vacuum cleaner."

So they forgot the car and the vacuum cleaner and went back to handstands and kisses and whatever else they could think of. Oh, they filmed themselves eating a meal. The tripod was set up and the table was set. It wasn't even dinnertime. But they ate a big meal together.

The dialogue was great: "Pass the salt, please."

"I really love the way you cooked the artificial asparagus."

"Could I have some more hothouse yams?"

Everyone pretended the food wasn't artificially produced.

The Days went for a walk to the park but decided against filming. There was a lot of fighting there and too many motorized toys.

They went back home and filmed a family discussion that went like this:

Chris Day: What do you like most about the end of the world, Hickory?

Hickory: I like the fact that there won't be any more school.

Camille: What about you, Willow?

Willow: I like the fact that we'll all go together.

"Hmm," said the father and stopped filming for a minute. Camille put her arms around the two kids. Chris put one arm around the whole family, held the camera at arm's length and filmed them hugging. Then he put the kids to bed and filmed them falling asleep. They looked so peaceful.

In the morning, Chris drove the video disk in to the entrepreneur.

Space Legacy was in an upclass neighbourhood with several preserved "living" trees. Day signed away most of his salary for the rest of his born days and got in receipt a guarantee that his disk would be sent off in a private-sector launch vehicle a week from Thursday, assuming the world lasted that long. It would be dispersed with a dozen other probes and headed toward the Horsehead Nebula.

"But there are no guarantees that anyone will ever see it," the entrepreneur said. He knew that it was just a courtesy on his part. No one who walked into the store ever changed his mind.

"But you can watch the launch on your TV at home. We'll pipe it on over channel 77."

"Thanks so much," said Chris and he went home.

Not long after the ginkgo trees stopped growing new shoots, a power failure somewhere in a far north alert station tripped some signal or other and there was a lot of confusion high up with the people who were still studying the best way to end the world. So things didn't go quite as planned. But the effect was good enough.

When Reese opened up the probe and saw the platinum disk, he knew that he was on to something big. He knew he hadn't been fishing emptiness for nothing.

He took it home and called around to borrow every sort of decoding instrument in the neighbourhood until he came up with something that gave him not only sound. But a picture. Reese sat down in a dark room and watched the picture begin to come into focus on the wall. He was alone and it was the biggest moment in his life. "Hi," a smiling man was saying to him. "We're the Day family and this is who we are." The camera work was jerky and a little out of focus.

Reese watched the image on the screen: a little girl skipping rope, walking on a balance beam; a boy hanging upside down on a swing set. People kissing, hugging, sitting down to a table and eating food. It went on and on but Reese was lost in the moment. And then the kids fell asleep.

The voice came back on: "I don't know if anyone will ever see this but we wanted to give it a try. We're the Day family and we live at 4700 Dutch Elm Street in Culloden. That's just off the Number 7800 Highway North. Well, good luck to you, whoever you are."

And then darkness.

Reese was so excited he forgot to eat for two days. He didn't know what to do so he went back out into deep space to fish for a while.

He had seen the most incredible thing he had ever seen. In his world, everyone lived alone. It was the way things had always been. They shared and borrowed like crazy, but none of the People had ever lived with another of the People like in the pictures on his wall.

After a week of fishing around in the emptiness and watching the video over and over alone in his fishery, he knew he had two things he had to do: first he had to share his discovery with the People. Then he had to return the find to whoever had sent it in the first place.

The People were not fully ready for the Day family. But the disk was dubbed and redubbed and found its way into nearly every home on the planet. Everyone watched it alone and, afterwards, cried or laughed or shouted or fell down screaming.

A girl walking on a balance beam, a boy riding a bicycle around in a circle, a man staring into the lens of a camera, the steering wheel of a car—but most of all, people sitting down to eat together, Willow and Hickory asleep and the quavering voice of a man at the end. And then the idea that they all lived together in a single dwelling.

Reese became a controversial figure for his find. Loved or hated, feared or emulated. More and more of the People went out to the fringes and began deep space fishing. That was not so strange at first.

But then some started going out in pairs.

The president of the People called up Reese, who was still anchored in the zone where he had first found the probe. This was an absolute first for Reese.

"You know what you have to do now," the president said. "Not that you haven't done enough already."

"I know," Reese answered, not surprised to get the reminder, even from the president.

"Well, a thing found is a thing found," the president said. "And now a thing has been borrowed and used . . ."

"And I need to return it."

"Right and thank you," the president said and bleeped off.

So Reese gave it a day to sort out particulars at home, to calculate directions and speed and all that. Many very famous People phoned up offering to help but Reese worked alone. No one had ever before had a destination to go to beyond the fringe. Many had gone deep space fishing but found nothing more than fragments. Reese had found a whole thing.

Time worried him a bit. How long had the probe been out there? What would he find on the other end? Would he even live long enough to return it?

But then he would watch the document again. The smiling, the hugging, the fun. It would be worth it to go to a place like that. Even if it had changed. Reese took a hot bath and dreamed he was in the backyard with the Day family.

The journey was not as long as expected. Soon he began to receive sound messages. Then video pictures too. All, he knew, were from years ago. But the closer he got, the more contemporary were the messages. One day he was hearing earth from thirty years ago, the next he was only a decade behind. Then it was last week and soon, yesterday, and before he knew it, he was right up to today.

But today there were no messages.

He circled the planet once and knew he had found the right place. But his heart was filled with sadness. Maybe the shroud was always there. Maybe it was a protective covering.

He came in low, began to read the land masses and oceans, but everywhere it looked more or less the same. Ash and rubble.

But there were figures walking about the rubble. They did not look quite like the Day family. And none smiled. He stopped and asked a man if he knew the Day family and where he could find them.

"Have you come to take us away?" the man asked, his face a palette of injuries.

"No, I just need to return something to the Day family."

The scene would repeat itself many times until he found a raspy shadow of a woman who said that she knew where Culloden used to be.

Reese thanked her profusely for her help.

And then, at long last he found Dutch Elm Street and he found the property where the Days had filmed the amazing gift.

The house was not there. Nor the permanent green grass. Part of the car, though, still sat in the driveway and someone had built a small stone fortress of some sort alongside of it.

"I'm looking for the Day family," Reese said. He tried to make himself sound cheery.

A woman's head poked out of the stone fort. "We're all that's left. What do you want?"

Another head poked out, this time that of a man.

Reese could only stare at them. He knew who they were. How could he help but not see children inside the faces.

"Willow? Hickory?" The words sounded hopeless to his own ears.

The two hunched figures climbed out of the stone fort and looked at him. He was holding out the platinum disk.

Reese saw the surprise, the fear. Then there was hope, and soon, resentment. It hit him hard. But he did not completely understand. Then it clicked. He had been tricked. The video had just been something false, something made up out of an imagination. It could not have been real at all.

Reese set the disk on the dented, rusting hood of the old automobile and turned to go. He had been made a fool of. "You should not have done this to me," he said in anger. "You should not have done this to the People." He turned to leave but then grabbed the disk again. He tried to smash it against a rock but his hand was grabbed by Willow.

"Wait!" she said. "Don't go."

Reese stopped and stood stone-still.

"Will you show it to us?" she asked.

"No," shouted Hickory. "It was not supposed to turn out like this. It was all supposed to end."

Reese looked puzzled.

"Nothing ever does end," she said. "It was wrong to think it would end so easily."

"I want to see it," Willow said. She was so thin and frail, she seemed to bend in the wind.

"I can show you," Reese said. He didn't know about the end, about what went wrong.

Reese stopped the video several times because it made Willow and, finally, Hickory cry. Reese could not figure it out. Hadn't they played a trick on him? Hadn't they made up ghosts for parents and imagined a house and a backyard, then planted the idea of living together in the mind of the People?

After two hours, Hickory and Willow got up to go. Reese took the disk and placed it in Willow's hand. She accepted it and held it to her chest.

"Why did you send that to me?" Reese asked Hickory.

"Because," Hickory answered, "we wanted something to last forever. We wanted something to last beyond the end."

"And now?"

"And now," answered Willow, "we have what we have. What we didn't know was that the end for us would go on and on. Like this."

"Maybe you are mistaken," Reese said.

"Please go," Willow said. "Thank you for sharing the Day family with us again. Just please don't show it to anyone else here."

The disk was still held firmly to Willow's chest.

· · ·

Reese returned to the comfort of the fishery. He rose from Dutch Elm Street and departed from earth. He set a course for deep space. He did not want to return to his part of Horsehead Nebula for a long time.

Eat, Sleep, Jump High for Smarties

by

R. P. MacIntyre

Oh, good, a pet story! Well, not quite. Or, at least, not your average pet story. But then Rod MacIntyre's young-adult stories are never *ordinary and never dull. He is always original and not a little twisted. And he wields a metaphor like a finely honed sword. (A lot better than the kids in Mr. Hawes's English class, as you will soon see.) As well, Rod is an intrepid explorer of emotional territories just off the edge of the map. His writing is thought-provoking, moody, sometimes dark, and in this case, funny, if you like your humour very well done!*

Kathy had this little dog, a miniature poodle whose name was Tupper. Normally I hate little dogs. They're constantly yapping and they bounce around like there's a tiny invisible trampoline under them all the time. But I didn't mind Tupper.

He was reasonably calm and quiet and was very businesslike. He wore a little gray suit and you could almost imagine him carrying a briefcase. Except he was a junkie. He would do anything for a piece of chocolate. He would spring five feet straight up and snap a Smartie out of the air like it was a Frisbee. Kathy said he reminded her of me, totally dedicated to money. I wish life was that simple—eat, sleep, and jump high for Smarties. Except it isn't.

I like money. Lots of it. Wads of it, bursting from my wallet. Money is good. I never have enough.

I like money so much, I'm even willing to work for it.

The first job I ever had was selling Kool-Aid, "Randy's Kool-Aid, 25 Cents a Glass." I set up my stand in some bushes behind the ninth hole on the golf course across the street. I was six years old. Business was so good, I decided to franchise. I set up stands on the sixth and twelfth holes too. I got my friends to run them. Then it rained for a week and I lost my business partners. On top of that, some big kids came and robbed me. I got out of the Kool-Aid business. It taught me an important lesson: there are things you just can't control.

By the time I was fourteen, I had two paper routes plus a lawn care business that netted me five grand a year. That's right, folks—five Gs.

So last year, for my sixteenth birthday, I bought myself a new set of wheels. My folks, in a mindless fit of generosity, sprang for half the insurance, which cost almost as much as the car. Well, it's not exactly a car and it's not exactly new. It's a Jeep 4x4. It's only seven years old, and in great shape. I got a trailer to go with it, so I can tow my mower in summer and snowblower in winter. Business has been good.

In the summer I put extra fertilizer on people's lawns and water them more so I'll have to cut them more often, and in winter I pray for those Arctic highs and B.C. lows to mix and make lots of snow. This disgusts Kathy. However, she likes the portable CD player I got her for her birthday.

I'm also working as a packer at Super Store (a.k.a. Stupor Store) for fifteen hours a week, which brings me to problem one: school is beginning to interfere with work. I mean, what does school teach you about making money? Especially classes like English.

Which brings me to problem two: Kathy. Kathy Stetson. Kathy's in my Biology class. And Language Arts. She writes poetry and stuff and gets it published in the school paper. It's always about death and war and other heavy topics. It doesn't rhyme, so I don't know how good it is.

I don't *want* to like Kathy, but I do. She wears black all the time, even though it's no longer cool. She's forever burying her nose in some kind of book, except when she's looking at you. When she does that, she has this little sneer on her lips, like there's something about you she finds *very* funny. She drives me crazy. So the first time I asked her out she said, "What took you so long?" She has this knack of making you feel like an idiot and like a genius at the same time. Women.

Kathy has this twisted view of the universe. She thinks that money is evil and that everybody should throw their cash into a great big pot and take what they need. She figures if everybody did that, there'd be enough to feed everyone on the planet. I suppose it's a good idea if all you want to do is eat, but I want to know where they're going to keep the pot and who's going to be the first to throw his money in.

Kathy also thinks you go to school for an "education," that you don't go for the piece of paper—diploma or degree— which makes you worth something in the marketplace. My argument is that an education is just fine, but you got to learn something. Something useful, not how a pig fetus gets rid of its waste products, like what we took yesterday in Biology class. I mean, what good, in everyday life, is knowing how a pig works? Zip. Nothing, as near as I can figure out. That doesn't stop Kathy though. She slashes away at pickled meat like some kind of demented butcher.

Mr. Hawes is our English teacher. He does his best to make it interesting for us. He cracks bad jokes, wears funny ties and encourages us to be creative. He is also quite short. So when he wants to make a big point, he'll stand on the waste basket. When he wants to make a bigger point, he'll stand on his chair. When he wants to make a *really* big point, he'll stand on his desk. Today he was practically hanging off the ceiling.

"Don't you guys *know* what a metaphor is?!" he screams at us. "Is it so *hard* to under*stand* what a *metaphor* is?" He is teetering from the edge of his desk. "We spend three days talking about it and you still don't *know what a metaphor is?*" The little vein in his forehead is pulsing purple. He's going to croak right in front of us, topple off the desk and die. And we will have killed him.

What has got him to this point is our stupidity.

Our class isn't big. There's twenty-five of us and we sit in four rows. I'm the third person in the third row. He started at the top of the first row reading the first person's attempt at writing a metaphor.

"This isn't a metaphor" he says, after reading it aloud. It was something about chickens. How they cluck.

The next one he reads is about trees. *The trees blow in the breeze, they bend, they bow.* "Trees *do* that, give me something they *don't* do."

Then someone's cat. *The cat springs like its leg is full of muscle.* Not a metaphor.

Then about a car. *It races, like a well-oiled machine.* "It *is* a well-oiled machine."

Then a rainbow, *shining high in the sky, like a big bow.* "It *is* a big bow."

He reads them, and after each one he reads, he gets madder. "Can't anybody in this room write a metaphor?"

The truth is that nobody can. Certainly not me. But not even Kathy. I feel sorry for Kathy. She writes a whole story.

It's about this guy who has an apple tree. And he collects all the apples, then eats as many of them as he can. But he's tired after all this eating and picking, so he wants to take a nap. But he's afraid that someone will come along and take his apples while he's sleeping. So he pees on them.

When he awakes from his nap, he's hungry. But he can't tell the difference between what's been peed on and what hasn't. So he ends up eating all his apples trying to find one that's clean.

Mr. Hawes reads this and the whole class laughs.

Mr. Hawes does not. "What's so funny?" he asks. He asks it in such a way that everyone shuts up. He looks around the room. It's so quiet you could hear a bird fart.

"It's not a metaphor."

"Yes it is," blurts Kathy.

Mr. Hawes arches his eyebrows, like this somehow makes him taller. "For what?" he asks.

"For *Life*," says Kathy.

Mr. Hawes's eyebrows sink to the middle of his nose. "Maybe it's a metaphor for *your* life, Ms Stetson . . ."

"A friend of mine," she interrupts. She doesn't exactly look at me, but I know of whom she is thinking. So does half the class. I hear a few titters. Neither Mr. Hawes nor I think this is particularly funny.

"Don't interrupt me. If I want interruptions, I'll call for them."

"Then they wouldn't be interruptions," interrupts Kathy, again.

This is when he flies off the handle. He climbs the waste basket and uses words like "attitudes," then the chair, with words like "respect," till finally he is tilting dangerously bluefaced from the desk with something about "thoughts, learning and creativity being the essence of life."

In the meantime, while he is ranting, I am writing, or rather, rewriting. I know that what I wrote in the first place is no better than what anyone else in the class has written. That *the grass grows green as Christmas trees* is not a metaphor. That if I don't come up with something good, we will either be attending the funeral of Mr. Hawes or he will have a major nervous breakdown and drag an M-16 into the class and fire at us, splattering pieces of our stupid bodies across the blackboard.

But I am hurt, a wounded animal scorned in public by the woman I love, and I am writing now from my soul, passionate and true. I ignore Mr. Hawes as he leaps from his perch and lands two desks in front of me. He reads another failed metaphor. We are one step closer to the M-16. He shreds the offending paper to shrapnel and flings it into the air. I keep on writing.

The bits of paper descend like snow, landing on our heads. The person in front of me has written his doomed metaphor into a notebook. Mr. Hawes rails, and fires it across the room. It splashes against the blackboard and slides dismally onto the floor.

I stop writing.

He snatches my paper from my desk. He snarls: "*The grass grows money green and mowed, spits spent clippings at me till I choke for a dollar.*" I have no idea what this means, but it is what I have written.

Mr. Hawes visibly pales, to a more natural colour. He reads it again. Silently. He stops shaking. He clears his throat. "A metaphor," he says, nodding his head.

The class roars approval, but they do it very, very quietly. In fact, you can't hear a thing.

"An image," he says, disbelieving. "This is good," he says. "This is actually quite good. Thank you, Randy. Randy is the only one in the class who knows what a metaphor is." His voice rises, along with his eyebrows. "*This, ladies and gentlemen, is poetry.* The metaphor for the greenness of the grass is money. And it is so overpowering, this greenness, in tiny ways, spitting clippings, that it chokes the writer. It threatens to kill him in revenge."

I had no idea it could mean all that. He continues talking, but I am not listening. I am trying not to smile. I am glowing inside. I have just done something that no one else in the class has done. *I have written poetry.* I have written words on paper that have power, that have life. That have *saved* lives—ours, and probably Mr. Hawes' too. I have made his day. He is concluding his speech.

"This, Kathy, is what your whole story could have been. But Randy did it in one short line. That's the power of a metaphor." Mr. Hawes is smiling now, happy once again to be a teacher, to awaken our minds, to broaden our horizons.

The only trouble is that Kathy doesn't want her mind broadened at the moment.

"There's no money in it," she says.

"What?" Mr. Hawes doesn't quite believe what he is hearing. Neither do I.

"I said the trouble with poetry is that it doesn't make any money." This sounds like something I would say, in fact, have probably already said.

"Do you mean to say it has no value unless it makes money?" Mr. Hawes asks, eyebrows up.

"No, but some people would say that," and she looks directly at me.

Which makes Mr. Hawes look at me.

Which makes the whole class look at me.

It's like a spell. Twenty-five pairs of eyes cut into me. My soul is bleeding out. They are peering into my measly moneysoaked soul. What's the matter? Are they forgetting? *I'm the one who wrote the poetry*. And all of a sudden I get this blinding flash. I look at my bleeding soul lying there on the floor and it has no meaning. All the money in the world stacked up together has no meaning. It's just a stack of money. But words, even two words, have more meaning than all the money in the world. And I know this to be the truth and at the same time I know that all the poetry in the world wouldn't buy you a loaf of bread.

"I don't know what to say," is what I say.

I've only been a poet for two days and I've already skipped one day of work. This, I believe, is what a poet would do. I can feel my hair growing longer, my cheeks sinking. I turn my jaundiced eye on everything and sneer. On everything, that is, but Kathy. For Kathy I just want to be a puppy dog. I want to sit on her lap and pant. I will cuddle and look cute. I will be happy there. I will not pee. I promise.

Except that now I'm a poet, Kathy doesn't talk to me. I mean, we go out but she doesn't say anything. She sits there, brooding. She gives one-word answers, "Yes," "No,"

"Maybe." I don't know what to do. If you're not going to talk to someone, what's the point of being with them? And now she's started taking Tupper with her everywhere she goes. She holds the dog on her lap and talks to him. She talks to him. This dog is where I want to be. I am beginning to hate Tupper.

I am driving down 8th Street with Kathy and Tupper. It is snowing. I am thinking, *snow, I hate snow. I will have to start my snowblower. But it is soft snow. The snow is like burnt clouds. Hot snow.* This is when I realize I am doomed. That if I am driving down 8th Street in my Jeep with my girlfriend and her businessman dog, neither of them talking to me, and I am thinking thoughts about burning clouds and hot snow, that there is no hope for me. That I probably really am a poet and that I will write great poetry that no one will read till I am dead. That I will live a totally useless but meaningful life.

I unwrap a chocolate bar, steering for a moment with my elbows. Tupper perks up. Kathy looks straight ahead. I take a bite of the bar. It's an Oh Henry! The system I have is to suck the chocolate, chew the peanuts, then get down to the fudgey centre. It lasts longer that way. I flip a chocolate crumb to Tupper. He snaps it out of the air.

"Don't," says Kathy.

I break off another crumb and do it again. Tupper is pleased.

"Don't," says Kathy, again.

I break off another piece, but before I do anything with it, Kathy grabs the whole bar from my hand and in one motion lowers her window and flings the Oh Henry! into the night.

Tupper follows it, hurling himself out the window.

I don't know if you've ever tried to hold a pet doggy funeral in the middle of winter, but there are certain problems. Problem one: digging a hole. Problems two to ten: consoling the pet doggy's owner.

In Kathy's backyard the snow was deep and I cleared a plot of ground about two metres square. Into the centre I threw a plastic bag of leaves left over from the fall, soaked it with charcoal lighter fluid and set it ablaze. This was to thaw the ground, though for a moment I thought of cremating the dog. The fire succeeded in turning the top two inches of soil into muck. Beneath that, it was still frozen hard as rock.

Kathy was in tears. Tupper's stiff little body would not be covered by two inches of mud. What did the poet do? He borrowed Kathy's dad's drill, fitted it with an extension, knelt on his knees and drilled into the frozen ground, chewing it up as best he could. Then he shovelled and hacked with an axe till there was a hole deep enough to fit the doggy's corpse. In it he first placed a box of Smarties, then lowered the dog on top.

Kathy could not look as the poet scraped the frozen earth back into the hole, covering the little dog.

As I packed the mound with the back of the shovel, an amazing feeling came over me, a feeling that I was burying me, and I could imagine how that shovel must sound if I were under the earth and how final it would be. That there would be no more. That the snow is cold, not hot. That I was burying the poet too. I wanted to dig the dog back up and lay my own head there. I dropped the shovel. I hugged Kathy in her black coat. We stood there in the frozen snow.

We stood there a long time, but it was Kathy who finally said, "Let's go." And we came here, to this muffin shop where we always go for coffee. Some friends join us. Kathy is telling stories of when Tupper was a pup. We are laughing. He once ate the tongue from her father's shoe, then spat it up. Back in the shoe. "He was just putting it where he got it from." Each story she tells is funnier than the last. Yet, while she does this, I am asking her with my eyes or with my mind or some way that I cannot see, *How come you aren't talking to me?* And in among her tales she answers, *Because I am the poet, not you.* There are things you just can't control.

The one story she does not tell is how Tupper would jump high for Smarties.

The "Scream" School of Parenting

by

William Bell

When I asked William Bell for a story for this collection, he got political on me. He had recently written a story he really liked, but the protagonist was a girl. I was looking for stories with boys in them. Bill admitted to being a little sorry to hear that. "It seems to promote the stereotype that boys only want to read about boys," Bill wrote to me. "Like all stereotypes, it's based on a truth, as my teaching experience tells me, but stereotypes need bashing, not promotion." "Hear! Hear!" say I. And the wonderful thing is that "The 'Scream School' of Parenting" is just a great read, whoever you are. I think that any boy will be able to relate to what Naomi is going through. Let's face it: we've all got parents.

I'm thinking of starting a Losers' Club at our school. I'll be president, secretary and membership co-ordinator, all wrapped up in one. I'll let in gangly, zit-speckled boys whose legs and arms have grown faster than their bodies (not to mention their brains), whose Adam's apples bob like golf balls, whose voices moan like cellos one minute and screech like cats the next. You know the ones I mean. They lean against the gym walls at dances, making sarcastic, sexist remarks and think that farts are funny. The females I accept will be like me, girls who hate their hair, who always feel they've chosen the wrong clothes for the day, who have no boyfriends, no boobs (maybe our first meeting will be about whether there's a connection), no life.

Okay, I'm feeling down. Way down. I just came from a Drama Club meeting where I found out I didn't get the part I auditioned for, again. This time it was Blanche in *A Streetcar Named Desire*. The drama teacher, Ms Cummings, a dumpy, mousy-haired hag who wouldn't know a good actor if she tripped over one, told me I missed the part because I hadn't mastered the "Nawlins" accent. Really, that's the way she says "New Orleans." As if she's ever been there. The real reason is because I'm small (Mom says "petite") and skinny (Mom says "slender") and my chest isn't noticeable from the audience (Mom says nothing). Cummings rattled on for days before the auditions about how she'd be looking for actors who can develop sexual tension. "You have to drip sensuality," she urged. "This is

Nawlins; this is the South—hot jazz, torrid, sweaty nights, passion," blah, blah, blah. I felt like saying, You try to pulse with sexual tension when you're almost sixteen and a boy hasn't looked at you in years and you've got a body like a rake handle.

Ah, who cares. It's my birthday and I'm going home to get dinner ready. I hope Mom and Dad make it home on time.

I climb the curved staircase, trailing my hand on the oak bannister, pad down the corridor to my room and toss my backpack on my desk. My CDs have been put away, my clothes hung in the walk-in closet. The bed has been made up, my TV and VCR and stereo dusted. I hate this. The cleaning lady has been in here again. I've asked Mom a million times to tell Audrey to stay out of my room.

I close the door and strip down to my underwear, tossing my clothes over my shoulder onto the carpet—take that, Audrey. I stand before the full-length mirror. What a disaster. Wheat-coloured hair. A plain, thin-lipped face, like the "before" picture in a make-up ad. A body straight and boring as a throughway.

"Naomi, I hate you! You're so deliciously thin," Gillian bubbled the other day as we were dressing for gym. "You could be a model!"

"For what?" I wanted to ask. "A Feed-the-Children campaign? Gardening clothes?"

In my shower, as the hot needles of water prickle my skin, I wonder if I'll feel different tomorrow. Some of my friends make a big deal about turning sixteen, but to me the only positive thing is that I'll be taking my learner's permit test soon. Dad promised to buy me a car when I get my permanent licence next year. That'll be great; I won't be trapped in an empty house any more. If only I had somewhere interesting to go. Or someone to go with.

I put the three steaks I took out of the freezer this morning in some marinade and set them aside. I'm planning my birthday dinner for six o'clock, so I have time to make a tossed green salad and prepare three big potatoes to be nuked in the microwave. To save time, I hung some bunting paper around the kitchen last night. Just as I'm taking off my apron, the phone rings. "I'm running a bit late, darling, but I'm pretty sure I'll be home on time," Mom says, breathless as usual. I can tell from the hollow rumbling in the background that she's calling from her car.

With my preparations done, I pop a can of cola and take it out onto the deck off the kitchen to enjoy the last warm rays of the sun. The planks smell of sawdust and resin and wood stain. Our house, situated on three partially wooded acres, is brand-new, designed and built by my father. It's very secluded—except for the decrepit houses behind us that were supposed to have been torn down a year ago to make way for a golf course. Dad and the country-club developers have been in civil court time after time. The owner of the old houses wants the tenants out but they keep getting delays. Dad's furious, calls them no-goods and welfare bums, taking him to court on free legal aid while he has to shell out real money for his lawyer. (He ought to hire my mother, but she's too busy.) He sank a fortune into our house but the view out the back, which should have included stands of young trees, streams and emerald fairways, is still a rural slum.

There are two semi-detached brick boxes. One stands empty, waiting for the wrecking ball. The second contains two families. Behind the deserted building a dilapidated shed slumps in the yard, along with an ancient Buick sagging on concrete blocks, two broken motorcycles with flat tires and, believe it or not, an asphalt-paving machine. The other yard is graced with a teetering pile of used lumber, two wheelbarrows without the wheels, a dog house without a dog and a yellow snowmobile seamed with rust.

There are three pre-schoolers, two boys and a girl, playing in this yard, yelling at each other at the top of their lungs as they pull a wagonload of stones across the bare, hard-packed ground. "IT'S MY TURN!" "IS NOT!" "I'M TELLING!"—that sort of stuff. These kids learned to communicate from the adults in the house—there seem to be about four or five of them—who are honour graduates of the "Scream" School of Parenting. They shout, holler, bellow, whoop and bawl at each other as if deafness was in their genes. Right now, for instance, the mother is sitting by the kitchen window. I can see the smoke from her cigarette curling up through the screen.

"YOU STOP THAT RIGHT NOW!" she hollers.

"WE'RE NOT DOIN' NOTHIN'."

"I'M TELLING YOU, STOP FIGHTING! AND SHUT UP YER DAMN YELLIN' OR I'M COMIN' OUT THERE!"

"I DON'T CARE!"

She doesn't come out. She's too lazy to haul her carcass off her chair.

"I'M GONNA COUNT TO THREE, THEN I'M COMIN' AFTER YIZ! ONE!"

The three brats ignore her.

"TWO!"

"THREE!" I almost yell, just to end the racket, but the kids continue to scream at each other until the girl takes a rock from the wagon and bounces it off the head of one of the boys. The other boy laughs. The screaming intensifies as I get up and step through the patio door into the kitchen. So much for country relaxation.

It's six-thirty and Dad is still at the construction site. He hasn't even checked in yet. I'm watching a sitcom re-run in the family room when Mom charges through the front door.

"Hello, Naomi!" she trills. Even after a day of phone calls, meetings, tension and deals—she's a lawyer in one of the big firms in the city—she looks attractive, stylishly dressed, her make-up and jewellery understated. Too bad I didn't inherit her looks. She plunks her briefcase down on an empty chair.

"Happy birthday, darling!"

"Thanks, Mom."

"Has your dad called?"

As the word "no" forms in my mouth, the telephone rings.

"Hi, honey. I'm just leaving the site now," he says. "See you in fifteen."

In the kitchen, I remove the salad from the fridge and put it on the table, then take out the steaks. Mom is perched on a bar stool at the counter across from me. I wipe the marinade off the steaks and lay them on a platter. Mom is fidgeting, tapping her lacquered nails on the side of her highball glass.

"How was school today?" she asks as she opens her appointment diary.

"Not so good." It's clear she's forgotten about the audition. "I didn't get the part, just in case you're wondering."

"That's a shame, darling. I'm sorry. I know you worked hard on it." She takes a sip of her rye and ginger. "So who's going to play Ann?"

"That was last year, Mom. This year it's *Streetcar*. Sarah Taylor got the part I was after—Blanche."

"Oh, well, Sarah's a nice girl."

Nice if you like stuck-up and obnoxious.

A chirrupy noise comes from Mom's jacket pocket. She takes out her phone and flips it open.

"Yes? Yes, I—Oh, God, I was afraid of that. Yes—"

While she talks I step out to the deck and pull the tarp off the barbecue. One of the adult-male screamers in the other yard is squirting lighter fluid on some balled up paper and bits of wood piled on a hibachi that's balanced on the end of a picnic table. He seems to be the dominant male of the household—a late–middle-aged scarecrow with stringy grey hair held out of his face by a dirty baseball cap, a gaunt face grizzled with a few days' growth. With a loud poof the fire bursts up from his barbecue, forcing him back. He takes a pull on his beer and stares at the smoky fire as if he's never seen flames before.

Starting our barbecue is a matter of turning the valve on the tank, switching on the dials and pushing a red button. Pop! goes the blue flame. I adjust the dials, lower the lid to let the heat build up and go back inside just as the scarecrow begins to bellow at the kids, who are digging a hole beside the snowmobile.

Mom flips her phone closed and puts it down next to her empty glass, frowning.

"What's up, Mom?"

If you're the daughter of a lawyer you have to be able to keep secrets. Mom knows I never ever pass on what she tells me about her cases.

"It's the nursing home action. It looks like we're going to lose—the first round anyway. Jack is with their lawyers now, trying to work out a settlement."

The Red Pines Retirement Community on the other side of town always seems to be in trouble for code violations. The firm Mom works for represents Red Pines. Her phone, a little thing, blue with a stubby black antenna, chirps again.

"Yes? Uh-huh. No, no way we'll agree to that. They're bluffing. No, I can't, not yet. Maybe later. I'll call you."

She flips it closed. "I think I'll take a shower and get into something fresh," she says, slipping off the stool.

In the other yard, my pyromaniac neighbour seems to have his fire under control. He has been joined by the dumpy woman, another cigarette dangling from her mouth, and two men. The four of them are sitting on kitchen chairs on their porch, drinking beer from bottles and discussing something with a lot of energy. Occasionally, a burst of laughter punches into our kitchen.

I'm tossing oil and vinegar dressing into the salad when Dad bursts in.

"Hi, kiddo, how's it going?"

My father doesn't look like a builder. He's small for a man—"Not short, on the lower end of average," he says—slim, with black hair and rugged features. He takes his phone—wood-grain finish, very appropriate—from the pouch on his belt and puts it on the countertop beside Mom's, then pulls an imported lager from the fridge and pours it carefully into a long, tapered glass.

"What a day," he sighs, a moustache of white foam over his lip. "Sometimes I wonder if those idiots can spell the word 'schedule,' never mind keep one."

He wipes away the foam with the back of his hand. "How's things with the smartest kid at Woodlawn High?"

"Okay, I guess." I wait, but he doesn't ask. "I didn't get the part," I tell him. "Blanche, in *Streetcar*."

"Shoot. I know you wanted that one badly. Oh, well, there will be other roles."

Maybe so, but I won't get them. I'm obviously going to go through life playing walk-ons. The microwave beeps, and I jab each potato with a fork to make sure it's done.

"I'm going to put the steaks on now, Dad, okay?"

"Great. I'm hungry as a wolf."

I take the platter of meat outside and slap the steaks on

the hot grill, where they immediately begin to hiss and splutter, then set my watch for two minutes.

"HATTIE, I TOLD YOU TO LEAVE HIM ALONE!"

"I DIDN'T TOUCH HIM!"

"YES YOU DID; I SAW YOU. STOP THE DAMN LYIN'."

"YOU'RE THE LIAR, NOT ME."

"WATCH YOUR TONGUE, MY GIRL, OR I'M COMIN' DOWN THERE AND WHACK YOU A GOOD ONE."

"BETCHA WON'T!"

The kid knows what she's talking about. The adults holler threats but remain parked in their chairs. Only a nuclear blast would budge them. Or a drained beer bottle. My watch beeps and I turn over the steaks and set the timer again.

Scarecrow is flipping hamburgers in a cloud of smoke. "SANDY, BRING OUT SOME MORE BEER WITH THE POTATOES."

"ALL RIGHT, ALL RIGHT," comes a muffled female voice from the house. "I ONLY GOT TWO HANDS, YOU KNOW. ONE OF YIZ COULD SET THE TABLE."

I lift the steaks off the grill with the tongs and turn off the barbecue, then carry the platter inside, slamming the patio door behind me.

At the table, Mom and Dad look anything but relaxed as they cut into their steaks.

"This is delicious, kiddo," Dad offers. "Best steak I've ever—"

A phone chirps. Both Mom and Dad look at the countertop where the two phones rest like little soldiers, ready for action.

"Do you think we could possibly get through my birthday dinner without your little friends over there?" I ask my parents.

"It's mine," Mom says, standing and snatching up the blue one. "Yes?"

"So are there any other parts in the play you can get?"

"Okay, that's a bit more reasonable."

"Not really, Dad. It's basically a three-hander."

"Oh. I've never seen that play. Never liked O'Neill."

"No, we won't budge on that point. We can't."

"It's Williams, Dad."

"Oh, yeah, right."

Mom sits down again. "I'm sorry, Naomi, but I'm going to have to go out later."

"Aw, Mom, it's my birthday. I rented a video and everything, that French flick you guys were talking about last week."

"I know, dear, but it can't be helped. I've got to be there; the whole thing's falling apart."

We eat in silence for a few moments. I'm doing a slow burn, wondering why I bothered to go ahead with this charade of a birthday party to begin with, but no one seems to notice. As if on cue, a phone squeaks.

"My turn, I guess," Dad says. Then, into the phone, "Magee here."

"I'll try to be back as quickly as I can, darling."

"What do you mean the insulation won't be there in the morning? They promised."

"Can we watch the video later, Mom?"

"Sure, that will be fine. I'm looking forward to it."

"But we can't proceed until the drywall comes. I was hoping to get it up and taped tomorrow."

"Okay. I guess I could work on my project until then."

"Oh, hell, you really think I need to come over there?"

"Is that the essay on teenage alienation?"

"No, I handed that in long ago. Got an A, too."

"Wonderful. I'm proud of you."

Dad plunks himself down in his chair. "I've got to slip out for a half hour or so after dinner."

Mom frowns. "Well, why don't you open your gift now, dear, just in case we're held up?"

The other yard is lit by a spotlight dangling from the clothes-line pole. The whole bunch of them are munching hamburgers, sloshing down the beer, yakking and laughing. I sit on our deck in the dark, holding my gift in my lap. It's a portable CD player, pink-pearl finish, with lots of buttons—all the features. It's expensive, a real gem.

The colour is different, but it's the same model Mom and Dad bought me for Christmas five months ago.

I hold it in my lap, my fingers caressing the smooth plastic. In the other yard, somebody turns on a radio.

Shonar Arches

by
Nazneen Sadiq

We've all heard it: how different things were for our parents; how, when they were kids, they were taught to respect their parents. It's so much harder to believe when you've never actually met those fabled grandparents. That was more or less my case; I moved to Canada from England before I was four and never saw my grandparents again. But if they had ever visited us here, I can well imagine my mother going kind of nuts, just like Amit's mother in Nazneen Sadiq's marvellously funny tale. And I can well imagine Amit's apprehension about his dida coming all the way from Calcutta. It's almost like an invasion! Dida, it turns out, has a surprise or two up the sleeves of her sari.

Amit scowled at the stalk of broccoli on his dinner plate. Then he narrowed his eyes, pretending they were laser guns. Zap! shot the beam, and all that was left on his plate were traces of melted butter.

"Eat your vegetables, Amit," said his father.

"I'm going to," he muttered in disgust. It never worked. Somebody, he thought, should arrest all the dumb farmers who grew vegetables. Meanwhile, the best thing that could happen was for Mom to be struck with a sudden case of colour blindness. Then she wouldn't see all the horrible green vegetables in the supermarket.

"Why can't we have french fries?" he grumbled.

"Because you had them yesterday," Mom replied.

"Why do we have to eat all these dumb things all the time?" he persisted.

"Amit!" snapped Dad, a warning note in his voice.

"Guess what's for dessert?" asked Mom, and Amit knew she was changing the subject. That was his mom all right! Whenever things got sticky, she changed the subject.

"I know a boy at school who choked on Brussels sprouts and almost died," he whispered to Mom.

"And his mother had probably made his favourite dessert too," she said, sounding sympathetic, but not looking it.

Knowing the battle was lost, Amit viciously speared the broccoli with his fork. "This stuff," he muttered, "could kill me."

"We'll risk it, son. I'm sure you're tougher than you look." The edges of his father's lips pressed away a smile.

Crazy, thought Amit. Sometimes parents were really crazy. What was so funny about watching your child kill himself over vegetables! He swallowed the entire stalk with a glass of water.

His mother said, "*Gulab jamuns*, Amit, that's what I made for you."

Amit tried to scowl at her, but the announcement really cheered him up considerably. He knew how long it took to make the special Bengali dessert. When he was younger, he used to watch in fascination as the round confectionery balls spun crazily in the sugar syrup boiling on the stove. But the best part was the taste. The spongy balls were smooth, creamy and never quite melted away. The syrup was piercingly sweet. Even a double fudge sundae didn't taste as good. But no way was he going to give Mom a break; he was going to let her sweat it out for making him eat broccoli!

"I'm going to have to bring Bob home from the office one day to eat your *gulab jamuns*," Dad said with a smile.

"Has he ever had them?" asked Mom.

"Yes. I took him to a Bengali restaurant for lunch one day, but they weren't half as good as yours."

Mom brought the glass bowl out of the fridge and set it on the dining-room table in front of Amit. "As many as you want," she whispered to him, and sat down in her chair.

Amit dug the spoon into the syrup and lifted two of the golden-brown spongy balls into his bowl. Then he ladled three large spoonfuls of syrup over them. The tantalizing smell of cardamom and rosewater filled the air, and for a moment he just sat there inhaling deeply.

"Get your nose out of that bowl, Amit," said his father.

"How do you get our food to smell so good?" he asked his mom as he passed the bowl to his father.

"Wait till your grandmother comes, Amit. Her food is even more wonderful," replied Mom.

"That's right, son. You're in for a real treat," agreed his father.

Amit didn't know what to think. He had never seen his grandmother before. She lived in a place called Calcutta in West Bengal, India. His parents had come from the same place, but he had only been two years old when they moved to Canada. He knew nothing about Calcutta, except what his parents told him. Mom went to Calcutta every two years to visit his grandmother, but this year she was coming to Canada for a visit. He could see that Mom was excited; she had been cleaning out the spare bedroom and running around the house rearranging things. The worst part was that she had started coming to his room and nagging him to tidy up.

"You have to get rid of all the junk," she said, pointing to his prize rock collection.

"Junk! Those are fossils, and some of them are millions of years old," he explained.

"Oh, well, then at least make them look neater," she replied.

"They're not supposed to look neat or anything. Anyway, it's my room!" he shouted.

"Don't you talk back to me," snapped his mother. "I would have had my face smacked if I had answered one of my parents in that tone of voice."

Here we go again, thought Amit. Now I'm going to get the lecture about how Bengali children were taught to respect their elders. Mom could be a real pain at times. She kept harping about Bengali this and Bengali that. Didn't she know he really didn't believe all the stories about prissy kids who never talked back? Dad was crazy. He had given in rather meekly when Mom had nagged him about his jumble of tools in the basement. These days, except when she was cooking, his mother had become some sort of building inspector! This grandmother who was arriving was creating a lot of flak....

"Don't forget to wear something nice, Amit," said his mother the next morning as he was getting ready for school.

Amit pulled his Star Wars sweatshirt over his head and asked, "How's this?"

"How about the nice plaid shirt I got from Sears?" replied his mother, walking toward his closet.

"C'mon, Mom, what's wrong with this?" demanded Amit as he tried to keep her from opening his closet.

"Amit, I want you to look nice at the airport for your grandmother," she insisted.

"So why don't you rent me a tux?" he said airily.

His mother grinned at him and then got that look in her eye which meant, you're not getting away with it. She whipped open the door to his closet and asked, "Where's that lovely shirt?"

"I think it's lost," said Amit hopefully.

"It has to be here somewhere." His mother was impatiently pulling apart the bunched-up hangers.

"I hate it. The collar is too tight," Amit said in a final attempt to stop her.

"No, it's not. Here it is! Oh, Amit, it's filthy. What have you done to it?" wailed his mother.

"I guess I forgot to throw it in the laundry." He tried to look apologetic. "I'm going to be late, Mom. I've gotta go." And he charged out of his room.

"We'll pick you up at two at school. Don't forget." His mother's voice followed him into the kitchen as he grabbed his lunch bag. He also heard something that sounded like "washing hands" behind him as he slammed the screen door.

Amit was scowling again. Instead of playing the first baseball game of the summer gym period, he was sitting in a traffic jam on Highway 401 on the way to the Toronto airport. He had complained to his parents, but they had hushed him, saying "This is your dida's first visit to our home, and that's more important than a baseball game."

He didn't even like the word *dida*. It was Bengali for grandmother. He didn't like the way Mom kept babbling on about her. It was almost as though she was the most important thing in the world. His best friend, Rick, had said at school that morning, "You won't catch me missing a baseball game for any old grandmother!"

One hour later a very plump woman wearing a vibrant blue sari rode up the escalator at Lester B. Pearson Airport. Amit had never seen his mother like this: she was jumping up and down like a kid, squealing "There she is, there she is!" Both his parents dashed forward. Dad took the two bulging bags Amit's grandmother was holding, and Mom flung herself into her mother's arms. She doesn't look like a regular grandmother, Amit thought to himself. Her hair was shiny and black, and she had podgy feet stuffed into the most delicate-looking sandals he had ever seen.

"Let me see him," exclaimed Dida as she advanced toward Amit with her sari sailing about her.

"Hello," said Amit, and he stuck out his hand.

"Such a little boy, Amit, my *khokhon*," gushed Dida, and she gave him a big hug.

It was the wrong start for Amit—first to be called a little boy, and then to be rammed against Dida's chest where he almost suffocated on mouthfuls of sari!

"What's the matter, aren't you feeding him?" Dida accused his mother.

As he pried himself out of his grandmother's embrace, Amit saw that all his mother did in reply was smile.

"Yes, she's been starving us for years," replied his father, and he gave Amit a sly wink. "Let's take you home," Dad said, and he started moving them toward the glass exit doors. Amit quickly stepped up with his father, leaving his mother and grandmother to follow. He could hear them laughing and talking, and for some reason it just made him scowl all over again.

Life, thought Amit to himself as he walked home from school a few days later, was just not the same. Dida had struck like a hurricane. She was everywhere. Chattering, walking into his room and pinching his cheeks, rearranging Mom's pots and pans in the kitchen, and cooking. Mom was doing strange things like sleeping in. He didn't want his grandmother frying eggs and forcing them down him in the mornings. He wanted his mother sitting quietly with him as he munched his cereal. If he hadn't put his foot down, he would have wound up with fish curry and rice in his lunch bag instead of a perfectly respectable cheese sandwich.

It wasn't that he didn't like traditional Bengali food, but Mom kept a mixed kitchen, and when she cooked Bengali dishes, she didn't make everything so hot that it scorched the roof of his mouth. His grandmother acted as though all their regular Canadian food was terrible. She kept taking over from his mother and churning out Bengali dishes. There were all sorts of people dropping in for visits, and Mom didn't seem to have much time for him anymore. Even his father spent a lot of time with Dida. He would start each evening by saying, "And how is so and so in Calcutta?" And Dida would go on forever.

It was as though they had a private world, and he was locked out. Dida treated him like a kid, thinking all he needed was to be fed. She never asked him any questions about school or his friends. All she did was talk about food and cook. One day he got into trouble by asking, "When is she going home, Mom?" His mother had called him rude and inconsiderate. Amit hadn't spoken to his mother for two days, and he couldn't remember ever having lasted that long.

I'm going to change everything today, Amit said to himself as he walked through the front door.

"Hi, Mom. Hi, Dida. I'm home," he called.

Nobody answered. There were sounds coming from the kitchen, and there was an oily, spicy smell everywhere.

"What are you making, Mom, chocolate brownies?" he asked sarcastically as he stuck his head into the kitchen.

"Hello, son. I'm learning how to make vegetable pickle." She gave it some complicated Bengali name.

"All fresh, nothing like what you buy in the shop," Dida announced smugly.

"Can we go to McDonald's tonight, Mom?" asked Amit.

"I don't know, Amit. A break might be nice. I *have* been busy all afternoon," replied his mother.

"Yeah, you haven't been out for ages. Besides, we have to show Dida what Canadian food is like."

"It's not Canadian; it's fast food," Mom corrected him.

"C'mon, Mom, even Dad likes it. He thinks McNuggets are fantastic."

"What's this, what's this McNugga?" asked Dida.

"It's a kind of chicken, Dida, and one million people have it every day," replied Amit.

"One million!" echoed Dida.

"Amit!" said his mother, flashing him an exasperated look.

"Sure they do, Mom, if you count the restaurants all over," Amit quickly added.

"This I have to see. So many people eating this food!" said Dida in amazement.

"Can I call Dad at the office and tell him, Mom?" Amit pleaded.

"All right. Maybe it will be good to get out of the kitchen," said Mom. "I think your grandson has just invited you out for dinner," she said to Dida.

"I must get ready; I must change my sari. Amit, I will wear my new silk sari," said Dida, and she started washing her hands at the kitchen sink.

"You don't have to bother, Dida. You can come as you are," explained Amit.

"Oh, no. This old sari is not good enough. When I go with my Amit, I must look good," Dida insisted, obviously horrified by the thought of appearing in an everyday sari.

"Hey, Mom, tell her. Nobody dresses up to go to McDonald's!" begged Amit.

Nobody, Amit realized, could tell Dida to do anything if she didn't want to. Here she was, sitting in the back seat of the car, all dressed up to go out for burgers. Her purple silk sari had bright yellow paisleys all over it. When she had sailed out of the front door, Amit was reminded of the old Spanish galleons. Her dark hair glistened with oil, and it was gathered in a bun at her neck. Tucked into the side of the bun were two small yellow flowers. She had even put on a spicy scent, which made Amit feel as though he was sitting next to a huge cinnamon danish, dressed in a purple silk sari.

She chattered away on the ride, looking out the window, shaking her head and saying it was nothing like her *shonar*

Bangla. Shonar meant golden. Dad had told him that was what most Bengalis affectionately called their land.

"Well, Dida, tonight we are off to the shonar arches," said Amit, feeling rather clever. Mom and Dad chuckled at his joke.

"Ah, yes," said Dida, but Amit knew she hadn't a clue.

The McDonald's on Yonge Street was a big one. It even had a kiddie section with a small merry-go-round and a slide. Amit had come here many times. He was looking forward to a Big Mac, fries and a chocolate shake. Chicken McNuggets were OK, but a Big Mac was something he had grown up with.

Everybody stared at Dida as they entered the restaurant. Amit's father looked for a table along the side windows. Dida didn't want any of that. She wanted to sit at a table smack in the middle.

"Here, Amit, now we can see everyone eating McNugga." She pulled Amit toward a centre table.

"McNuggets, not McNugga," Amit hissed at her. He was beginning to feel a little embarrassed.

"Where's the menu?" asked Dida as she plonked herself on a chair.

"It's on the wall, but we can tell you what to have," said Amit.

"A fish fillet for me," said Mom.

"Fresh, is it fresh fish?" asked Dida suspiciously.

"You have to have a Big Mac, Dida." Amit leaned over to her.

"Nothing too big," said Dida, and she patted her stomach. Everybody laughed. Dad gave Amit a twenty-dollar bill and said, "All right, Amit, you know what to get for everyone."

"Two Big Macs, one fish fillet, nine Chicken McNuggets, four fries, two coffees, and two chocolate shakes," Amit rattled off at the register.

"Coming up!" said the cheerful blonde girl behind the counter. A couple of minutes later Amit staggered up to their table with a loaded tray.

Dida's eyes widened. "So quickly. They cook so fast."

"Yup," said Amit, feeling as though he had scored a minor victory. "OK, Dida, here's a Big Mac, fries, and a chocolate shake for you." He placed the food in front of her.

"Also some McNuggas if you want to try them," said his father, and he winked at Amit. Even his mother sort of chuckled as she bit into her fish sandwich. Dida lifted the Big Mac, glanced at Amit, and took a bite. Lettuce and dressing dribbled over her fingers, and she looked startled.

"Lots of napkins, Dida, you've gotta have lots of napkins," mumbled Amit with his mouth full. He pushed some toward her. Dida took two more bites of her hamburger while all three of them waited expectantly.

"It's soft. Everything is soft, yes," she said, nodding her approval.

Amit was stunned. Dida liked her Big Mac! He felt as though he had hit a home run.

Dida put down her hamburger, wiped her fingers, and took a sip of her chocolate shake. It was a small sip, and nothing came up the straw.

"You've got to really suck it up, Dida. It's very thick," Amit explained, a little surprised at his helpful tone.

Dida tried again, and her eyes popped as the cold shake flooded into her mouth. Then she gave a wheezy sort of giggle. "This is melted ice-cream, Amit. You're going to get your grandmother fat." She wagged a finger at him.

Dida tucked into her Big Mac, doused her french fries with vinegar, sipped her "melted ice-cream" in great big gurgles, and kept asking Amit whether a million Big Macs were being eaten that very evening. Her eyes travelled across the other tables, and she smiled at anyone who looked at her. She's having a good time, Amit thought to himself in amazement. And so am I! This was the first time Dida had made him feel important. All the questions she asked about the food were directed to him. When Dad pushed some McNuggets toward her, she looked at Amit and said "Are they good?" She dipped her fingers in the sauces, and even took a bite out of Mom's fish fillet. Amit felt something warm blossoming inside him.

"I have to wash my hands, Amit," she said when she was finished.

"How about another one, Dida?" asked his father.

"Well, maybe one more ice-cream drink," she agreed, flashing Amit a shy grin. "But first I have to wash my hands."

"I'll show you where," said Amit, jumping from his chair.

"Amit, I would like to go and tell the cook the food is good," whispered Dida to him as they walked toward the washrooms.

"Oh, well, er, OK, I guess we can do it." He shook his head in disbelief. What a mind-blowing request! I should

have ducked out of that one, he thought, as his grandmother disappeared into the washroom. He remembered
how embarrassed he had felt earlier on, when they had
entered the restaurant. But something had changed since
then, and he was almost starting to enjoy his grandmother.

Dida charged out of the washroom with her purple sari
streaming behind her like a banner. She took Amit's arm and
walked up to the counter with him. Amit cleared his throat
nervously, took a deep breath, and said, "My grandmother
would like to thank you guys. She really digs Big Macs."

"Hey, that's neat. Hi, Grandma, thanks!" said the cheerful teenager who had served Amit.

Dida patted the girl's hand and said, "You're a good girl.
Food is soft and good, but McNugga sauce"—she shook
her head—"not hot enough for Dida from Calcutta." All
the kids behind the counter laughed, and so did Dida.

"Hey, lady, do they have McDonald's in Calcutta?"
asked a tall boy behind the counter.

"No, but I will tell them when I go back," replied Dida.

By this time some of the kids who served behind the
counter were gathered in front of Dida. Amazing. There
was old Dida shooting the breeze with the McDonald's
kids. Maybe, thought Amit, this is the first time anyone has
thanked them like this. He looked over toward his parents;
his father gave him a questioning look. This time it was
Amit's turn to wink.

That night Amit was rearranging his rock collection
for the hundredth time when he heard someone come into
his room.

"Amit, I have something for you." It was Dida, holding a photograph in her hand.

"Oh, hi, Dida. Who's in the picture?" He stepped closer to her.

"I brought some old family pictures for your mother, but this one is for you," she replied, holding out the photograph.

Amit held it under the table lamp and bent down to look at it. It was of a man holding a little girl on his knee; she had something in her hand.

"My father and me," Dida said softly behind him. "One day he took me to the city and got me a paper cone filled with something cold. When he put it in my hand, I almost dropped it, Amit. It was a paper cone filled with white snow. There was a little wooden stick stuck right in the middle of the snow. Then he told me to eat it. It was the first time I had ever eaten ice-cream. I will never forget how delicious it tasted. Tonight you made me remember that time."

Amit swung around and saw that Dida had closed her eyes and had a dreamy expression on her face. He could actually see her as a little girl eating her first ice-cream. Something tingly ran through Amit. It wasn't a bad sensation at all.

"So you see, you must have the picture. It will remind you of me," she said, opening her eyes abruptly.

"I have something for you too, Dida," Amit heard himself say. He walked over to his rock collection and picked up the three-cornered knobby one. It was bluish-purple and shot through with a mustard streak. This was his "pesky" rock. He had almost twisted his ankle when he tripped over it during a hike with his Cub patrol. The strange yellow streak had fascinated him, so he had quietly put it into his pocket and called it the "pesky" rock. "For you," he said, putting it into her outstretched hand.

"It will always remind me of you," replied Dida, closing her fingers around the rock.

"Yes," said Amit, knowing he had scored a home run. But Dida was the one who had pitched a straight ball.

Duncan's Way

by

Ian Wallace

This is another family story. It's set in Newfoundland, a place that more people leave than ever come to stay. Duncan's family has lived there forever. If you've been lucky enough to visit that fabled island, then perhaps you'll understand why leaving is the very last thing a native Newfoundlander would ever want to do. It certainly isn't what Duncan wants, and so he sets out to do something about it.

Ian Wallace is best known as a fine illustrator of picture books. Duncan's Way *may be his very best picture book yet. But the text of the story is so poignant that I think it stands on its own.*

For seven generations the men of Duncan's family fished in broad wooden boats off the coast of Newfoundland. Painted the colours of sealskin, fresh cream or lupins in June, the longliners were christened with the names of the women whom the fishermen loved. But the boats no longer returned with their holds laden. The days of plenty were over. The cod had disappeared from the ocean's depths, and with them went a way of life.

Duncan and his father stood watching a lone kittiwake circle the abandoned fishing stages that dotted the shore.

"C'mon, Dad," he said. "Let's go do something. Anything."

There was no reply. In the eighteen months that his father had been out of work, Duncan often found him just staring at the sea.

"Didya hear me, Dad?"

"Yeah, sorry. Not now. Maybe later."

"Yeah. Like maybe January when the snow's flying around our ears."

Duncan stormed from the yard, past the empty homes of friends and neighbours who had packed up and moved away. Beyond the windswept church, he stopped where the cemetery rolled to the sea. He came here whenever he needed to sort things out. He wasn't afraid to be among the graves.

He crouched low, his fingers tracing the chiselled letters on his great-grandfather's headstone. Then he took a harmonica from his pocket and played an old fishing song.

His dad hadn't always been silent and sad. Mostly Duncan remembered him whistling and singing and joking and teasing. But that was before the foreign factory ships had sucked the cod from the ocean. Or the seals had swallowed them up. Or men like his father had overfished the stocks. Or whatever reason you believed about why the fish were gone.

He confronted the North Atlantic. "My dad was born to the sea. Like his father and all the fathers before him." He smacked the harmonica against the palm of his hand. "I'm gonna get him back there!"

When he returned home his dad was sitting on the sofa, watching a game show on TV. Some guy had just won a huge jackpot and was going wild. Duncan could tell his father was envious.

Without warning, Luke, his brother, snuck up behind him.

"Go out for a little one-on-one, dipstick?" he whispered, and bounced a basketball off Duncan's back.

"You're not the boss of me!" He jabbed his brother hard in the ribs.

Luke laughed. "Ooh, tough guy!" The ball whizzed by Duncan's ear. It hit the far wall with a solid smack, dropped to the floor and bounced around the room. Their father didn't look away from the TV. He just put another handful of popcorn into his mouth.

His mother came through the back door from her job at the grocery store.

"Oh, do these little piggies ache," she said, kicking off her shoes. She gave Duncan a hug. "And how is my little fella?"

Duncan groaned. "I'm not your little fella, Mom. I'm eleven and a half." He started to pull away.

She kissed the top of his head. "You'll always be my little fella."

While his mother fixed supper, Duncan set the table.

"I was thinking about Dad," he told her. "About how he needs to get back to the sea."

"That won't happen for a long time, my son. Nobody knows when there'll be enough cod to fish again." She flipped thick slices of bologna in the sputtering pan.

"But he does nothing except watch TV or stand at the side of the road talking to his buddies." His mother's body tensed. Duncan's eyes scanned the six loaves of bread on the counter. The four partridgeberry pies. And the plate of tea buns. "And bake."

"Baking is hard work, too!" she snapped, and turned off the stove. "Supper's ready."

When the dishes were done, Duncan and his mother and brother went up the shore. The largest iceberg they could remember had floated into the bay and grounded. It sat so naturally there, shimmering in the darkening water, that Duncan hoped it would never melt away. In the quiet, his mother spoke.

"You were right, Duncan. We need to get your father back to work. Lord knows I've tried to think of every possible way. So's he." She looked out at the iceberg. Tears welled in her eyes. "Your dad and I have decided to leave Newfoundland."

The words were finally out. The ones Duncan had been dreading. The same words that many of his friends had heard before their families packed up and left the province. "There's no future for us here," they'd said.

Duncan tried to speak. To his surprise, words wouldn't come. He turned to Luke for help, but his brother looked like a guy who'd had the wind knocked out of him.

"We can begin again in another part of Canada," she said. "Just like your friends."

Duncan couldn't imagine giving up the sea for flat fields of grain, city skyscrapers or snow-covered tundra. And he couldn't imagine his father doing it, either.

"Lots of people are finding ways to stay," Luke blurted. "Bud Penney turned his garage into a video store."

"And lots haven't," she replied sadly.

Duncan regained his voice. "We can't leave. We've lived here forever."

"We don't have much choice. Time and money are running out."

Duncan slept fitfully that night. His stomach began churning when he thought of moving away. But mostly he thought about his father's boat and the boats of all the cod fishermen sitting idle at the wharves. He imagined countless others in outports strung along the coast like knots on a fishing line. All of them sat idle, too.

Early the next morning Duncan untied a dory from its mooring and, starting the motor, set out across the bay. The cold saltwater was rough beneath the boat, swelling and splashing over the hull, clean across his face.

Finally he reached the far side.

He arrived at the home of Mr. Marshall. Over several summers he and the retired fisherman had jigged for cod and played their harmonicas together. Duncan found him in the basement working on his model trains, one of them a replica of the *Newfie Bullet*, which no longer existed.

Duncan watched with delight as two trains sped through vast forests before scaling cliffs that snaked along the coastline.

Mr. Marshall gave him a turn at the controls. With the blast of an air horn the locomotives slowly gathered steam. Everything Duncan had been thinking about for the past eighteen months spilled out of him like a dam bursting.

"The disappearance of the cod is affecting us all," Mr. Marshall said when Duncan stopped talking. "I don't know that you or I or anyone can get your dad back to sea."

Mr. Marshall got down from his stool. He motioned Duncan to follow. They circled the miniature landscape. Then suddenly Mr. Marshall hit the ocean with his fist, picked up a tiny wooden boat and tossed it to Duncan, who caught it on the fly.

"What is a boat, if not for fishing?" he asked.

Duncan turned the boat in his fingers. "It's a way to get from place to place. Or a way of taking things to people. Or people to things."

"Darn right," said Mr. Marshall, and he thumped his fist on the ocean a second time. The trains sped past, heading in opposite directions. A steam whistle blew. "So, boy, if there aren't any cod to fish, what do people need that your dad can take to them by boat?"

That was the toughest question Mr. Marshall had ever asked him. Duncan was lost for an answer.

"I told you, my dad does nothing except watch TV or talk to his buddies." Mr. Marshall looked disappointed. Duncan's face flushed red with embarrassment. "And bake things we love to eat. Mom says he's the best baker in the province."

Mr. Marshall nodded. "So . . . ?"

Duncan didn't know what to say. A harmonica began to play in his head. Then he heard Luke's voice: "Lots of people are finding ways to stay." The trains slowed to a halt.

Mr. Marshall moved along the coast. He unloaded baggage and parcels, mailbags and lumber from the boxcars at two outports. His face bore the same contented look that Duncan's father got when he was baking.

"If a garage can be a video store," Duncan began slowly, "can a boat be . . ." He set the tiny fishing boat back in the ocean. "A bakery?"

Mr. Marshall smiled. "Possibly."

As he headed home the wind off the North Atlantic stilled. The waters of the bay became calmer. And Duncan's plan became clearer. Excitedly he revved the motor and swung wide around the iceberg.

His family was sitting at the kitchen table when he raced through the door. He brought a map from his bedroom. He traced the coastline, stopping at each outport.

Slowly, thoughtfully, Duncan revealed his plan. He saw his brother's eyes brighten.

"We could stop at a different place every day," he told them.

"A bakery boat?" His mother tried out the words.

"There's bound to be at least one folk festival up the shore this summer," Luke offered. "And think of all the family reunions. That crowd from the mainland sure would be hungry."

Duncan leaned closer to his father. "If you bake it, Dad, we'll sell it from the docks."

The boys were silent, waiting for him to say something. Anything.

"A bakery boat, John?" his mother said.

"It's not a bad idea," he said finally. "Maybe we'll have to give it a try. See if we can make a go of it." He gave Duncan a wink. He looked out the window. "By sea."

In the days that followed, Duncan's family visited every outport along the eastern shore to plot a baker's route. They went to the bank, where they took out the last of their savings and secured a loan to turn his father's boat into a floating bakery. They outfitted it with a secondhand oven and stove, a refrigerator and freezer, and all the gadgets and utensils that a baker would need. They painted the longliner from bow to stern the colours of a buttercup, and changed its name from *Barbara's Pride* to *Duncan's Way*.

Duncan painted a large sign in bold letters that said BREAD 'N' BUNS BY BOAT.

One clear July morning, they got out of bed when fishermen normally rise. Their family and friends saw them off. They set sail with a light wind at their backs. Duncan's mother was at the wheel, guiding them down the rocky coast. Duncan and Luke helped their father knead dough for bread and buns, mix batter for cakes and roll pastry for pies.

"We'll make a great team, boys," their father said as he put the first loaves into the oven.

Duncan played an old fishing song on his harmonica. His family sang boisterously along. And they joked and teased one another just like they did in the days before the cod went away.

from

The Dream Carver

by
Joan Clark

There were fishermen in Newfoundland a long time before Duncan's family settled there. In 1960, on the northern tip of Newfoundland's Great Northern Peninsula, archaeologists found the remains of a Norse settlement that dated back almost a thousand years. Greenlanders arrived in the New World five hundred years before Columbus, but they weren't the first—not by a long shot. Newfoundland was already inhabited by the Osweet, the original "redskins," so named for their custom of rubbing their skin and hair and even their tents and utensils with red earth and grease.

In Joan Clark's fascinating novel The Dream Carver, *Thrand, a fourteen-year-old Greenlander, is captured by the Osweet. He cannot understand why they hold him captive, why they feed him, why they don't just kill him, which is what his own people would have done to a* skraeling, *as they call the island natives. There is a lot he cannot understand about these* skraelings, *but for now, all he wants to do is escape. Unless he gets back to the settlement soon, his father and the other Greenlanders will have to leave without him. The thought of never seeing the blue and white world of Greenland again fills him with grim determination.*

In my dream I am lost in a forest where everything is red: the trees, the rocks, the lake. Drops of blood fall from a ruddy sky. Moving through the forest are the ghostly figures of people who are completely red, even their eyes are red. They drift through the forest as if it weren't there. They pass through trees and rocks instead of going around or above. They walk on water and fly through the air. These are the undead, the ghosts who occupy an invisible world. I know I'm dead, that I've somehow wandered into a world of red ghosts. I open my mouth and scream.

"Wobee," a voice says. "Wobee."

I open my eyes and see the old woman bending over me. I close them again and return to the forest of ghosts. A ghost drifts through me like red smoke. I shiver from the coldness of its touch.

"Wobee," the old woman says again and smiles. I notice her teeth are white and stumpy, worn down to the jaw. She puts a warm hand on my forehead and rubs it back and forth. I don't want her to touch me, she may be a ghost, but I can't force her hand away since my own are bound. She continues to rub my forehead, all the while speaking her unfamiliar tongue. Does she know how afraid I am of strange forests, coming as I do from a country where trees are scarce? If I could tell her about the ghosts, would they go away? Maybe the old woman understands my fear because after a while, I close my eyes and instead of drifting into the bleeding forest, I lock myself into untroubled sleep.

When I waken again, she's still there, smiling. She pats my head and says, "Wobee," as she does every day.

Today she adds something. She pats her own head and says something that sounds like "Imamasduit." She says this over and over, always patting herself as she speaks. When her husband comes in, she pats his head and says, "Bogodorasook." She does this several times more. I think she's telling me their names and that the name they are using for me is Wobee. I pretend not to understand, though I do. Nor do I tell her my real name. My name, Thrand, which I have taken for granted since I was a child, has become more important to me than it has ever been before, because except for my clothing, it is the only thing I now possess.

Imamasduit takes a skewered fish from the fire and holds it out to me. I elbow myself into a sitting position and hold the stick between my hands. The fish skin is crisp and black from being close to the fire. She watches while I tear the skin away from the flesh with my teeth. I'm hungry but I make myself eat slowly so I can see the bones. I'm halfway through the meal when Bogodorasook beckons Imamasduit outside. After Imamasduit disappears through the tent flap, I reach for a cup of water while trying to hold on to the skewer. To my dismay the rest of the fish slides off the stick and into the fire. No, not into the fire, to one side of it, which means that if I can retrieve the fish before it burns, I can finish my meal. I am hungry enough to want to try this. The skewer isn't long enough to reach the fish but there's a large poking stick nearby, to one side of the stone fire ring. My hands have grown clumsy and stiff from being tied—which is why I dropped the fish. But if I can get hold of the stick, I might be able to work the fish out of the stone ring and onto a rock.

I grasp the poking stick between my hands and try to manoeuvre the fish to the edge of the fire. In doing this, a flame licks my deerskin bindings and sears the underside of my wrist. I drop the poking stick and press my wrist against my mouth, using my tongue to soothe the burn. Then I examine my wrist. A welt is rising but it's not very large. The underside of the deerskin is completely black. I notice a hole in the binding where the flame has eaten through. If I could make the hole larger, I could weaken the binding. Over and over, I hold my wrists close together then force them apart to weaken the tie but this doesn't work. Perhaps I can break the deerskin by rubbing it across a stone. I hold my wrists on either side of a fire stone and rub the binding back and forth. The welt hurts every time it touches the hot stone, but I ignore it and rub harder. Harder, faster. Then I look: the edges of the hole are thinning! I rub and rub, back and forth. I feel the deerskin tearing. Finally it breaks! I'm free! Quickly I crawl to the tent opening and peer through the flap. No one is close by. I hear voices but they seem to be coming from the woods behind the other tents. Ahead of me is the empty stake. Beyond that, near the water, one of the women is bent over the racks where the fish are being dried, close by the sea. The boats are shore hauled close by the racks. If I can slip between the trees to the right of the tent, I can crawl through the underbrush to the beach without being seen. I hear voices behind the tents off to my left. It sounds as if a meeting of some sort is underway: that must be where the old woman has gone. I'll never have a better chance to make a run for it than now. I crawl through the tent opening, cross the grass and plunge into the woods. Once under cover, I look out. The woman near the water is still bent over the fish racks. Apart from her, no one's in sight. How lucky for me! I lose no time in crawling through the underbrush to the stony shore. The woman has her back to me which means I can creep up to one of the boats and get inside. I flatten myself on the bottom of the boat and wait, willing her to move away.

After a while, someone calls the woman and she leaves the racks to join the others. Now is my chance. I get out of the boat. Because it's made of tree bark, the boat is light enough for me to lift into the water without making much noise.

The camp is on one side of a fast-flowing tidal river moving toward a bay. On the other side of the bay, opposite the tents, are several large islands which are thickly treed. I intend to avoid these, since reaching them would mean crossing a broad open space where I could be easily seen if my captors looked that way. Instead I paddle close to shore, using the shelter of rocks and trees, heading toward the mouth of the bay where there are more islands. Fortunately, the tide is going out, which means the boat is carried forward with the current despite my clumsy efforts at paddling.

Soon I've reached the end of the river and am well into the bay. The current slows and I paddle harder to make up for the loss of speed. I keep my eye on an island which is farther out. Compared to the others in the bay it's small, but because of the lay of the land I don't think it can be seen from the camp. If I can reach it quickly and paddle around to its other side, I'll be invisible to anyone looking out to sea. This is my best chance to outsmart my captors who when they come after me, will likely assume I'm following the shore. Leaning forward, I paddle hard, straight across the bay without looking left, right or behind until I've passed the end of the small island and am on its other side, out of sight of the camp. I stop to rest. My chest heaves and my skin is wet from the exertion, but I'm charged with energy and excitement. A short rest before I continue. I can hardly believe my luck! I notice the small island has birch trees growing on top.

Straight ahead are two large islands with sea birds flying above. In a short while, I'll head for those islands. They are farther away than the distance I've come, and to reach them I'll have to cross a stretch of open water that will put me in view of the camp. But once I've made that crossing and am on the other side of the islands, my passage across the bay will be blocked from view. If I can reach the other side of the bay by nightfall, I'll beach the boat and follow the coastline north until I come to Leifsbudir. I pick up the paddle and begin again.

I've barely started the crossing when shouts come across the water from the camp. My captors have discovered my absence! I look at the sea-bird islands. They are steeply cliffed and bare of trees. Even if I reach them, I can see no place to land. Should I take the risk and go on? Already my arms and shoulders ache from paddling this far. My captors are strong paddlers and will have more energy than I. There's no doubt they would catch up to me before I could reach the shore on the other side of the bay.

Reluctantly I turn the boat around and head toward the small island I left behind. The birch trees will provide shelter and hide me until night. When the moon is up, I'll cross the bay. Meanwhile my captors won't know if I'm on one of the islands or if I've beached the canoe somewhere and gone ashore into the woods.

There's no beach on the island. I step onto a rock, pull the boat out of the water and lifting it to avoid the sharper rocks, haul it into a thicket of alders until it's hidden from view. Bending low, I find the cover of a dwarf spruce and look around. The island rises into a small hill. I climb toward a grove of birch trees on top. A voice reaches me from across the water, on the opposite shore. At the top of the hill, between the birch trees, are mounds of reddened stones. They might be cairns. If they are, they're unlike the high stone markers we build in Greenland. These cairns are low and narrow like graves. Whatever they are, I avoid them, for the reddened stones are clearly the work of my captors, which means this island is being used by them, perhaps as a burial ground.

I've made a mistake coming to this island. I should have taken my chances and kept on paddling toward the seabird islands. But it's too late to change my mind. The best thing I can do now is hide here and rest until night when, under cover of darkness, I can continue my escape.

Near the birches is a large spruce whose lower branches are so heavy and thick they lean on the ground. The branches overlap each other in such a way that they could cover my body completely. I flatten myself beneath the branches where they are thickest. The ground is damp, fragrant with the smell of spruce needles. I lay my cheek against the needles and try to loosen the fear gripping me. It's no use. As long as I'm being hunted, my body will be as tight as a bowstring. Now that I am lying down, weariness overtakes me. My limbs have become so heavy, I feel I will never be able to lift them again.

The air is windless, empty of all sounds save the cries of distant sea birds. After a while, I hear a light splashing noise. It could be the lapping of a wave against a rock. There it is again! I listen closely. The splashing continues, even, measured. My pursuers are paddling past! I'm sure of this though I can't risk crawling out to look. I lie beneath the branches, still and tense. After a time, the splashing ceases and my body loosens somewhat. My pursuers have moved on.

All afternoon I lie on my belly beneath the spruce. Most of the time I hover between wakefulness and sleep, not daring to sleep lest my pursuers return. Apparently there are no birds or game on this island for I hear nothing close by except shufflings and stirrings of what I take to be mice.

At nightfall, a light breeze disturbs the trees. The leaves of the birch trees rustle. Above me the spruce creaks. I have never been near trees at night and am uneasy with the sounds. I turn over and lie on my back so I can move the branches and look about. It's too early for the moon, but far away I see the flickering stars. I close my eyes and doze while around me the birch leaves flutter and shake. Deep inside its trunk, the spruce groans. Unwillingly I slip into a dream.

All around me are talking trees. I've been captured by forest giants who can see through their skins. Every leaf and needle is an eye. The long arm of a spruce reaches down and presses my arms and shoulders to the ground. I try to get up but I'm unable to move. Needles prick my arms and legs.

Tree fingers grope across my face. The fingers are wet and red. A drop of blood splatters my forehead. Above me, the spruce sways and groans like a grieving ghost.

The spruce has me pinned to the ground. I can feel tree roots creeping over my skin. They are circling my ankles and wrists, binding them tight.

I hear a whisper. It's as faint as the water shifting against the shore but shaped like a voice. It seems to be coming from inside a mound of reddened stones. Within the mound is a severed head. The head is talking to me.

"Wobee," the head whispers, "you killed me."

Whose head is it?

The spruce giant tightens its grip on me. Fingers cover my nose and mouth. I can scarcely breathe.

Above me in the sky the stars are red.

RanVan:
A Worthy Opponent

by
Diana Wieler

As a writer, Diana Wieler really seems to know what makes a guy tick. All of her protagonists are male and they're all memorable. I'm a big RanVan fan. Ran is just his video-game code name; in real life he's Rhan Van, and in real life he hasn't been scoring any free games lately. Things aren't ever easy for Rhan and Gran—the only close family he's got—but Rhan always manages to make it worse! It's not just attitude, although he's got attitude to spare. He's angry, sure, but there is a lot that's good and noble inside him, too. There are three RanVan novels in all and they're all great. This excerpt is taken from the second in the series, RanVan: A Worthy Opponent.

O, valiant warrior, we've long awaited your arrival! Our benevolent ruler has been overpowered by his evil twin and now serves the forces of darkness. Together the brothers are invincible. Their magic holds sway over both the planet and its inhabitants. Our world is in chaos.

Rhan Van gripped the edges of the game console. He'd wandered into the arcade almost idly, a walk to stretch his legs after three cramped days on a Greyhound bus. But dozens of screens glowed brightly in the dim room, and the air was alive with the searing of lasers. At the back of Captain John's he'd come across this game, Gemini Planet, and he'd forgotten about walking anywhere.

He'd liked the graphics instantly. The preview scroll showed the landing of a small dragon-winged craft on a planet sharply halved in black and white. In the next frame the pilot stepped out onto a shadowed landscape. His flight suit was inset with metal plates, but it looked like a knight's armour to Rhan.

The brothers do not rule the sun! Their powers are greatest during the hours of Descent; your own rises during Ascent. The shifting polarity of the planet can be your greatest ally, or your peril.

In the corner of the screen Rhan could see the numbers clicking off at unnatural speed—an hour's worth in the time it took to draw a breath. When 23:59 kicked over, the dark background began to lighten, lush plants grew over the barren rock. The pilot was changing, too. Dull metal gleamed silver and the spaces between the plates began to glow—a liquid, electrified blue. Rhan's heart leapt. It was his colour.

Earn the five rings of Ashtar, hidden above and below ground. They will give you the strength to destroy the evil twin and release our king. But pursue your foe with care: the brothers are identical. Your choice will lead either to glory or to night neverending.

Great, Rhan thought. The guy you have to rescue looks exactly like the guy you're trying to kill off. And the privilege of saving the planet wasn't cheap either. Four quarters to start, two to continue. His mind reeled thinking what it would cost to learn the moves, never mind get good at them.

But he wasn't just anybody. Under the code name Ran-Van he'd blazed a lot of different video battlefields in his career. He was coordinated and he learned fast—better than fast.

"Don't mind me. I love to watch amateurs get fried by this thing."

Rhan spun around. A young man was leaning against a pillar, arms folded over his chest. He seemed slightly older than Rhan—seventeen, maybe—and he was taller but lean. At first glance Rhan thought the stranger was bald, but then he noticed the white, almost translucent fuzz over his skull. He could have been an android, except for the eyes: bright and steady, intensely alive.

"What makes you think I'm an amateur?" Rhan said.

The stranger suddenly flipped a dollar coin at him. "Go for it," he said.

The challenge was sharp in the air. Part of Rhan wanted to dive into Gemini Planet then and there and blast the microchips right out of the thing. But reality set in. He didn't know the first moves on this game, and he wasn't about to die horribly for this jerk's entertainment.

Rhan tossed the money back, just as fast. "Sorry, I'm not taking students this year."

The young man almost smiled as he tucked the coin in his pocket. He gestured at the scores monitor that had just come up on Gemini Planet's screen. It listed the top twenty players, under their code names.

"That's funny," he said, "because I know everybody up there and you're not one of them."

"I'm incognito. Keeps back the crowd." Rhan was curious now but he tried to be casual. "So where are you?"

No change of expression. Rhan scanned the list of code names.

"DayGlo?" he said, picking one from the middle. There was no response. "Hakker? Merlin?"

"Today I brew, tomorrow I bake . . ." the stranger said.

Rhan stared. For an instant he thought he recognized the curious phrase. But then it was lost.

"Figure it out, *amateur*," the stranger said. "Use your brain, if you can." He slipped easily through the players and into the mall.

Just then, the lights flickered rapidly.

"Time, guys!" the attendant called.

Rhan blinked. Damn! The place was closing and he hadn't played anything. As he left the arcade he gave

Gemini Planet a backward glance, the word "amateur" curdling in his stomach. He was pretty sure which monitor RanVan was going to conquer first.

Outside Captain John's, Rhan paused to light a cigarette. Around him the mall was a din of rattling screens and doors as shops closed up for the night.

Across from the arcade, a small cluster of guys in sports jackets had formed a ring out from a bare wall. Rhan remembered passing them earlier, at the mall entrance, and he'd given himself a mental warning. Sixteen years in Vancouver had taught him to thread his way around the various packs that staked out the malls and school courtyards. If the circle closed on you, you'd lose something: jacket, shoes, money. Or you'd just lose.

They had quarry now. Shoppers heading for the doors gave the group a wide berth. The attendant from Captain John's wandered into the doorway to watch.

Then, the first shove. The ring of jackets broke for an instant and Rhan caught a glimpse inside. The little guy in the Toledo Mud Hens baseball jacket barely came up to their chins. He was just a kid! In a panicked push he tried to force his way out of the circle and was yanked back, hard. The cluster tightened again.

Rhan looked left and right, his pulse in his temples. The mall was full of people. Why didn't somebody do something?

He thrust his cigarette in the ashtray without looking at it. He could feel the familiar roar beginning in his veins, the first gust of energy shaking him awake. He was needed here. When he started to move, the rush intensified, each step accelerating the next, like running down a hill.

There's five of them—five on two. Think fast! What have you got, RanVan? Something, anything!

The element of surprise. Rhan hit the leader at a dead run, a shoulder check into the broad back that sent them both sprawling onto the polished floor. But the impact had wrenched the circle apart. The others stumbled, dazed.

"Go!" Rhan called.

The kid bolted for open space. Rhan scrambled to get up, but he felt hands seize the back of his jacket. A blaze of fury drove up from his stomach. They might take him, but RanVan the Defender wasn't going down without a fight.

The instant he was hauled to his feet, Rhan whipped around with his elbow up—and drove it into the security guard's stomach.

Rhan Van had turned sixteen on Halloween, on a Greyhound bus travelling from Vancouver to Thunder Bay. He had dark hair to his shoulders and metal frame glasses. He wasn't big but he prided himself on being quick, nimble.

Riding home in the police car Rhan knew he'd have to be more than nimble to wriggle out of this.

The cruiser hesitated in the parking lot of the Trail's End Motel, which had been Rhan's new address for less than five hours. The officer looked over the line of ten faded clapboard cabins.

"Which suite did you say your grandmother was in?" he asked.

"We're not in a suite. We live in the house," Rhan said irritably from the back seat. "My gran's cousin owns the place."

They pulled up to the main doors, a reception area that had been built on the front of the old two-storey house.

"You know, this really isn't *necessary*," Rhan said. "You don't want to shock her or anything. She's got a bad heart." Not really a lie. Didn't everybody over sixty have a bad heart?

"Uh-huh," the officer said, unimpressed. "Let's go, son."

Gran came to the door in a housecoat, an imposing five foot eight even in slippers. Her wild white hair was rolled up in curlers and tied with a blue kerchief. She listened intently but didn't say much. That, Rhan knew, would come later.

"There aren't going to be charges laid," the officer was telling Gran, "but there could have been, if you get my drift. I think the security guard is being very nice about this. Maybe it was a misunderstanding, but assault is assault."

"It wasn't assault. It was a rescue," Rhan said.

"And I thought you ought to know what kind of crowd is up there at the mall. We've had one bad incident after another: fights, theft. It's not a group I'd let my kid hang around with."

"I'm not hanging around with anybody. I just got here! I told you, it was a rescue!"

They both glared at him. Rhan folded his arms over his chest and shut up.

When the policeman left, Gran said nothing. All the way up to his room on the second floor, she didn't speak. Rhan tried to rehearse his argument in his head but found he couldn't concentrate. He knew he was in for it. Why didn't she just start already?

When the door closed, he turned to her. She was wiping at her eyes with a tissue.

"What the hell. . . ?" Rhan started, alarmed.

"Well, what do you think?" Gran said. "I open the door and all I see's a uniform."

"I was right there behind him," Rhan said.

"I couldn't see you. And no cop ever brought me good news."

It was true. With a pang Rhan realized what she must have thought in those few seconds—that he was hurt, or worse. The scare wasn't completely gone from her face.

"I'm sorry," he said.

Gran tucked the tissue into her pocket. "Seems like you got a lot to be sorry for tonight."

Rhan sighed. "Look, what was I supposed to do? Stand there and watch this kid get beat up—?"

"No," Gran cut him off. "But you don't have to jump in with both feet. What do you think security guards are for? Why didn't you just go get one?"

Rhan didn't answer. In the mall that thought hadn't even crossed his mind. He sat down on the bed. It was hard and spare, like the rest of the little room. There was an old brown dresser and a wooden chair.

Gran was looking out the window. "Like it isn't hard enough to be here in the first place?" she said. "You don't know what it did to me to ask that woman for a place to stay."

"You're the one who keeps saying it's only temporary," Rhan said.

"And it is," Gran replied with conviction. "Believe me, Zoe was the last resort. If the Devil himself had come up with a better idea I would've considered it. It just all happened too fast."

Only two weeks earlier Gran had been the caretaker of the ramshackle six-plex where they'd lived in Vancouver. When it was sold, she'd lost her job and her home in one swoop.

"That Zoe has to see you trucked home by the police," Gran continued, "like some common hooligan . . ."

"Right. I'm an *un*common hooligan."

"Don't get smart. You know what I mean. It scares me, this temper of yours."

Rhan got to his feet. "It's not temper . . ."

"You're belting people for fun?"

"It was an accident, for Christ's sake!"

"You gotta be standing on the track to get hit by the train," Gran shot back.

Her blue eyes were clear now. Rhan turned away.

"Sometimes you make me proud and sometimes you just make me wonder," Gran said after a moment. Her voice softened. "Kid, I need you to grow up."

The fiery knot in his throat was sudden, unexpected. When he heard the door close, he dropped onto the bed again.

Rhan Van had known he was a knight for a little over a month. There had been a girl in Vancouver and he'd thought she was in trouble. Wanting to help her, trying to save her, he'd discovered something in him that was extraordinary.

He wasn't exactly sure how he did it, but when the power overtook him, amazing things happened. In the past few rollercoaster weeks he'd pushed over a wall with his bare hands and saved a man from plunging off the third storey of a house. The night he and Gran left for Thunder Bay, he'd stopped a robbery with a well-aimed can of soup.

The transformation was always brief, but in his mind's eye he could see the electric blue energy running over him like armour; he could feel it zinging through his veins. In those moments he was RanVan the Defender. He was somebody who could help, who could make the difference. It was the greatest feeling in the world.

Even tonight, before everything got so screwed up.

He winced. He remembered the jarring impact, and the way the old security guard had crumpled and fallen to his knees. Over and over Rhan had said he was sorry, babbling on, shocked. He hadn't known he could hit anyone that hard.

Somehow he had to get a grip on this. He was still a knight, he just wasn't . . . finished. He needed training—a teacher or something. But he didn't know where to look, and it couldn't wait.

He stood suddenly and rummaged in the dresser drawer for a notepad and pencil. He hesitated, then started to write.

1. Perfect existing skills. That was the biggie, Rhan thought grimly. He had to figure out how to control the power. He couldn't let it get away on him, like tonight. There had to be a way to help people without hurting anybody.

2. Determine parameters. Being a knight was so new, maybe there were parts he hadn't discovered yet. What could he do and what was impossible? He had to know where the edges were.

3. Pain. A whole category in a single word. Rhan knew he had too many mortal genes to be impervious to pain, but he figured a real knight would be pretty nonchalant about it. It was a mark of the breed.

4. Select quest. That was a future thing, distant and blurry, to look at once he'd conquered everything else. Knights always had quests—golden fleeces, holy grails. It was the journey that started the great adventure of your life.

Rhan read his plan over and over, feeling a strange tingle. Words became different when you wrote them down. It wasn't just a list anymore; it was a vow. And a vow was something you kept ... or else.

But he had no idea what "else" might be.

Bush Boy

by

W. D. Valgardson

While most Canadians live in cities, most of Canada is wilderness. I live on 76 acres of bush in eastern Ontario. But the bush that is the setting for Bill Valgardson's "Bush Boy" is a denser, darker place, more dangerous with the threat of snags and blowdowns and cougars. That's where young Jamie finds himself. He knows his way around the woods, but he's scared this time, and with good reason. There is something even more dangerous than a cougar out there with him: you could say, the most treacherous thing on the planet. Another human who doesn't want Jamie around.

"Hey, Bush Boy, what're you doing?" Lance called over the noise in the hallway. People were pushing past. Others were opening and closing their lockers. A few of them turned to look at who was doing the yelling.

"Bushby," Jamie replied.

"That's what I said, Bush Boy. What's your old man up to?"

"Picking mushrooms," Jamie said. He didn't like talking about it. Everybody knew his dad had been hurt when a snag fell on him. Snags were called widow makers. They hung up in the branches and could drop on you without warning.

His dad was getting better but he wasn't going to be logging for awhile. When he could, he picked mushrooms and gathered salal. Anything to make a few bucks and to keep busy. There was worker's compensation and Jamie's mom had her job at the grocery store, but they'd explained to him that things were going to be tight for awhile. He'd had his heart set on a dirt bike, but he wasn't going to have one unless he found some way to get it for himself.

Coming from anybody but Lance, being called Bush Boy was good for a punch in the arm. Lance could get away with it because they'd been friends when they were little and lived next door to each other. There was a creek that ran through their backyards, and they spent a lot of time playing together, even though Lance was two years older. Jamie had named himself Bush Boy then. He saw himself as

Tarzan of the northern forests. Only Lance knew where the name had come from.

They'd had a tree house and a swing made from a rope and a tire. They'd swing as high as they could and yell at the top of their lungs. Lance had even talked Jamie into jumping off the swing into the creek. He'd broken his ankle that way.

Lance always had great ideas for adventures, but before they were over, Jamie always seemed to be in trouble. There was the time Lance suggested they borrow a rowboat to go crabbing. He forgot to mention that he hadn't asked permission. They both ended up sitting on a bench in the police station until their parents came to get them. That was when Jamie's mother and father suggested he find someone his own age to play with.

His parents weren't unhappy when Lance's family moved to Duncan. They were gone for three years. When they came back, they bought a house on the west side of town. Lance had his own crowd now, and they didn't want someone younger hanging around with them.

Since he'd returned, Lance had been wearing a wool poncho. He had his head shaved on both sides. The rumor was that the stud in his left ear was a real diamond.

"We're going dirt biking," Lance said. "You want to come?"

Jamie knew Lance had a new dirt bike. He and his friends had been racing over the hiking trails. They weren't supposed to because it tore up the thin topsoil and caused the ground to wash away. When someone complained, Lance shrugged it off. "What're you going to do about it? Arrest me?" He knew people would grumble but they wouldn't actually do anything. The local Mountie was busy giving out speeding tickets and reporting accidents.

Jamie desperately wanted to try out Lance's bike. He imagined himself flying over the bumps and sliding around the corners.

Stupid snag, he thought. *Stupid tree. Stupid father for not getting out of the way fast enough.* Then he felt guilty. His dad was lucky he hadn't been standing one step over. The snag would have come right down on top of him instead of just giving him a glancing blow.

The bell was ringing for the last class. The crowd started to thin out as people went to their classrooms.

"No, I'd better pick 'shrooms," he said. "Thanks."

Lance laughed. His two friends laughed with him. They always laughed when Lance laughed. If Lance frowned, they frowned. They walked on each side of him, pushing people in the hall out of the way. Jamie thought of them as Dopey and Grumpy. Their real names were Donald and Gerald.

When Jamie got home, he made himself a peanut-butter-and-banana sandwich, wrapped it up and put it in his pocket. He added a soft drink and some trail mix. He picked up his white bucket from the garage. He rode out on his bike. The place where he picked was three kilometers out of town. When he got there, he stashed his bike in the bush. Mushroom pickers kept their areas secret. None of them wanted to find a good place and then have someone else come and pick it.

His dad was driving back and forth to Victoria for a few weeks to do physio, so Jamie was on his own. The problem was they hadn't had much rain. The forest was dry and that meant the mushrooms weren't sprouting up like they normally did. Also, Jamie got paid by weight. In dry weather the mushrooms barely weighed anything. In wet weather they were large and heavy.

Unfortunately, there wasn't anything else to do to make money. Once a week he rode his bike up and down the highway, picking up bottles and cans for the refunds. That made him a few dollars but it wasn't steady. Besides, the store would only take forty-eight cans a day. The fact that his mom worked there meant he couldn't try taking in more than the maximum.

Picking mushrooms was hard work. There was no flat area here. Just steep cliffs and ridges. He started just off the roadside, scouring the ground for the light golden color of chanterelles. They were the only mushrooms he picked. There was no making mistakes with chanterelles, his dad said. Nothing else looked like them except the false chanterelle. It sort of looked like a chanterelle, but when you looked at it closely you could see that instead of the smooth shape of the real chanterelle, the false one was twisted.

He worked his way back and forth along the slope, moving gradually upward. He was looking for a drip line. That was where little waterfalls and steady trickles of water poured down the slope during the winter rains. They carried the mycellium down and then mushrooms sprang up along the water's path.

In spite of being teased occasionally about being a bush boy, Jamie hadn't really been far off the road by himself.

The forest was so thick that you could get lost just past the edge. The slope was covered in moss and ferns. There were the red rotting stumps of first-growth cedar that had been cut down many years before. Some of the oldest ones had rotted completely away and left large holes in the ground. Others were so soft that when he grabbed the wood, it came away like wet wool.

The chanterelles grew in the strangest places. Sometimes under logs. Other times under the moss itself. To find those, he had to watch for a hint of yellow showing through. Then he carefully pulled away the moss and eased out the mushroom. After that he didn't move again until he'd looked all around. He knew that where he found one, he'd find more. Seeing them was hard, though. When he first went with his father, he couldn't even see the ones that were under his feet.

The forest was so quiet it was spooky. Jamie could hear the rasp of his jacket. Overhead, the branches moved slightly, making a creaking sound. He was tempted to use a game trail rather than pull himself up the slope by holding on to bushes and trees. Climbing the game trails was much easier, but he didn't want to take a chance of meeting a cougar head on. There were lots of them around. Two had been spotted in people's yards in the last month. In July one had grabbed a kid staying at a nearby summer camp. The cougar had got him by the head and was trying to drag him away when the camp counselor bashed it on the head with a large stick.

After three hours, all he'd picked was about a kilogram of mushrooms. In a good year some people picked twenty or thirty kilos in a day. That's what he wanted. He wanted to go down to Joe's and have him weigh up the mushrooms and say, "That's a good day's picking."

He had to face up to it. There wasn't going to be any good picking until it rained. He bent back his head. Through the tops of the trees all he could see was blue sky.

When he got home his mom was sitting in the kitchen having a cup of coffee. She was staring out the window at the ocean. Usually when she did that, it meant something was wrong. He got himself a glass of milk and sat down with her.

"I got laid off," she said. "The mill's closing for two months. The price of lumber is down. Business is going to drop off. They're not waiting for it to happen."

The next day he kept looking at the sky, hoping for clouds. Usually in September it rained nearly every night. Instead, the sky was the same pale, whitish blue it was in summer. There wasn't a cloud to be seen.

A good rain was what he needed. The kind that started during the night and kept on for days until the forest floor was soaked and little waterfalls were tumbling over the cliffs.

He was leaning against his locker, hoping for rain, when Lance punched him in the arm. "Make a fortune, Mushroom King?"

Lance leaned close, glanced around to see if anyone was watching, then put his hand in his pocket and eased out a roll of bills. The outside bill was a fifty.

"You and me," Lance said, "we're friends. Twenty bucks for helping me out tomorrow."

"What about school?" Jamie said.

Lance shrugged. "Fine. I'll ask someone else. There's plenty of people want to make twenty bucks. Tell you what. I'll throw in an hour on my dirt bike. I wouldn't do that for anyone else."

"I don't know," Jamie said. Lance moved his lips but didn't make any sound. He didn't need to. Jamie knew exactly what he was saying. "Wimp."

The next morning Jamie started for school, but instead of going inside, he crossed over the soccer field and met Lance and Dopey and Grumpy among the trees at the back.

"What're we doing?" Jamie asked.

"Just going for a walk in the forest. Just like picking mushrooms."

"How're we going to make money that way?"

"Don't sweat it," Lance said. "You get twenty bucks no matter what. We do okay you get more. Maybe fifty. How often do you make fifty bucks? Here, guaranteed, ten bucks." He reached into his pocket and took out his roll of bills. He pulled out a ten and gave it to Jamie. "We're friends. Friends trust each other, right?"

They cut back through the trees to the edge of town. The three of them had their dirt bikes stashed in the bush. Jamie got on behind Lance. They led the way, racing over a logging road until they were in an area Jamie didn't know. They stopped and pushed the bikes off the road.

They hiked a game trail for half an hour. The ground was steep. They crossed one ridge, went down the far side, then up another ridge. Jamie felt in his pocket. He'd brought his father's compass with him. It was easy to lose your way in a place like this. Once you lost it, it was hard to get your sense of direction back. Moss grew everywhere, not just on the north side of the trees. The trees blocked out the sun. Even on the top of a ridge the forest was so thick and the ridges so uneven that you couldn't see the ocean.

"That's cougar scat," Jamie said. He bent down to inspect it. "It's fresh."

"You're always worrying about something, Bush Boy. You think a cougar's suddenly going to appear and chomp on us? We've been here lots of times. Never seen a cougar. Never seen a bear. Never seen no dragons."

"Never seen no cops, either," Grumpy said.

"No helicopters," Dopey added.

They started laughing but Lance waved his hand for them to be quiet. He pointed to one side of a blowdown. They were at the top of a ridge and looking down the slope.

The blowdown was the biggest Jamie had ever seen. There had to have been a twister. Trees were uprooted or snapped off and piled on each other at every angle.

Jamie hoped they weren't going into the blowdown. They were very dangerous. He'd been going to look for mushrooms in one once and his father had called him back. When he'd wanted to know why, his father had said, "Let's just stop for a break and watch." As they rested, they heard a sudden creaking, and one of the trees slipped under the pressure and sprang loose.

Lance led them to the blowdown, then along its edge. Dopey had been carrying a pack sack. Lance took it and handed it to Jamie. He motioned for Jamie to follow. Dopey and Grumpy brought up the rear. Lance crept forward until they came to an area that was more open.

"Now you earn your money, Bush Boy."

"What do I do?"

"There's a plantation there. Lots of lovely plants just ready to be harvested. You pick the leaves and put them in the sack. When it's full, you come back. You get a full sack, you get your fifty."

Jamie didn't move.

"What's the matter, Bush Boy? Scared?"

Jamie was scared. Everyone knew there were marijuana plantations around. People were always joking about it. But the mushroom pickers, if they stumbled on one, left right away. The growers used government land because that way if the Mounties found the plot, no one could be charged. The trouble was, anyone could come and pick the plants. There were stories of long-haired types sleeping right in the middle of their crops when they were ready for picking. They carried machetes and guns.

"You gonna buy a dirt bike picking bottles? You want something, you gotta take some risks. You fill the pack and you get a bonus. A hundred bucks total."

A hundred dollars, Jamie thought. There was a sign up at the grocery store advertising a second-hand bike for $185.

He grabbed the pack sack and crawled forward. Then he stopped.

Some things, he thought, weren't worth doing. That's what his dad had said when they were out picking and they saw a doe. Jamie had told his dad to shoot it, but his dad said there were some things that weren't worth doing. He'd brought a gun because there were cougars in the area, not to shoot a deer out of season.

Jamie was just starting to crawl backward when he heard someone yell. Behind him he heard Lance say, "Get out of here."

Jamie glanced back. He just caught a glimpse of Lance and Dopey and Grumpy as they fled. He stood up.

The grower had been looking at the other three. Now he saw Jamie and turned. He was carrying a machete. He swore and charged. There was a large fallen-down tree behind Jamie. He dropped to his knees and scrambled under. The grower had to climb over the tree. It slowed him down and gave Jamie a bit of a lead.

Jamie couldn't think. He ran into a tree, got knocked sideways, stumbled and kept running. There was no way that he could outrun his pursuer.

The blowdown was directly ahead of him. He plunged into it. He scrambled onto a large tree and ran along the trunk, grabbing at the branches to stay upright. Behind him he could hear the grower swearing and yelling. There was no time to plan anything. He had to keep jumping from tree to tree.

All at once the tree he was on moved, and with a yell, he fell sideways. He thrashed through the branches. When he hit the ground, he scrambled forward on his hands and knees until he hit his head against a root. He lay there, his heart pounding. All around him the branches crisscrossed. Here and there openings appeared.

He tried to control his breathing. His chest ached from running. He could hear the grower walking along the trunks. The blowdown was like a maze. There was no way of knowing which direction was which in the tangle of branches and trunks.

Jamie was just starting to crawl away when overhead he heard a boot scuff on a log. He looked up.

The grower was standing directly above him. He swung the machete and chopped off a branch. It looked like he was going to climb down into the tangle.

Just then there was a crack. Jamie knew the sound of a tree pulling loose. The grower paused.

"I know you're there somewhere," the man yelled. "If I catch you, you're dead meat. You've been picking my crop for the last couple of weeks. You come back and you're dead. You hear me? You're dead."

With that he disappeared. Jamie didn't move. He wasn't going to be tricked. In a few minutes, he heard the boots scuff wood close by. He'd been right. The grower had been pretending to leave. Now he really left, his departure marked with curses and threats that gradually faded.

Jamie didn't dare climb back onto the logs. At least here he was safe for the moment. If he had to he could stay until it was dark. Then he could creep out of the blowdown by the light of the moon.

Suddenly he remembered the cougar spoor. Jamie looked around. The branches seemed to form an endless series of caves filled with shadows. In amongst the branches he wouldn't have a chance if a cougar was prowling. Staying where he was didn't seem like such a good idea.

Then he remembered his father's compass. He would have to go around and through the trees, but it would keep him going in the right direction.

He took it out. It wasn't broken. It had a strong metal case and it would take more than a tumble off a tree to break it.

He wormed his way through the branches. Sometimes he had to crawl on his stomach. Sometimes he crawled on his knees. Sometimes he was able to stand upright. Finally, he was peering from the edge of the blowdown. He looked around, then slipped into the forest.

When he got back to the road, the three bikes were gone. Lance hadn't even waited to see if he was okay.

Jamie didn't get home until supper time. The school had called to see why he wasn't in class. He told his parents he'd gone dirt-bike riding with Lance. He was grounded for a week and his mother gave him a lecture on all the times he'd got in trouble with Lance in the past.

"There are times . . ." she said. Since he wasn't going any-where except school for a week, his father handed him an ax and suggested he work his way through the woodpile.

On Monday he saw Lance and Dopey and Grumpy huddled at one end of the hall.

"How are you, Bush Boy," Lance said. "We looked for you but you didn't keep up. You've got to learn to move faster."

"He said you've been picking his crop for weeks. You knew he would be watching."

"No hard feelings," Lance said. "Sometimes things happen. Here. For your trouble."

He held out a ten-dollar bill. Jamie looked at it, then at Dopey and Grumpy. They were both grinning.

He'd had some good times with Lance—jumping off roofs, climbing over the fence into the salvage yard to see what they could find, riding their bikes off the end of the dock. Every time he'd held back, Lance would charge ahead, yelling, "Wimp. Wimp."

If the two stooges hadn't been there, Jamie might have asked what had happened. Lance probably would just have smiled with the left side of his mouth and shrugged his shoulders. They'd both have known the question wasn't just about Lance running and leaving Jamie alone.

"I don't want it," Jamie said. He took the ten Lance had already given him and held it out. When Lance didn't take it, Jamie let the bill drop to the floor.

They stood there staring at each other. Lance looked to the side.

"Ah, what do I care. Come on, you guys," he said to Dopey and Grumpy. "You make your choices, Bush Boy." He turned away and retreated down the hall, becoming smaller and smaller until he and his pals turned the corner and disappeared.

The Tiniest Guitar in the World

by
Martha Brooks

There are all kinds of girls who play electric guitars and play them well, but the irresistibility of that instrument is still something you could say was a "guy thing," without sounding too sexist. Maybe that's what makes Donald Petrie do what he does in "The Tiniest Guitar in the World." It seems an unusual idea, even to him, and proves to be a first-class challenge. But there are more challenges ahead, as he must defend his actions. This is a story about differing perceptions and a story about caring. It's a story about "travelling on into the light," which, not incidentally, is the title of the anthology from which the story is taken.

Martha Brooks, Budge Wilson, and R. P. MacIntyre are the three writers who, I think, are probably most responsible for putting short stories for kids and, especially, young adults, back on the bookshelves of this country.

I am following Fletcher P. (Flint) Eastwood down the hall. I've been ordered to his office, where we will sit and the lid on his good eye will jump up and down like a butterfly in a frenzy before he'll calmly ask, "What's up, Petrie?"

I will respond politely, "Nothing, *sir*," because my father went to an army academy and he taught me that this always makes a good impression. It also drives Mr. Eastwood crazy. The way I say *sir*, he can't find any fault with.

He's built like a retired football player and sort of bounces when he walks. His suits—all three of them—fit too tight in the jacket and too loose in the pants. There's a little ring of blondish gray hair that sits on his ears like a costume store bald wig, and the skin on top is firebrick red. Which is why we call him Flint.

His dinky office smells of eraser crumbs and old coffee and unidentifiable aftershave. You might say it's like a second home to me.

We get inside. He closes the door. "Sit," he says to the orange chair in front of his desk.

I sit down and kick at a paper ball near my feet. Beside it is a paper clip. I pick that up so I'll have something to fiddle with.

Flint settles in behind the desk, sighs, wipes his face with a wrinkly hand. I shoot a look at him in time to catch the butterfly-in-a-frenzy eyelid maneuver. His chair makes that old familiar squeak as he leans dangerously far back.

He pauses, then comes forward fast. His elbows hit the desktop with a hollow sound like distant drums.

"What's up, Petrie?"

I've twisted the paper clip so that it's like a square with half the top missing. "Nothing, *sir*."

"Goddamn it, Donald—don't patronize me. Mrs. Lindblad *saw* you outside at noon."

"What? Sir?"

"You and your friends. Robert Isles and that . . . Goran fellow—Chris. Loose brown cigarette papers. Does that ring a bell?"

"Loose *brown* cigarette papers?"

He leans in on me. "Are you boys selling drugs?"

The paper clip now resembles a mutilated snake.

"Put that thing down and answer me."

I toss the clip. It bounces off the desk leg and veers back, tangling itself into the laces of my boot. "No, sir," I mumble, pulling it off.

The worst thing about somebody making up their mind that you're a liar is that you can tell the truth until you're blue in the face, but they aren't going to believe you, anyway.

"What's that? What did you say?" He's practically lying on his desk.

"I said, no, sir."

"Dammit, look at me when you answer."

I look. The other eye is glass. The color doesn't quite match his good eye.

"No . . . sir."

"You know, Donald, I can't think of a single other person in this school who spends more time in this office, but it never seems to faze you."

He talks to me a lot about stuff not fazing me—my poor grades, my total disregard for the school's dress code, and my being a disturbing influence.

"You were *seen*, Donald. Outside, at *noon. Rolling marijuana cigarettes and selling them to the seventh-grade boys!*" At noon. Outside at noon. Robert Isles, Chris Goran, and I found a dead squirrel. It was flattened—fairly fresh roadkill. Its mouth was open, its teeth bared. Its right arm stretched up past its ear. The other hung down around its belly. Goran starts joking around that it's lip synching. Isles is sucking on a can of root beer. Goran holds up the squirrel. Makes its left paw twitch frantically up and down. Isles spews root beer all over the ground. And that's when I get this unusual idea.

Goran's little brother, Paul, walks by with Simon Wiebe. We make them go into their classroom and bring out a pair of scissors. And what happens next is pretty amazing. Everybody hangs around watching. It's about the most creative thing I've done since I was a little kid.

"Donald, I've given you more warnings and second chances than just about anyone in the history of this school," Flint says, fishing around his shirt pocket under his gray pinstriped suit jacket. He pulls out a fresh pack of gum. "What is it you care about?" He picks at the outside wrapper. "I'd really like to know." He can't get the tab undone. He finally mangles it open and offers me a stick.

"No, thanks, sir. It's bad for my teeth."

Patiently smiling, he takes a piece of gum for himself. He's going to act all buddy-buddy now. This is the ace up his sleeve, as they say. Sometimes you go to see the vice-principal or a counselor or whatever because you really need help. I don't know if they think you *enjoy* asking for help, or what. But you're depressed. They offer you a piece of gum. You tell them your problems because who else have you got to turn to—your mother? Then they offer you some turd piece of advice that messes you up even more because on top of everything else, you now have to worry about this new evidence they have on you, and about how they'll use it against you whenever they're in the right mood and you're in the wrong place.

So much for the buddy system.

Flint leans his arm on the desk, his chin on the palm of his hairy hand. It's his I'm-open-to-anything-you-have-to-tell-me-because-I'm-a-reasonable-caring-human-being position.

"Have you given any further thought to what you might do after you leave school?"

He's leading up to my becoming a drug dealer. Or to washing dishes at Mr. Steak for the rest of my life.

"Well, sir, lately I've been thinking seriously about marine biology."

"I see." He chews away. Waits for me to continue. We've been over this ground before.

"I worry about oil spills. Stuff like that."

"Stuff ... like ... that," he repeats, drawing out my words like my life is some kind of free-for-all display. He wisely nods. Puckers his lips. Sniffs. I know what he's going to say next and that it will make him very, very happy to say it.

"You are aware, of course, that you'll have to finish high school first. With good grades. Just when were you planning to get those?"

I feel a little nauseated. A little hot. A bit enraged. "To *get* them, sir?" I say innocently.

He slams down his hand flat on the desktop. I must jump about ten feet.

"Don't be smart with me! I've given you hours of my time. I've tried to reach you. I've been lenient with you. I've done everything I could to be the best possible friend I can. And I *am* your friend, Donald. But today just takes the cake. What are we going to do about it?"

"We?"

"Don't you know I could have you arrested right now? For trafficking? Don't you know that?"

"I wasn't selling drugs. And there's no such thing as brown cigarette papers. Name one time you have *ever* seen a brown cigarette paper, sir."

"Well. She was obviously wrong about the color," he says, like he's thinking for the first time since I walked in here that he might be losing ground.

"She didn't see brown cigarette papers today," I say in a soft, respectful tone. "What she saw was a brown root beer can being cut up and rolled."

I sit back and wait to see what he'll do next. His face shows a real struggle. He's madly trying to stuff back whoever it is behind the vice-principal mask he dons every morning as he's getting that fat knot into his silk tie.

"A root beer can?"

"Would I make up such a thing?"

"Possibly. This may sound like a dumb question, Donald, but why would you be cutting up a root beer can?"

I take a deep breath. Might as well tell the truth. Who knows? He just might believe it.

"I was making an electric guitar, sir."

"Go on." He's got this steady bead on me, like if I blow this one I'm a dead man.

"A very small electric guitar. Not a real one, you understand, but something that looked like one. For a dead squirrel, sir. I made it so it would look as if he was really playing it. Sort of caught forever in the moment, if you know what I mean—kind of like a statue."

Flint crinkles up his forehead and allows this to register. He takes his pencil and sort of dances it between his hands. He then plops it into a stained white mug along with the other yellow pencils and cheap blue pens.

"Where is this squirrel?"

"He's lying on his back, sir, out in the school yard. I can show you if you like."

"And the guitar?"

"It's here in my pocket. I didn't have time to set him up yet, so to speak." The cold aluminum warms quickly in my fingers. "I actually didn't know if I felt like just leaving it out there, either. The guitar, I mean." I hold it out to Flint.

He takes it and studies it for a minute. Then he sort of sags over his desk.

"This actually resembles a guitar," he says, looking up at me with wonder on his face.

"Yes. I know it does," I say, suddenly very happy. It's only at this exact moment that I realize that it does. And that it's actually beautiful to look at. I start to laugh. My eyes smart.

"No. I mean truly it does," he says, pointing to the delicate strings. "How did you do those?"

"I cut the can up really fine there. I mean at that point of making it."

"You must have a *very* steady hand. This stuff looks almost *shaved*."

"Well, I did sort of shave it. It was a kind of experimental shear-and-shave sort of thing."

"Does it actually fit the squirrel?"

"Yes, it does. We tried it out. It looks very lifelike."

"Believe me," he says, still looking at the guitar, "I know more than you think I do about what you're going through. You have an original turn of mind, Donald. If you could only find a way of using that to your benefit, instead of always using it like a suit of armor, then you'd have a sweet life."

"A sweet life?"

"Yes."

I wait for him to elaborate on this. He doesn't. He hands back my guitar. He plays with a pile of papers on his desk. "I pulled you out of your last class," he says, finally. "You might as well go on home now."

"Really? Thanks."

Flint's biggest problem is that he still likes kids, but we've finally worn him out.

I pause at the door, and on a kind of whim I say, "You really should be looking into another line of work, Mr. Eastwood. Something that makes you feel happier."

"That would be terrific, Don," he says tiredly. "If I could only find the energy."

"You'll figure something out," I say.

I close the door as soft as a feather, so as not to jar his nerves any further.

I start down the hall. This is a small private school. I've been coming here ever since three-quarters of the way through first grade. The elementary school and the junior and senior high schools are separated by double glass doors. I don't often have a reason anymore to be in the elementary part. But as I slide between the doors, I'm glad I came. I've entered another world—it's a trip back. Colored construction paper taped to the walls, framed decorated poems entitled "What Is Spring?" Some little kid has pasted cotton balls onto brown crayoned lines to show that SPRING IS PUSSY WILLOWS!

I'm thinking about my second-grade teacher, Miss Huska. She had black hair and green eyes and I fell in love with her on the first day back to school after Christmas vacation. My dad had left on New Year's—packed up as much as he could get into his big brown suitcase and left for good, and even though I didn't know exactly what was going on, like that I wouldn't see him from then on except sometimes in the summer, I felt sad and sick. At recess, when everyone else went outside, Miss Huska let me stay with her, indoors. That was when I decided to invite her to have lunch with me.

In the smaller grades, the teachers would sit down and have lunch with a student if they asked. First you had to write out a formal invitation (to improve your writing skills), and then they would write back. When I handed her my invitation with a picture of a lady and a boy eating lunch in their bathing suits (beside a big sand castle), she laughed and said, "Thank you, Don. This is for *me*?"

She always said, "This is for *me*?" like you'd just handed her a million bucks.

After the bell rang, we all sat in our desks for art class. Miss Huska smiled when she gave me her reply, which read, "Dear Don: Yes, I will have lunch with you. Thank you for your gorgeous picture! And thank you for inviting me. Yours truly, Miss Huska."

That morning, in art class, I repeated in my mind the word *gorgeous*, like a prayer, as I made her three lime green tissue-paper roses. She put them in her pencil can, where they stayed for months and gradually got faded by sunlight until we were let out for the summer.

Outside the second-grade room, which used to be Miss Huska's class, a boy is sitting in the hall, on a sunny spot, his legs sprawled. He's flicking his chewed-up pencil against his knee. The door is closed, but I can still hear the voice of his teacher on the other side, raving on about arithmetic.

I shove my hand into my jacket pocket. I feel the feather-light strings of the guitar. The kid looks really bored, waiting by the door until his punishment is over. I push against the toe of his shoe to get his attention. He's skinny, with a grown-out brush cut. I hand over to him my work of art.

He looks at it, turns it upright, raises his eyebrows like a TV cartoon. He smiles. He has the kind of teeth that'll need braces in a couple of years.

I'm beginning to wonder if he appreciates what I've just handed him. I remember reading somewhere that art doesn't become art until it goes out into the world.

"It's yours," I say.

Even as I say it, part of me wants to take it back. It looks better and better in his hands. I can't believe I've created something so ... gorgeous. That I actually did that. Finally I say, testy as hell, "Do you want it, or don't you?"

The kid pulls it to his chest, and my heart sinks. Then he gives me the craziest wink and starts madly fingering that tiniest guitar in the world like he's some big-time rocker.

He gets so involved that he doesn't even notice me leave, my boots clacking down the hall.

Outside, the sun is bright and the air is cold. On my way through the school grounds, I pass the squirrel, on his back, forever playing the invisible guitar. I'm grateful to him. Maybe I should make more stuff out of rejected junk material—a sort of personal statement on overlooked beauty.

I lean over, touch my right hand to my forehead, and salute him. After that, I turn and head home into the strong spring wind.

Sun Dogs

by
Rick Book

There is something that unites Canada from coast to coast, something bigger than the railroad, bigger than the CBC. And that's winter. You might think, reading this collection, that I was trying to hide the fact; the summer stories outnumber the winter stories three to one. But Rick Book's "Sun Dogs" kind of evens things out all by itself. It's a real bone-chiller. As anybody who lives here knows, you don't mess with winter. Especially in Saskatchewan, which is where Rick grew up and where he sets his tale. You might want to have a cup of cocoa handy while you're reading this. Maybe a nice comforter, too.

Wisps of snow swept across the flat white fields. They swooped down through the ditch, parted slightly for bristles of fireweed and thistle that the mowers had missed in the fall, then licked across the frozen gravel road with ragged tongues. Sometimes in bad weather, when the fields and road and sky are like one seamless white carpet, the weeds are the only way you can tell where the road ends and the ditch begins.

Mom was driving. We were coming home from church in Lashburg, my sisters Nicky and Tracey-Lynn in the back seat. It was March and we were itching for spring after months of short dark days and numbing cold. But spring was just a faint scent in the air on certain mornings, and this morning it wasn't there at all.

"Sun dogs," I said to Mom, who was pressed up against the wheel, straining to see the road. They were shimmering white spots hanging low in the sky on either side of the sun—light refracted by ice crystals. It meant the air higher up was cold. At ground level it was ten below, almost balmy by Saskatchewan standards.

"Weather's going to change," said Mom. She raised her eyes to look at the sky, then dropped them quickly back. "We could be in for a storm." An abandoned red brick church loomed out of the whiteness on our right. In summer, after suppers, I often rode my bike there, pried open the door with a screwdriver, and played "Bumble Boogie" on the old pump organ. Mom slowed to turn left. We were a mile from the farm.

"So what'd you think of Harry's sermon today?" The white Fairlane chugged around the corner. Mom pressed the gas, gripping the wheel tightly as she picked up speed. The girls were arguing over which Beatle was better looking.

"Don't know, haven't thought about it," I lied.

I'd been paying more attention to the fact that Anna-Maria was in the choir. I liked her, had actually sung some hymns out loud thinking it would score a few points. But then Harry'd started talking about sin, something I knew a little about. He had fixed me with a steely Christian gaze and asked in his thick Dutch accent, "Vat if every time we did sometink wrong, we pounded a nail into a door?" He paused to let us squirm a little, then drilled a look right through me. "And if every time we did sometink right, we pulled a nail out?" We were quiet as barn cats, waiting for the thundering fist of a punch line. "Yet even if we pulled out all de nails, we'd have still a door full of nail holes." There was much coughing and rustling after that, and later the collection plate was overflowing.

"I guess he was saying behave yourself if you want to keep your front door looking nice," I said. Mom laughed, her blonde hair poking out from under a burgundy paisley scarf. I figured mine probably looked more like a screen door.

Maybe it was the weather, maybe it was because it was Sunday, but when we got home I was restless. Dad was sitting at the kitchen table reading a *National Geographic*. The coal-wood stove was going. He didn't go to church much, said he worshiped at the church of the great outdoors. Which was a good idea in summer. I went upstairs, put on jeans, thick wool socks, a heavy wool sweater. "I'm riding down to the river," I said as I strode into the kitchen, grabbed an apple and opened the fridge to get some cheddar cheese.

Mom looked up from cutting celery. Tuna sandwiches for lunch. "You think that's a good idea? You saw those sun dogs." *Why is it when parents ask a question, there's always an opinion behind it?*

"Hell. Radio didn't say anything about a storm. Might be three days before anything happens."

"Stop swearing in my kitchen." Worry flashed across her blue eyes like the aurora borealis, her knife poised in midair. "You know how unpredictable the weather is." She turned to Dad, up to his eyeballs in some Mayan dig. "Bart?"

Dad lowered his magazine. "He'll be fine." He looked at me. "Just hightail it home if you see anything coming, okay?"

Nicky flounced in. She was thirteen and looking for action. "Can I come, too?"

"No, stupid. You don't even know where I'm going."

"Don't call your sister stupid." Dad was glowering now.

"Right." I nodded, turned and headed for the door, reaching up on my way by the fridge to grab some matches from the old tin match dispenser. It was the smartest thing I did that day.

"Come on, Scamp," I said to our beagle. "Let's go." But he just lay there and wouldn't budge. *That's a new one,* I thought and walked out the door.

The sky was the color of bath water. The sun glowed dimly like a pale moon with two small discs on either side. I wondered, as I walked to the barn, how the ice crystals in sun dogs stayed up in the air when snowflakes and hail didn't.

Paddy was at the fence by the barn paddock, ears forward, head up and over the top rail like he knew something was up. I whistled. He whinnied back. Paddy was a Palomino quarter horse, a gelding. I'd bought him for $275 a couple of years ago, money I'd made from summer jobs, mowing ditches for the municipality, digging culverts into roads with a pick and shovel. He sure was a pretty horse. Not big, but he had a nice golden coat with white mane and tail and forelock, and a white blaze down his nose. Dad said Paddy didn't know he was a horse at all. Thought he was a human or maybe the world's biggest lapdog.

He snorted with that little tremolo through the nose that horses do, and I snorted right back in the way that people with horses do. I opened the fence, grabbed Paddy's halter and walked him out to the front door. I went into the barn and got the bridle and saddle and blanket. The blanket had been my grandfather's. The saddle I'd bought from an old cowboy out east of town. I was tightening the cinch when Paddy cranked his head around. His nose went right to my jacket pocket like a bee to a flower. He'd found the apple.

"Hey, you fat four-legged thief," I laughed, offering him the McIntosh from Ontario. He took the whole thing in his mouth like a Lifesaver. Paddy looked a little ratty with his long winter coat, and his hooves needed clipping. I figured I'd curry him when we got back.

I swung up in the saddle and settled into the butt-worn seat, enjoying the creak of the leather, the warm smell of horse. We walked past the house and down the lane, then west between the fields toward the river, the South Saskatchewan River. There aren't many rivers in this province and I always felt lucky we had one just three miles from the farm. It was like a magnet for our family, summer and winter—a destination when there was nothing to do and nowhere to go. Every year we made bets on when the ice would go out. Sometimes we could hear the groaning of ice from the house and, once, the roar of it as a jam broke and swept downstream. I wanted to be there if it happened again. At least I wanted to see what condition the ice was in. I nudged Paddy in the sides with my work boots and he grudgingly started to trot.

We weren't exactly horse people. I was a little scared of Paddy, afraid of falling off and getting hurt. It had happened a couple of times at a dead gallop and I'd limped for weeks. Paddy wasn't broken in. He just tolerated us until he didn't want to anymore, then he'd head for the barn. We'd hired this cowboy once to come and break him for us, a little Japanese guy named Snowball. He was a cruel bastard. He raked Paddy's sides with his spurs, trying to get him to buck. After about five minutes Paddy's sides were covered with blood. Dad was so mad he was shaking. He told Snowball he'd shoot him if he didn't get off. I put ointment on the wounds, but the spur marks were still there. So we babied Paddy even more after that.

We followed a prairie trail down between two stubble fields. The straw from last year's crop stuck through the snow like an old bachelor's three-day beard. Straight ahead

I could just make out the hills on the far side of the river, a dark bluish smudge below the thin gray line of horizon. "It's colder than I thought," I said to Paddy. I pushed my brown Stetson down farther. "Wish I had my green toque." I slowed Paddy to a walk and did up the top button on my heavy denim jacket. I was glad for the fleece lining and my wool long johns.

"Damn!" I was looking down at the snow sifting through the stubble. The wind had changed. In just a few minutes it had swung around. Now it was blowing from the north. I turned in the saddle and looked back home. We were still about two miles from the river. "Better not be long," I said and gave Paddy a little kick in the ribs with my heels. I figured horses are like motorcycles. You have to kick 'em through the gears one at a time. Paddy broke into an amble but shook his head and sidestepped like he didn't want to go anywhere but back to the barn.

"Come on, you old plug, or I'll haul you to the glue factory." Paddy compromised with a trot while he was thinking it over, and when I kicked him again he consented to a canter.

Suddenly a white spot straight ahead of us exploded out of the snow and ran. Snowshoe! Paddy jumped, went straight-legged, came down hard on all fours. He twisted sideways to the left and launched himself into a gallop across the field. I grabbed the horn to hang on, dropped the left rein. Runaway! I leaned forward, reached down, tried to snag the rein as it lashed the air. Paddy stepped on it once, twice. It stretched, then snapped loose, whipped forward past his ear.

The ground below raced by, a blur of seething, plunging white. My head was full of the sounds of leather, horse hooves beating the frozen ground beneath the crusty snow. Finally I grabbed the rein, leaned back and hauled in hard on both reins. Paddy slowed, then lurched to a stop and stood there, belly heaving under me, blowing steam out his nostrils. My heart was racing, blood pounded in my ears. "Paddy!" I yelled. "Haven't you seen a stupid rabbit before?"

With that out of his system, Paddy settled into an easy lope. In a few minutes, we were out of the fields and weaving through sagebrush and buffalo-berry trees. As we passed, the wind blew icy combs of hoarfrost off the branches. We headed west to a barbed-wire fence, then followed it until we reached the gate. It was open. There were no cattle out here in winter. We rode through. Soon we were in the hills— khaki green in summer, now white and round and smooth, gouged with ravines where old creeks had carved their way down to the river. I angled south toward the Seaton ravine, just a dip in the land full of chokecherry bushes. As the ravine deepened, the bushes became gnarly gray sticks of maple, then poplar and finally willows by the water. We walked along the ridge, and from on top of Paddy I could see the river. The ice was cracked like a hard-boiled egg. Pressure ridges crisscrossed from one side to the other half a mile away. It looked ominous—like a rattler ready to strike.

We followed the ravine and where it widened finally, we angled down a big hill to the bottom, where Paddy waded through chest-high drifts to reach the shore. Cakes of dirty ice full of wind-blown sand had pushed up on the frozen banks, had bulldozed young willows and driftwood into piles. We stopped. Paddy sniffed at some ragged cattails while I sat there taking in the scene. I thought of the early explorers seeing this for the first time, cataloguing each geographic feature, each sensation and thought for their journals and maps. Did they think it was an empty, lonely and bleak land? Or did they think, like the Indians, that it was beautiful? The Plains Cree had been here for ten thousand years. It was their garden, a gift from the Creator. I imagined a hunting party and I was one of them. On pinto ponies, with strings of dead snowshoes and white-tailed deer dangling head down across the horses, we returned to our tepees hidden from the wind in the deepest coulees, where sweet plumes of woodsmoke rose in the air.

Paddy snorted. I snapped back to reality. Out on the river white waves of snow were drifting across the ice, curling over the ridges. The wind had picked up! The far shore had disappeared. I looked up. A mass of low clouds, dark with snow, was barreling along the river toward us. My heart jerked into high speed, a surge went right to my legs and hands. *Storm!* I'd stayed too long! I looked up at the sun dogs. "Dammit, I'm stupid."

Dad's words poked at me. "He'll be fine. Just hightail it home if you see anything coming, okay?"

"Come on," I yelled to Paddy. The tension in my voice surprised me. "Let's get out of here." I pulled hard on the right rein. Paddy wheeled around and I kicked, nosed him toward the snowdrift we'd broken through just minutes before. Paddy wanted to follow our tracks along the side of the ravine where we'd come down. But I was in a hurry now. I wanted to get to the top of the hill and run like hell for home. I kicked Paddy again and yanked left on the rein. "We're going straight up, big guy. Let's go."

Horses, like dogs or any animal, can smell fear. And they sure know when a storm's brewing. Paddy charged the hill. I leaned down close to his neck with the reins held tight. We were halfway up when it happened.

Crack!

There are certain sounds I'll never forget as long as I live: the thwack of a baseball into my glove, the puck on my stick in an empty rink, Paddy's leg snapping. A small wet sound, like a carrot breaking.

Before I knew what it meant, Paddy was falling forward and sideways to the right. And I was flying over his right shoulder, watching in slow motion—his mane, his shoulder rolling, the saddle falling away under me. I landed in a fury of writhing snow and mane and leather reins. Paddy screamed, a horrible high-pitched sound I'd never heard before. I scrambled to my knees. He was laying with his back to me, thrashing, his legs flailing the air. His right front leg had snapped, above his hoof, just above the fetlock. It was swinging back and forth like a cloth on the wind each time he kicked. I threw myself onto Paddy's neck, spread my arms over him. "Paddy, Paddy! Don't!" I yelled.

But his mouth was twisted, his eyes bulged wild with pain. Paddy jerked his head, rolled, struggled to get up. He lost his balance, put his weight on his broken foreleg. It bent over at right angles in the snow. Paddy screamed again, but stood and hopped wildly up the hill on three legs, fell again, rolled, hooves stabbing the air, chunks of snow flying. The saddle slipped down his side, stirrups kicked out, reins whipping the air around his head. I scrambled after him, yelling, falling in the snow. Paddy turned and lunged back down the hill. Half hopping, half slipping, his nostrils flared, his eyes huge. He came right at me. "Paddy!" I jumped and rolled out of the way. Paddy brushed by, the saddle hanging under him now, stirrups banging his feet, kicking up snow. Paddy lurched toward the willows, down where the snow was deep in the brush in the bottom of the ravine. He ploughed in, falling on his side, thrashing. Again he struggled to get up. A few more lunges. Then finally he stopped, up to his chest in the soft deep drift.

I ran and slid down after him. "Paddy, Paddy." I was crying. Paddy's head was bowed, his sides heaving. I walked up slowly, waded up to my waist in the snow. I put a hand on his rear. He was sweating, in shock, in danger now of getting a chill that could kill him. *Kill him! He's broken his damn leg!* My mind was going a hundred miles an hour but I couldn't think. I just needed to get up by Paddy's head, grab the reins, calm him down, stop him from hurting himself anymore.

I worked through the snow beside him, keeping my hands on Paddy's flank, talking to him in a low voice. "Paddy . . . take it easy, big guy."

Slowly I ran my hand along his neck, touched the side of his face. "Atta boy, take it easy. It's okay." I saw why his head was bowed. The reins were caught on something in the snow. I bent down, pushed the snow away with my gloves. And then I saw his leg.

"Ugh." The sight of it sucked the air right out of me. The leg was folded forward at an awful angle. The jagged broken bone had punched through the skin, had poked bright red holes in the snow. I could see white tendons glistening. *Why isn't it gushing blood?*

"Careful, big guy, don't worry. I won't hurt you." I brushed the snow away and found the rein snagged on a branch. Slowly I pulled it out of the snow, talking all the while. "When we're outta here, I'm going to fix your leg and give you the best meal you've ever had in your life, Paddy boy. Chopped oats and mash with apples, lots of nice fresh hay. You like that, big guy?" I stood up slowly, let the reins fall. Paddy was still breathing in short jagged gasps. I kept one hand on his flank and moved back to undo the cinch.

"Gotta get this saddle off. Then you'll feel better, won't you?" The saddle was jammed in the snow under Paddy so the D-ring of the cinch was now up on his back. I undid it and carefully pulled the saddle out from under him, then tossed it and the blanket into the snow.

I stood there for a minute to catch my breath, to think. The awfulness started to sink in. *We're in big trouble.* I checked my watch for the first time that day: 3:30. It'd be dark in less than an hour. I couldn't leave Paddy and go for help. We were three miles from home and there was a blizzard coming, maybe minutes away. Anyway, I wasn't dressed for walking home, and only dead men go walking in a prairie blizzard. If there was a whiteout I could stumble around in circles until I froze to death. The wind had picked up. And snow was falling. It was too late. I was frozen with fear.

I imagined Mom and Dad at the kitchen window, maybe the upstairs bedroom, faces full of worry. "Maybe Dad will come in the tractor," I said out loud. But that wouldn't do Paddy any good unless he brought the stoneboat. And there'd be no reason for him to think of that. I knew what I had to do. I just didn't know how.

"Gotta get you out of this deep snow, boy."

A gust of wind swooped down the hill, lashed us with snow, dumped snow down my neck. *My hat!* Panic welled up inside me again. I guessed I'd lost it when Paddy went down. Somewhere on the hill. I was sweating, too. *I could die out here if I don't find it.* It seemed like such a trivial thing, but in winter small mistakes can kill you. "Be right back, Paddy."

I shivered as I climbed up the hill through the mess Paddy and I'd made in the snow. I stopped where I thought we'd been when it happened, kicked the snow around with my boots and found something else I was looking for. I dropped to my knees and swept away the snow with my hands. A badger hole, much bigger than a gopher hole, with a frozen pile of dirt at his doorstep. It had been hidden under the snow. An ugly black hole in the white. *Maybe this will kill my horse.* Maybe—and I could hardly even think this thought—*maybe it'll kill me.* I stood, eyes squinting, tears streaming down my face. I looked up at the sky and yelled, "GODDAMN YOU ALL TO HELL!"

I'd never felt so empty and alone and afraid in my life. I dropped to my knees and buried my face in my leather gloves. Shame splattered me like battery acid. *This wasn't His fault, you idiot. This was* YOUR *idea in the first place.* YOU *stayed too long.* YOU *chose to charge up that hill like some TV cowboy.*

There was no time for that. I got up, spotted my hat at the bottom of the hill by some bushes. I scrambled down, shook the snow out and put it on. The band was cold and wet. I was shivering. Fear, like ice-cold water in a metal tank, rose inside me.

Can't let that happen. Gotta stay calm. We gotta get out of this.

Paddy hadn't moved. His slumping back was covered with a thin layer of snow like icing sugar. I brushed it off, put my hand on him. He was shivering, too. I waded up to his head in the trampled drift. "Gotta make a path for you boy. Gotta get you into these trees, into some shelter." Even the word *shelter* seemed too much to hope for. It was getting dark quickly now, and at night there would be no shelter anywhere from the cold. The sky was gray-black. Snow swirled overhead and sifted down the messed-up hill. Our tracks, all signs of Paddy's accident, would soon be gone. A magpie shrieked in the wind. I looked around, saw nothing but the twisted tines of trees reaching up to the passing sky.

I began to clear a path in front of Paddy. I pushed through the snow with my legs together, beating the snow down with my boots. I pushed snow to the sides with my arms and gloves. We only had about fifteen feet to go. But the question was: would Paddy move? Would he hop on one front leg? Or would he freak out again and hurt himself more?

Paddy looked like a broken old toy, his body sagging. He barely raised his head as I approached. "Hey, big guy. Got to move you, just a bit. Then you can rest."

He leaned his head against me as I talked, as I stroked the velvety side of his nose. "I know you don't want to move but we have to. I'm so sorry." My eyes were about three inches from his big brown eye. *Come on, buddy,* I said with my eyes to his. And then, as if in answer, Paddy raised his head and snorted.

I grabbed the reins. "Okay, Paddy, come with me. Come." I pulled on the reins slowly. They went taut. Paddy did nothing but look at me with his sad eyes, bottomless, full of pain.

"Come on, big guy. It's your only chance."

And then something seemed to happen inside of him. I can't say what it was. It was almost like he roused himself, got bigger. Paddy started to move. Slowly he raised his right leg, the broken foot dangling. And then he hopped on his left leg. Three hop-steps, then he stopped. The right hoof hovered above the snow. Paddy was breathing hard again. The vibrations must have hurt like crazy.

"I'm so sorry I got you into this, Paddy. Good boy. Just a few more like that." I gave the reins another tug. Again I sensed a rising in him. He neighed, not a shrieking neigh like before, but still there was pain in it. He took another hop-step and then another, and in a minute we were in the trees at the bottom of the ravine.

"Atta boy. What a great horse you are, Paddy boy. Okay, this is where we're spending the night. I'm going to build you a shelter right here, but you've got to lie down right now."

I was running out of time. It was almost dark. I needed to find wood and brush, to put up something to keep the snow and wind off us. All the time, just under the surface, fear was rippling, cold water in a black tank, fear that none of this was going to do any good, that I was going to lose my horse.

"Now, Paddy, lie down." I pulled the reins. "Right here, Paddy boy. I'm sorry, this is going to hurt again. Come on, lie down." For a horse that wasn't trained, he seemed to know what I wanted. Maybe he sensed that this was his only chance. Slowly Paddy folded his hind legs under him and sat down in the snow. Then he dropped his front quarters down, neighed again at the pain of it and flopped over onto his side, breathing hard.

I dropped to my knees by his side, brushed snow away from his head. I stroked his cheeks, patted his neck. "You are the bravest horse in the world." Paddy just lay there looking at me. Gently I took his bridle off.

Then I went to work. I stood, wiped the snow off my jeans, frozen stiff from the knee down. I fished my jack-knife out of my pocket, the bone-handled knife Grandma had given me for my birthday last year. My fingers were freezing. I fumbled with the big blade, finally got it open and cut the reins from the rings attached to the bit. I found a small tree growing, an inch thick, bent it over, broke it off. Then broke it again into five lengths a foot and a half long. I knelt by Paddy's broken leg.

"This is going to hurt again, Paddy boy. But I've got no choice." I brushed the snow away from his leg, saw the white jagged cannon bone jutting out of the torn skin. I pushed my hands under his leg in the snow. "Sorry." With my right arm wrapped around it, I pulled on Paddy's hoof. He snorted, that was all. The bone disappeared back inside the skin. I pulled again, then pushed at the crack with my left hand, pushing the bones together.

"I sure hope that's better, big guy. 'Cause I don't know what the hell I'm doing." Gently I placed the sticks around his leg, then wrapped the rein around and around them, slipping the ends under themselves to hold it tight. "It's not too pretty but it might work." *And this from a guy who can't stand the sight of blood!*

"Okay, gotta get moving."

I saw a couple of small trees, dead and leaning over. They were about three inches thick. I snapped them off from their frozen, rotten roots, then dragged them over to Paddy. I held one end up and put my boot on the tree, broke it into pieces four feet long. I put three of them by Paddy's head, grabbed one half of the remaining rein, lashed the poles together at the top so they formed a tepee. Paddy lay still, watching with one wary eye. "Atta boy. You rest. I'll have this up in a minute."

I took three more short poles and made another tepee near Paddy's rump. I got a ten-foot pole and laid it across the two tepees, so it ran above Paddy about three feet high. I needed a bunch of short poles now, branches, bushes, anything to lean against the long pole and make a roof over Paddy and me.

But I had run out of time.

The storm descended like a hammer, driving away the last shred of daylight. Wind whistled through the treetops above us, pellets of wet snow stinging like tiny bullets. Paddy raised his head and whinnied. "Down, boy. It's okay." But it wasn't. The saddle! I'd left it out in the drift. I ran to get it, stumbling and tripping through the brush in the dark. The saddle was already covered with six inches of snow. I felt around for the blanket. Got it! I lugged them back through the bush to our campsite. "Campsite!" I said out loud.

I pulled the saddle alongside Paddy's head, propped it up in the snow with the leather seat facing into the wind, the sheepskin on the underside next to Paddy's head. Maybe it would keep some of the wind out of his face. I grabbed the horse blanket. "Okay, big guy." I unfolded it, laid it across Paddy's wet neck, across his legs and withers. Paddy opened his eyes.

"That's for you, buddy."

I had to finish the shelter. There was no choice. My leather gloves were wet, my fingers were stiff with cold, my toes were tingling. I'd have to stop soon and bang them to keep them from freezing, just like when we played hockey at Uncle George's slough and it was thirty below. Snow blew down my neck. *Why didn't I bring a scarf?* Mom would have the last laugh at that one. All my life she'd been telling me to wear my toque and scarf. And all my life I'd laughed and walked out the door.

I felt my way around in the dark like a blind man, rummaging through the bush, breaking off branches, crawling back with them, leaning them against the pole above Paddy. It was slow work and it wasn't doing a thing to keep snow out. Every few trips, I'd check on Paddy, say hello, wipe the snow off. Sometimes Paddy shuddered. But he didn't move and he didn't make a sound.

When I had enough branches on the roof, I scrambled back to the brush at the edge of the trees. I dropped to my knees and tore at the bushes. Hunched over in the driving snow, I half hauled, half dragged armloads of them back. I laid them sideways to the other poles, pushed them tightly together, trying to thatch a roof. I was dog-tired but I couldn't think about that. I had to get the shelter built. Or Paddy and I might never see daylight again.

It was hard to keep track of direction in the dark. Once I thought I was lost and an electric shock of fear went through me. I stopped. *Don't panic. Don't move until you figure out where you are.* I looked for a minute, eyes straining against the snow, the dark. And there among the dark shapes of the trees, I saw the darker roofline of our shelter. *Better not let that happen again.*

Once I'd covered the back of the lean-to with brush, I started on the two sides. I was exhausted now, running on fear. When I couldn't pull or break any more bushes, I went behind the shelter and started scooping wet snow onto the roof with my gloves, then my hat. I was lucky—if you could call it that. It was a March blizzard and the temperature wasn't as cold as in January or February. I packed the wet snow and kept shoveling until I had created a solid wall on three sides of Paddy.

I crawled around to the front of the shelter, shaking like a loader motor. "All right, Paddy. I'm here now." Paddy didn't move. I couldn't see his face in the dark. I crawled between his front and back legs, up to his belly, swept the snow off him and patted him. "So what do you think, big guy? Think it'll keep us going till morning?" Still no sound, no movement. I sat down in the snow and leaned against Paddy's belly, careful not to touch his leg.

I was finished. I'd done all I could do, but I'd paid a terrible price. My hair was soaked with snow and sweat. I'd lost a lot of body heat. I was shaking; my teeth were chattering. I pushed my cold wet hat down, reached inside my jacket and pulled up the collar of my sweater. I tugged at my jacket collar and scrunched up my shoulders as far as I could. I had to do something about my toes. I made fists and pounded my knees, driving vibrations down into my boots to increase circulation. It helped my fingers, too. After a few minutes I could feel them again, a throbbing pain. I had my back to Paddy, was leaning against his belly like a sponge trying to soak up warmth, even give him some of mine. "Maybe we'll save each other, Paddy old boy."

In the dark, snow flitted around us like blackflies. Drifts piled up. I could feel them on Paddy's hind legs. The sound was a roaring hiss, like a whisper turned up full blast. Branches creaked, pellets of snow blasted the trees above. "Jeez, Paddy, I wish you'd turn up the heat."

And then a beautiful thought popped to the surface like a loon: "I've got matches!" They were in my shirt pocket. I'd planned to smoke a cigarillo, which I'd forgotten. "We'll be all right!" But a blast of wind snuffed out hope before it could ignite. *I'll never be able to light a fire in this blizzard. Maybe, if the wind dies down, if we live that long.* My spirits sank as I slid down inside myself, searching for warmth, solace, something.

In the black and awful dark, the answer slowly revealed itself. I thought about Harry's sermon—was it only this morning? I wondered what time it was. I couldn't see my watch in the dark. I wondered how much time I had, we had. I felt Paddy's chest, could feel the warmth, the faint thump of his heart. I thought of nails in the door of my soul.

I thought of the stories I'd grown up with: dead hunters too drunk to get their car unstuck down by the river, found frozen the next morning in the shop of an abandoned farm, tar paper wrapped around their legs, piles of wooden matches at their feet. Their hands had been too cold to light them. Or the farmer, lost in the whiteout between his house and the barn, found by his wife the next morning, a frozen sculpture hanging on a barbed-wire fence. He'd missed his barn by twenty feet. *Am I about to pay for my sins? All those nails in the door? Will they find me curled up and frozen to my dead horse? Will the coyotes find us first?*

I started to count nails. I'd been rude again to Nicky this morning. When was the last time I'd been nice to her? I guess it was when she was three. I put the head back on her doll and gave her a kiss on the forehead and for some reason said, "Don't tell Mom." Since then, I'd made her life miserable. Pushed her down a hill and through a fence on her tricycle. It had taken twenty-three stitches to close up her leg.

It was always something like that: a live mouse down her back; a dead chicken thrown into the girls' playhouse. Big brother stuff. Still, sitting there, I felt sick about it. Tracey-Lynn was still too young to have gotten the full treatment. But I had called her ugly lots because she wore glasses. And I called her stupid when she practised the piano. Mom was furious because Tracey-Lynn was just starting out. Otherwise I ignored her. Come to think of it, I didn't know my younger sister at all.

Mom! She'd be sick by now. I could just see her crying her eyes out, with all the lights on in case I was walking home in the blizzard. They'd be on the phone to all the neighbors, trying to figure out if we'd made it somewhere and what to do because we hadn't. They couldn't go out until the storm ended. It made me crazy. *It must be hell for them.* I thought of all the times I made her worry. Like when I hid in the doghouse when we had a house full of company for Sunday dinner. I didn't come when I was called. They searched the farm and even the dugout. Women were crying and men were grim—until they heard me sneeze. I got a licking that night and no food.

I thought of Mom and her garden, how hard she worked to weed and water it. And how much I hated it, how much I complained about weeding. "I notice you never complain when you're eating," she said one day in a fury. She was the one who said I could get straight A's if I wanted. I was always surprised how disappointed she was when I brought home mainly C's and B's. I knew I could do better, but Dad was right. I was lazy.

"You were a harder worker when you were ten than you are now," Dad had said not long ago. We'd been hauling wheat, shoveling in the bin, buried up to our asses, working around those rods that hold the granaries together. I'd been out with the boys the night before, sampling lemon gin and cheap cherry brandy.

I wasn't raised to be a farmer, but I was expected to do my share of the work. And yet, all I could think about was baseball or hockey or football, whatever sport happened to be in season, and when I wasn't playing or practising or fooling around with my cousins or chasing girls, I was in my room or in the bunkhouse with my nose buried in a book. The thought struck me that I wasn't much of a son. And in a horrible moment, I wondered if Dad was lonely for me. "Ohhhh," I moaned, deeply ashamed.

Paddy answered with a snort. He stirred. I could sense him half raise his head. I rolled over, shocked to discover how stiff I was, locked into a crouch beside him. "It's okay, Paddy. You all right? That's a good horse." And then, "I love you, Paddy." Again my mind filled with regret. I thought of how little I rode this horse, this guy I'd worked so hard to get, had begged for, for so long.

"You've got to take care of him," they'd said.

"I will, I will," I'd promised. And I thought of how ragged he looked. Hadn't been brushed in days, maybe weeks. His hooves needed trimming, needed a farrier to get them back into shape. "I don't deserve you, Paddy. You're so incredible, I don't deserve you." I leaned into Paddy's side, my face up against his wet shivering belly.

"When we get out of here, I'm going to spoil you rotten, big guy." I stroked him, brushing off more snow. For some reason I thought of my teachers and the fat old geometry teacher I tormented.

"She's just trying to teach me something that might be useful some day, and all I do is make life so miserable for her she probably can't wait to get home." I was talking out loud now, getting sadder by the minute, horrified at my life as a big dumb jerk. And now I was going to die, maybe, in a goddamn snowdrift.

The icy, creeping regret, the fear, the cold—it all made me sleepy. The howling wind was like a numbing lullaby, the snow a soft deadly quilt. *Well, maybe people who die in storms get this way. They just slip away in a dream.*

I can't fall asleep!

I jumped up, or at least tried to. I crouched in front of the lean-to, tried to straighten. I was so stiff and cold. My toes were numb now, my fingers, too. "I'm freezing to death!" My words seemed mumbled and very small. I had to do something. *Is Paddy dying slowly in the dark, too?*

He could die right here and I won't even know it! I knelt down again and crawled to Paddy's head.

"Paddy, Paddy. You okay?" I felt his face, brushed a pile of snow away from his ears. No answer. I bent down lower, put my ear to his nose. He was breathing!

"Don't die on me, Paddy. Please don't die. I'm so sorry I got you into this mess. I'm so sorry." Paddy answered with a small short sniff. It was a sweet sound.

"Okay, guy. Great. Now I gotta look after myself for a bit."

I got up. I started jumping up and down, spreading my legs one time, bringing them together the next, each time swinging my arms out to the side. What was this exercise called? *My mind. I can't think. I can't remember.*

And then I laughed out loud. I thought of my Uncle Norman. He would have had some wry comment that'd have me keeled over, laughing my guts out. Tears filled my eyes and I started jumping faster. I could feel my toes again. My fingers were hurting, which was a good sign. I wondered what time it was. *How long until morning? What if it's a three-day blizzard?*

Maybe it's what happens to people caught in disasters. They start making tough decisions, but by then the decisions aren't so tough. The idea just came. Maybe it had been there, lingering in the dark for a while. But I knew what I had to do, knew what would increase my odds of seeing daylight.

"I'm so sorry, big guy. I have to do this." I sat down on the snow between Paddy's front and hind legs, pulled his saddle blanket over my shoulders, left some to cover his legs, his withers. I worked my boots between Paddy's hind legs, where his balls would have been. He didn't move. I curled up, leaned sideways against his belly. My arms were folded against my chest, hands holding the blanket up close to my neck. That was awkward. I pulled them out, pressed them up against Paddy's belly. Better. My left side was almost warm. But the right side of me was freezing.

I can turn around later. I guess that's when I fell asleep.
Fitful images flew at me. People leering. A hockey coach
yelling, "Back-check!" Mom peering down. "You should
have got straight A's." Harry standing in the pulpit with wild
hair and a gigantic hammer, spitting nails from his mouth.
A Christmas tree. All my family. Colored bubbles of laughter rising inside the lights. Grandma saying, "I wish you'd
taken time to see me more." Dad with his shovel, frowning,
up to his neck in wheat, drowning, yelling, "Shovel harder!"
The farrier with his leather apron, his pick in Paddy's hoof,
snarling at me, shaking his head. The vet, all dressed in
white, with a huge needle spurting death, plunging it into
Paddy's neck. The stuff spraying out Paddy's nose, his crying eyes. Splashing in my mouth, tasting like vinegar. I went
down, down into soft clouds, drifting through whiteness. I
was snow falling, falling in silence, into nothing.

I woke with a jerk. "Huh!" Panic. *How long? Am I frozen?
My feet? Are they okay? My hands?* And then, relief. I was.
Did I just drift off? It feels like longer. Those awful dreams! I
sat up. Something was different. I looked around. Still pitch
black. *Paddy! Is he dead?* I tore off my glove and put my
hand against his side. He felt warm. He was breathing. And
then I heard it—Silence! No wind howling. No hissing
snow. The storm had passed. Hope surged inside me. "I can
make a fire now, Paddy boy! We've got a chance." And then,
"Hang in there, buddy. Hang in there."

This was going to be tricky. I had used every scrap of
dead wood I could find to build the shelter. It was too dark
to go very far. All I could do was feel around in the snow

and find wood I'd missed. I started out on my hands and knees, dug down in the snow in front of our shelter. This would be the fire pit. Every twig, every little branch I put to the side in a pile. The ground at the bottom of the hole was covered with frozen leaves. They'd be wet. I'd have to put down a layer of wood and build the fire on that. *How many matches do I have?* Not many. Just a careless handful.

I crawled around in the snow, finding nothing at first. Then, bingo! A big branch under a foot of snow. I pulled at it. Judging from the weight, a long one. I pulled it up through the snow, followed it along by feel, hand over hand, snapping off branches as I went, holding onto them, afraid to drop them in case I might not find them again. It was good to do something, to feel hope again.

There were lots of twigs. I dragged the branch back to the shelter, pulled the thick end away and put the smaller branches near the fire pit so I could break them off and set the fire. My hands were still stiff with cold. My gloves were almost useless. If it hadn't been for the wool lining, I'd be a goner. Still I had to have everything ready before I risked taking them off and fumbling with the matches.

I thought of a Jack London story. A prospector had been caught in sixty-five-below weather; his foot had gotten soaked in a creek. It was so cold he couldn't handle the matches. And when he finally got a fire going, snow fell off an evergreen and doused it. His dog sat and watched while he froze to death. I took my gloves off carefully.

I laid a row of small sticks across the bottom of the fire pit on the ground. Then a pile of twigs on top of that. There was grass in the snow. I pulled that, too, and rolled the blades of grass around my fingers into balls. Carefully I built a tepee of tiny sticks over the grass, then put bigger and bigger sticks on top. The larger ones I set to the side. I got my jackknife out and grabbed a bigger branch. Feeling my way in the dark, I carefully peeled the bark off, then dug in with the blade, carved a sliver of wood so it curled up. Slowly I moved the knife a little, dug the blade in and made another sliver. I did this over and over, sometimes slipping in the dark, trying not to cut myself, stopping to warm my fingers. In a few minutes I'd made a piece of tinder just the way Dad had showed me. But we'd never done it in pitch black before. And not in winter. I laid the stick down on the twigs so the flames from the grass would catch the shavings.

My fingers were numb. I tucked them into my pockets to warm them up before I tried the matches. I realized suddenly how precious these matches were. One little stick with chemicals on the end could mean my life and Paddy's. I fished them out of my shirt pocket and counted them. *Seven. Lucky number.* Hunched over the fire pit, I waited until my fingers were ready. Something made me look up. The trailing end of the storm system was passing by. Through the dark trees, between the clouds, I could see stars. And to the west, on the edge of the clouds, a silver rim of moonlight.

I struck the match on the zipper of my jeans. It flared up with a tiny flash, the light surprising after working blind for so long. Quickly I cupped my hands around it, moved it down into my fire pit and touched it to the grass. There was a brief hiss, a puff of smoke, and the match went out. *One down six to go.*

And that's when a coyote yelped. Another one answered. And not far away, I stopped, held my breath for a second, reminding myself that coyotes aren't wolves. They're scared of people, too. *But how hungry are they? Another good reason to get this fire going.*

"Damn!" I dropped the second match in the snow. I'd held it too close, burned my fingers. I was nervous now. The third just flared and went out. The tether on my lifeline was getting shorter. I felt in the dark and opened the sticks in the pile a little to allow more air in. I moved the tinder stick down closer to the grass. The fourth. My hand shook. I struck the match and quickly angled the head down so the flame would burn upward on the stick, anything to give it a better chance. I moved it down to the tinder. A wisp of smoke, a curl of wood glowed red and then another. Suddenly a little flame licked up no bigger than a candle. I held my breath. Slowly, like a surgeon, I eased some grass and a twig toward the flame. They caught.

In a minute I had a small fire. There was no time for relief. I felt for the sticks I'd set aside, grabbed them, banged the snow off, then carefully placed each one, blowing gently on the flames, nursing them along. The wood was wet. Tiny wisps of steam rose up. I started stripping off the bark. Quickly I cut into the sticks with my knife, opening them up to expose the dry wood inside. It took five minutes, maybe more, of coaxing. Finally I had a fire. I reached for more wood. Bigger pieces. And then the first "snap" told me the fire was real. I piled everything I'd found onto that fire. I built a log house around the flames so as they rose, they dried the wood, warmed it, then ignited it. Sparks rose into the black and with them, my hopes. I held my fingers right in the flames. They were so cold I couldn't feel any pain. I rubbed them. Only then did I allow myself a brief sigh of relief. Maybe we'll live after all.

But I needed more wood. The flames were a foot high now, and for the first time since dusk I could see trees around us. And the drifts of snow that the blizzard had built. *My God! We're surrounded!* The lean-to was buried in snow, more like a cave with snow blown and curled in drifts around the sides enclosing us. I could see Paddy dimly, a white shape in the shadows. Not moving.

"Paddy? Paddy, boy? Are you still with me, big guy?" My breathing stopped again as I bent over him. Waiting.

His head stirred, his eye opened. "Oh, God, Paddy. Thank you. Thank you for not being dead."

I rolled out of the way so he could see. "Look, we've got a fire, bud. This'll keep us going till morning. Till they come."

I stood up. The fire made wild dancing shapes on the closest trees but hardly a dent in the dark wall behind them.

I walked up to a small birch I hadn't seen before and pushed it. It didn't give. I tried another tree, a thin maple. It creaked. I grabbed it, rocked hard and snapped it off near the base. We were in luck. It was maybe twenty feet tall, the top out of sight in the dark. I pulled it beside the fire. I braced one end between two trees and stomped on it. It wouldn't break. I pulled it right over the fire so it would burn the tree in half. I'd feed the two ends into the fire later. A lazy man's fire.

The fire was going well now. But my hands and feet were still freezing, and clearing skies meant the temperature would drop. I stopped, crouched close as I could to the fire to warm my feet. I held my soaking gloves right in the flames. Steam swirled off them. The heat felt so good on my face. My eyes glazed over for a second as I stared at nothing. And then—*Where are those sparks? In the trees, just beyond the light. Did I see something? Coyote eyes? Shit. Couldn't be. Don't they know we're not good eating?*

Maybe it was just sparks; maybe I was too tired. The flames licked up into the darkness, two feet high, cracking, the wet wood hissing. *My watch! I'd forgotten. Five-thirty! Could it really be? Still two cold hours till light. Not enough wood. Maybe we won't make it. So sorry, everybody. So sorry for everything. Maybe no chance to be better.* My eyes were heavy. They wanted to close. I pitched forward, jammed my hands into the snow to keep from falling into the fire. *Got to have a nap.* I crawled back away from the pit, back into the shelter, tucked my boots between Paddy's legs again and huddled against my half-dead horse. "Just a little rest. I'll get more wood in a minute, Paddy boy. Don't die on me now. Please don't die."

Out of the corner of my eye, the last thing I saw, in the black wall beyond the trees, were twin sets of yellow glowing, reflected firelight dancing in the dark.

. . .

A buzz, low like a mosquito on a hot summer night. It wouldn't go away. It got louder and louder. And then, a roar. My eyes opened. Blinding white light. Blue. The roar still there. Then a flash of red above the trees. A huge wide wing of red! *Gunnar!*

His plane filled the ravine with sound. Searching for me. It disappeared over the hill, the sound with it. I was alive. "Gunnar!" I tried to yell but all that came out was a ragged croak. I tried to get up, but I was stiff and cold to the bone, my pants frozen solid. Paddy was covered with snow. *Dead?* The whole world white, with shadows, a thin wisp of smoke from my fire almost out, smoke still curling up, as if from a cigarette, to the blue above. My heart was pounding.

"Paddy. Paddy. They found us." I rolled away from Paddy, staggered to my feet, almost falling into the fire. I staggered like a drunk toward the path I'd made last night. But there was no path. It was gone. Instead, a wall of white ten feet high. I turned and ran, stumbling to the other side, the leeward side of the ravine, ploughed through the trees, then the brush, out into the full sunlight. The sound again. The plane was coming back. I launched myself at the six-foot snowbank, half crawling, half swimming across the top. I was yelling. I don't know what.

The plane was lower this time, a hundred feet up maybe, carving a red circle in the blue sky. I could see Gunnar at the window. I stood at the bottom of the hill, yelling, waving both hands above my head. Gunnar waved, dipped his wing and disappeared again. *He sees me.* On my hands and knees, I scrambled up the side of the ravine to the top. Gunnar turned, was coming back, the red wings tilting gracefully, silver skis glistening in the sun. He was lower now, maybe fifty feet, buzzing me. I was waving, crying, shrieking. The roar drowned out the sound. I saw him open the window and throw something out. A string of white unraveled like the tail of a kite and streamed down in a long thin, white line—toilet paper!

I started laughing. Gunnar and Maggie were Dad and Mom's best friends. They lived just a couple of miles away. Gunnar often dropped a roll when flying over our farm. We'd run out and get it because there was always a note on the end that said "Coffee's on" or "Let's go golfing." Slowly the ribbon unfurled toward me. I ran to get it as Gunnar turned to make another pass. The streamer crumpled into the snow. I picked it up, hauled it in like fish line, looking for the end. And the note. In a hasty scrawl, he'd written, "Thank God you're alive."

There was another sound. I looked up. A tractor, a green John Deere, was coming along the crest of the hill toward me. They must have seen Gunnar turning, seen the toilet paper. And on the other side of the ravine, two yellow Ski-Doos appeared. I waved again. The tractor was just like ours. I couldn't tell who was in the cab. I stood there waving. And then—as it came closer—I could see. It was Dad! And Mom was there, too, perched beside him. The big diesel engine belched smoke as Dad hit the throttle. The big black tires spun as they came toward me. They stopped.

My uncles, George and Norm, roared up right behind them on their snowmobiles.

Dad opened the door of the cab. He was smiling, his bottom lip quivering. Mom was bawling her head off. The heat from the engine, from the cab, hit me like a warm soft wall. "Paddy broke his leg," I cried, yelling above the roar. "I'm sorry. We stayed too long and he broke it in a badger hole. The storm came and I couldn't leave him and I don't know if he's alive but I built a shelter and later a fire when the wind died down and he's down there now all covered with snow—"

Dad jumped down and wrapped his arms around me in the biggest hug I'd ever had. Mom climbed down with a quilt in her arms. She threw it over my shoulders. "Eric, we thought you were dead." Tears streamed down as she touched my face. "Aren't you frozen?"

"You're a sight for sore eyes, boy," said Uncle George in his big black snowmobile suit. "You okay?"

I nodded. I couldn't feel my feet though.

"What's the matter? You think we're all getting too much sleep around here?" Norman laughed as he threw his arm around my shoulder. "Better get into that cab and get warm."

But I couldn't. Not yet. "Paddy's down there," I said pointing.

"He alive?" Dad asked.

"Yes. Maybe. I don't know." And then, "I think I killed my horse."

"You get in the cab," said Mom. "I've got lots of blankets in there. We'll go check."

"No, no, I want to go." I grabbed a blanket from her. "Come on."

Fear again, rising up, drowning hope, as I led them sliding down the side of the hill. Norm, his face grim now, with a .303. We waded through the snow and into the little camp that had been our world for the longest night of my life. Paddy was just a snow-covered hump in a sea of drifts. There was just a small, dark space between him and the roof. Only the saddle, sitting oddly on its side, suggested there was something there. I ran to Paddy and knelt down.

"Watch his leg," I said to Dad beside me. I brushed some snow away. Dad grimaced when he saw the splint. Paddy's head was covered. I gently brushed it off.

"Paddy? Paddy, boy. Wake up." His eyes, his ears, his mouth were full of snow. Ice had formed around his nostrils. I brushed snow away from his eye. It stayed closed.

Oh Paddy, please, wake up, I prayed. I brushed the snow from his ear. And then, it twitched.

"He's alive!"

Paddy snuffled. A tiny beautiful sound. Then . . . he opened his eye.

I looked up. Four adults stood there, grinning, wiping tears from their eyes, Norm with the rifle by his side.

"You won't be needing that," I said. "I'm going to make sure of it."

Naska

by
John Cuthand

This is a fishing story from the other side of the pole! John Cuthand, a Plains Cree from Saskatchewan, beautifully takes us down, down, down into the depths of the South Saskatchewan River, there to see the world from the point of view of a hunter so powerful she knows no enemies but the "bright burning sun"—Naska, the northern pike.

There is a great tradition in Canadian literature of animal stories. It is a distinctly Canadian genre, popularized around the turn of the century by such writers as Sir Charles G. D. Roberts and Ernest Thompson Seton. But of course, animal stories are a great deal older than those written by transplanted Europeans. There are bountiful First Peoples stories from every corner and every tribe. There are creation myths and trickster tales and wonder tales preserved orally

down to the present day; they are truly a national treasure.
John Cuthand carries on the tradition with this original and
moving story.

Her home was the deep water pools of the South
Saskatchewan River. Here among the water plants, rocks
and sandbars she passed the day and avoided the only
enemy she ever knew—the bright burning sun. She hunted
alone and without remorse, for such is the way of the big
northern pike.

Her name was Naska. She was in her prime, weighing
over thirty-five pounds and stretching almost a yard. Her
shining, well-muscled body was white on the bottom, a
mottled green and white along the sides and dark green on
top. Her mouth was a maze of needle-sharp teeth. Smaller
fish avoided her. And only the hard-shelled painted turtle
could afford to ignore her approach.

When the hot summer sun drove her into the deepest
reaches of the river, she would hover, her fins circling, facing the current a foot or so above the bottom. It was here, in
these long hours, that the waters told her stories. The river
sang as it flowed over and around the deep water rocks. It
spoke in the soft rustle of the water weeds and in the gurgle
and murmur of water pouring around the few scattered
boulders breaking the glassy surface.

The voice said, "I am the ancient daughter of ice mountain, born when the freezing sky allowed him dominion

over the south. I am the blood of ice mountain, born from his death before the warming sky. I am ancient and I am mystery. I am swift-flowing water. I am Saskatchewan."

In the black of the late night she rose with the morning star. She fed until the star was high and fading. When the first rays of the shimmering sun cast long shadows, she herself was like a shadow sinking into her deep water pools. She surfaced with the setting of the sun, fed, then slid deeper when the night became black.

On cloudy days she ranged beyond her familiar haunts. In the fall, with the gradual cooling of the water, her range extended farther still. In winter, when the ice sealed off the surface and the sun no longer warmed the water, she roamed as she pleased. She much preferred the colder water. In mid-summer she was sluggish, but that was also the time when the river sang to her.

One time it told her ice mountain had never been entirely defeated by the warming sky. "He rules still in one quarter of the sun's cycle. He covers me with his cloak and speaks to me in the booming thunder of my cracking ice mantle. He is father. In his death I was born. In his rebirth I die. I am ancient but he is ageless."

In the time of the full moon Naska would rise and seek different prey. The moon's glow concealed her, but she could see them. They were the night creatures that live between water and land. For them the beckoning, seemingly peaceful waters held terror. Quick, violent death came with a splash and a swirl of black water. Where a gosling or a baby muskrat once swam, all that remained was an expanding ripple.

The big fish did not think in terms of right and wrong. Hunger, insatiable hunger, drove her and she killed only to live.

Among her moonlit prey the story spread of a water demon in the form of an enormous fish. The story was told in the haunting lonely laughter of the loons, the croaking chorus of the frightened frogs and the chatterings of the milling ducks. The moonlight sighting of a long, shining back lolling over the water drove them farther down the sandy bank away from that terrible place. The hunted lived in fear and they feared her most of all. If Naska knew of their fear, she didn't care. Generations of her kind before her and from her had ruled and would rule the river's waters. For the river in its mysterious way had willed it so.

She had been the mother of many. Perhaps some were among her kill, for the female pike takes no part in the raising of her young. Perhaps one or two would grow to her size if they survived the slaughter of the first years. One and one alone, however, was destined to become mistress of the river. The river in its way had willed it so. Naska was the survivor and heir of a mother who once ruled these waters as she did. This she did not know. She knew only that the river was her home and the river's spirit her sole benefactor.

One night, when the autumn moon was full and the great fish was on the hunt, a wandering band of antelope came to the river's edge. They waded out into the shallows and were drinking their fill, when their sharp-eyed leader spied a great shining back coming toward them. He watched intently, expecting an enormous snake, for snakes were creatures they knew well. A great finned tail curved upward, then sliced down, scarcely breaking the surface. "This is no snake," thought the antelope, "it is a creature solely bound to the water spirit."

The great fish felt a curious pulse from the shallows and veered toward it. This was not the fluttering sound of webbed feet, her usual prey. It was the feel of something large, many large creatures.

The antelope, alert as always, sensed that something very alien was close. They stiffened, raising their heads to sniff the wind. Only the leader gazed at the smooth, flowing water directly in front of them.

Naska followed the river bottom and rose as it rose. She came as close as boldness could take her before caution and the rising river bottom forced her off.

The leader was the first to notice the ruffled water above the shallow-running fish. The V-shaped wake came directly toward them, then moved away in a sharp curve. The antelope were nervous but their curiosity got the better of them. They watched in fascination as the dark shadow beneath the now churning water glided by, first one way then another, more slowly and closer with every pass.

Naska could not see straight ahead, because her eyes were on either side of her head. Cruising first one way then another allowed each eye to scrutinize in turn. The antelope froze in place, only their eyes tracked the meandering fish.

The shadow slowed, then hung motionless, her body curved in an arc, head and tail lowered—the defiant attack stance of her kind. Her cold, unblinking eye peered from beneath the water. The antelope peered back. Both sensed danger, but both were too fascinated to turn back. Neither one moved. All was quiet and still except for the murmuring water and the distant night sounds. The stand-off was finally broken by a single curious antelope advancing a few hesitant steps. It paused in mid-step, ears forward, eyes shining. The dark shadow turned to meet him. The pronghorn's nostrils flared. Genuine fear was rising in him now, in spite of his curiosity.

In this position Naska could not see, but other more acute senses compensated. Her body felt the change in water pressure. Sensitive pores surrounding her mouth tasted the water. The tingling of these senses was her warning, but she wasn't quick enough. Her world exploded. The pronghorn struck with slashing hooves. He felt his first strike hit, then searing pain gripped his left front leg. He turned and leapt to the river bank. The others, as if one, instantly followed.

The herd left the river valley, trotting toward the rising morning star, now above the high prairie hills to the east. One limped, streaming blood from a deep gash to its front leg.

The pronghorn's slashing attack had cut deep, narrowly missing Naska's spine. Her reaction had been fast: a violent counterattack followed by a darting retreat. She left tasting blood.

The fight was brief but the effects devastating. Naska's needle-like sharp teeth had torn flesh as she shook her massive head from side to side. The pronghorn's small hooves, honed to a fine edge by climbing the rocky high ground, cut and crushed. Naska was lucky to be alive.

She retreated to the safety of deep water where, unmoving for many days, she nursed her wounds.

As she hovered, death close at hand, the river spoke to her again. "My riddles are written in your colours and patterns, in the coiled shell of the water snail and in the advance and retreat of my morning mist. All is there for those who seek. The willows know and bow before the river winds. I am as the veins of their stems and that of the animals. My sisters both young and old bring life to the land in the endless cycle of wind and water. We are ancient and honour only ice mountain and his creator. My father feels the deep stirrings of growth again. His advance will come soon, with the passing of ten thousand cycles of the sun. Death is always close at hand, but you, my defiant one, will live to hunt again."

The cold water of winter revived her. For the remainder of her days, though, she wore a distinct crescent-shaped scar high upon her back.

The spring brought high murky water. The great restless river cut new channels and deep holes. Fish, both hunter and prey, sought the sanctuary of the river's deepest pools. A strange truce resulted. Clustered together in desperate, common survival they faced into the current, awaiting the river's ebb. They ignored one another, choosing not to eat until the peril passed. Overhead, the river carried a deadly cargo of uprooted trees and smaller debris. In another time the fish would welcome the shade and shelter of a beached river log, but for now the debris was an adversary to be avoided. The gentle river was showing its wrathful side.

Naska's strong body was rocked by the swirling water and her sensitive gills ached from the heavily silted water. In time the river subsided. The fish returned to their former roles. Hunter stalked prey and sought the safety of weed beds and shallow water. Naska hunted with renewed vigour over a territory she now knew only by instinct. For the river bed had been forever changed by the river's rampage.

Just as the butterfly changes and renews itself in the cocoon so too did Saskatchewan in the cleansing flood of the early spring. Life more bounteous than before returned with the subsiding waters.

The spring also brought subtle but significant change. The fishes of the north moved south, and Naska challenged their invasion. Goldeye, pickerel and the odd wandering pike all bore the tell-tale wounds of Naska's wrath.

One day a new threat appeared. It was a creature she had never met before. It was big and moved slowly like a log carried by the current. Her other senses told her it was a living being.

At any other time her actions would have been predictable. But this intruder made her pause. It was bigger than she, much bigger. She approached slowly, her back arched and her broad tail making slow, deliberate sweeps. The stranger kept to its slow, steady course along the river bottom, unconcerned by her approach. Naska's fury rose. Her body tensed, then she shot out of the gloom in dauntless attack. Her jaws did not grip. The intruder was far too large. She came at it again and again. Her teeth broke on a craggy back. The fight was entirely her own. The giant fish did not fight back. Almost with contempt it seemed, the giant continued its fluid movement slowly and methodically down river.

Naska launched a final attack. By luck or misfortune she struck the giant's tail fin. She felt flesh tearing, then saw the huge fin sweeping toward her. A powerful blow stunned her. She recovered in time to witness the long tapering tail of Namew the sturgeon vanishing downriver. Their chance encounter was over.

The ice mountain's rule had come and gone many times before Naska grew too tired for the hunt. The smaller fish grew bold and she found it hard to catch them. Almost in disdain they drifted by her jaws, only to dart away when she moved to attack. What once took but an instant was now painfully slow. Her lightning-quick reflexes were gone. Her meals became slow-moving crayfish and frogs. On her last hunts, in complete contempt, the little fish followed her, seeking the remains of what little food she could find but not swallow. Naska's body ached and she spent much more time in solitude on the river bottom. Here she awaited the return of the comforting voice of the river spirit, but no voice was heard.

The time came when the moon was full and no shining back was seen breaking the river's surface. The moon waned and the night creatures along the edge of the land and water felt safe.

The morning star was at its highest point and the eastern sky was bright with early dawn. The sun rose red and fairweather clouds of violet and gold floated across the sky.

Naska's movements were slowing. Her gills once flushed with red blood grew pale and sickly. She didn't know why, only instinct drew her from her hovering place to the weed bed. With painful effort she closed her tired mouth over a single water plant. Then with a turn of her massive head she pulled it free. Straining against the current, she carried this hard-won prize back to her chosen place. No prey had taken so much effort as this simple task.

She faced into the current for the final time. The rising sun now bathed the river bottom in a soft halflight. Only the dying remained. Her gills stopped moving. Her mouth opened and closed a final time, freeing the water plant. Her tired body shook with her death rattle. She briefly drifted with the current, then rose slowly toward the sun. One eye saw blackness, the other a brilliant broken circle of light. The light grew in intensity. A bright light she would only see once filled her being. Then all was blackness.

Wind and current brought the limp corpse to the water's edge. It drifted to a sandbar where it rocked back and forth with the lapping waves. The birds of the air feasted. Before the coming of the next sunrise, mighty Naska's body was reduced to bones and a toothy, grinning skull.

The night creatures, once timid of her mere approach, now rejoiced in her death. And so began a night of steady tattoo, celebrating the end of their once formidable foe.

The frogs croaked together of a great victory, but theirs was not a valid boast. Only death had won.

In the spring the rushing water swept the bones along the river bottom where they collected in a shallow river hollow. Swirling silt covered them. A stand of water plants began to grow thick and lush from the calcium-rich sediment.

Along the wandering river, in the back water of a shallow place, small fish—the survivors of uncountable hatchlings—flittered among weeds, pursuing water bugs and minute creatures. Others much larger but no older, stalked tadpoles. They all feared the deep water where the larger fish lurked ever hungry for a meal of their kind. In time, the pull of instinct or perhaps destiny called the bold one to the deep, alluring water. She paused at a lush stand of water plants and hovered beside it. The water-filtered sun, moving in zebra-like patterns over her back, shone on a curious crescent-shaped birth mark. The singing river called her in the soft rustle of the water weeds and in the gurgle and murmur of water pouring around the few scattered boulders breaking the glassy surface.

The bold one swam deeper, down a sandy decline, past the last of the weed bed, and into the unknown reaches of the deep calling river.

Copyright Acknowledgements